a bo

SO WRONG IT'S RIGHT

USA TODAY bestselling author
julie johnson

Cover design by: ONE CLICK COVERS

Subscribe to Julie's newsletter: http://eepurl.com/bnWtHH

For the perfectionists.

"I cannot fix on the hour, or the spot, or the look or the words, which laid the foundation. It is too long ago. I was in the middle before I knew that I had begun."

———————

Jane Austen, Pride and Prejudice

PROLOGUE
ZEN AF

I GENERALLY THINK of myself as an even-tempered person.

Calm.

Composed.

Collected.

Cool under pressure.

Hell, I teach yoga, for god's sake. And if ever there was an occasion to *not* be cool, it's when you're in a 105 degree Bikram studio with your whole body weight resting on your elbows and your legs bent backwards over your head in an inverted *sayanasana* pose.

Talk about getting bent out of shape for no reason...

Sorry.

What was I saying?

Oh, right.

Me.

Sedate, serene, steady-as-she-goes Shelby Hunt. The quiet woman who lives on the quiet corner of the quiet tree-lined street in the quiet Boston neighborhood. The very picture of suburban bliss, with her two-hundred-dollar haircut, a walk-in-closet full of designer clothes, a new car in the driveway every year, and a handsome, successful husband in her bed every night.

It's such a pretty lie, even *I* almost believe it.

Almost.

The truth is, there's nothing remotely perfect about my life, or than man I've spent the past decade sharing it with. And there's certainly nothing even *slightly* quiet about the past few days, given the sheer hell that's broken loose...

But I'm getting ahead of myself.

Before I fill you in on the series of unfortunate events that have, for all intents and purposes, flipped my whole world on its axis, I need you to understand something. I'm not some swooning damsel who faints at the first sign of danger and waits for a man to swoop in and save her. I am no delicate flower, wilting in the heat as soon as things don't go my way. It takes a lot to get me worked up; to ruffle the glossy feathers I take such painstaking effort to present to the outside world.

I mean...

I *meditate.* I *garden.* I own not one but *two* aromatherapy candles. (Granted, I only burn them once a year since they smell a bit like patchouli and make my eyes sting... But that's not the point.)

What *is* my point, you ask?

Simply this: that I, Shelby Hunt, have never been the kind of woman who screams or throws tantrums when life doesn't go her way — which, despite what an outsider might think looking in on my seemingly perfect life, is more often than not.

I take things as they come and don't complain, because, in my experience, complaining rarely accomplishes much of anything. Why bitch over life's many unfortunate twists and turns when, instead, you could take all that useless angst and channel it into something productive? Like, say, the ability to breathe deeply through a head-to-foot *sirsa padasana* pose, even after your pelvis has lost proper circulation from contorting into a veritable pretzel?

See — I'm *totally* chill.

Cool as a cucumber.

No.

Cooler than a cucumber.

Placid as a pickle. Even-keeled as an eggplant. Untroubled as a... a...

Curse the lack of produce beginning with the letter U.

Whatever. Fruits and veggies aside, my point remains.

I am zen. *Zen as fuck.* It's not easy to rattle me.

And yet, I must admit...

Today, I am rattled.

I am not calm.

I am not collected.

I am not cool.

Honestly, though... can you blame me?

I am, after all, currently locked in the trunk of a car with my hands bound together by zip tie and my mouth covered in duct tape, being taken god only knows where by god only knows who, for god only knows what purpose. (Call me crazy, but I have a hunch it doesn't have to do with my rather impressive yoga skills or my impeccable home decor taste or my unparalleled fashion sense.)

The car jolts to a stop.

Trying not to pee my favorite pair of Lululemons, I hear a door open and attempt to draw from that bottomless sense of calm that's gotten me through some rather sticky situations in the past. Like that summer afternoon I blew out a tire on the highway in my two-seater convertible and nearly bit the dust beneath the carriage of an eighteen-wheeler. (Thank god for airbags.) Or the day of my wedding when a flock of pigeons shat all over my ten-thousand dollar white dress as I walked from the limo to the chapel. (Looking back, that was *definitely* an omen from the universe I shouldn't have ignored.) Or Christmas morning, when Paul hurled my favorite Tiffany-style lamp against the wall six inches from my head in a blind rage. (See what I mean about ignoring that bad marriage omen?)

All those times, I managed to make it through without much more than the faintest uptick in my resting BPM. And yet, as I listen to the crunch of boots on gravel approaching the trunk, I feel my heart thundering like a battering ram, hard enough it could splinter my ribs and tear itself right out of my chest.

My deep breathing techniques have officially fled.

My chakras are decidedly unbalanced.

I am full-on, no holds barred *freaking the fuck out.*

It's almost ironic. I mean...

Who would've ever in a million years thought *I'd* wind up here?

Sedate, serene, steady-as-she-goes Shelby Hunt.

Putting the *om* in *OMG, I've been kidnapped.*

CHAPTER 1

NAMASTE (IN BED)

ONE WEEK EARLIER...

"NAMASTE."

Releasing a long breath, I open my eyes and watch as fifteen intermediate-to-advanced yogis bow back at me. With murmured thanks, they begin rolling up their mats and heading for the exits. I wave when I spot a few regulars in the group, mixed in with a healthy number of new faces. My class has grown more and more popular, these past few months. I'll have to start turning people away if Aimee, the studio owner, doesn't give me another time slot. Plus, I can't lie — it would be nice to have something else to occupy my pathetically under-scheduled Saturdays.

A girl can only spend so many hours binge-watching Netflix alone before her brain starts to atrophy... along with certain other sorely-neglected body parts south of the waistline...

I don't bother looking for my friends in the crowd.

They're not exactly what you'd call *athletic* — unless running through the mall in pursuit of a shoe sale counts as cardio. (I'm looking at you, Phoebe.) Besides, they've all been so busy for the past few months, I'm lucky if I even get to see them at our occasional girl's nights. Without margarita pitchers and gossip to entice them, there's approximately a zero percent chance of getting them to show up at one of my sunrise fitness sessions.

Maybe if I start serving bottomless mimosas after class...
I sigh deeply.

It's not that I don't understand *why* my besties have been MIA as of late. Our twenties have been a whirlwind of job changes and life shifts, new relationships and apartment moves, lavish weddings and squirming babies. Plus, unlike some of us, my friends actually enjoy spending time at home. (It probably helps that they have men who worship the ground they walk on — albeit, in fabulous footwear — waiting when they step through their front doors.)

What a novel concept: actually wanting *to spend time at home...*

"Thanks for a great class, everyone!" I call as my students filter out the front exit into the parking lot. "Hope to see you next week!"

When the door finally swings shut behind the last girl, I glance around the empty studio. It's a familiar mess — foam blocks and free weights scattered haphazardly across the hardwood. I flip on the stereo and hum along to the refrains of an '80s love ballad as I stack the equipment in the racks on the left side of the room. My mind makes a slow loop through my daily to-do list.

Stop by the Farmers Market.
Long run along the Charles River.

Cook that new butternut squash soup I've been meaning to try.

Eat a bowl alone while watching a rerun of Chopped I've already seen twice before falling into my empty king-sized bed, pretending not to notice the crushing sound of silence in my empty house.

And repeat.

I'm stacking the last of the free weights when I catch a glimpse of myself in the floor-to-ceiling mirror dominating the far wall of the studio. Bare feet, high ponytail, pink sports bra, black leggings. My posture is tense despite the past two hours of deep breathing exercises. My bow-shaped mouth is set in a frown. My light brown eyes appear flat and empty. God, I barely recognize my own reflection.

When did I become this unhappy stranger staring back at me?

Maybe around the time I served my husband Paul divorce papers six months ago. Or maybe further back, when he stopped coming home for dinner, or sleeping in our bed, or spending any time with me whatsoever. Then again, if I'm being totally honest with myself... maybe it happened long before then. So far back, I'm almost afraid to look, for fear of what I'll find. Because the stark naked truth of the matter is...

Maybe I've never been happy with him.

Not ever.

Not one year, not one day, not one hour.

Not one single second of this marriage.

I'm so caught up in my own thoughts, I barely register the sound of the studio door swinging open until I catch a blur of movement in the mirror on my right. Spinning around, my mouth starts running on auto-pilot before they've even cleared the threshold.

"Sorry, you've just missed our morning session. The next class is core aerobics with Aimee, but it doesn't start until noon..."

I trail off, sucking in a sharp gulp of air as I get a good look at the men who've just stepped inside. My tongue feels suddenly made of lead, unable to form words as my eyes scan them from head to toe. Which, frankly, takes quite a while because *holy shit* these men are enormous. Well over six feet tall with brawny builds to match, I'd guess they're somewhere between thirty and forty but it's hard to tell with their hair buzzed so short and their faces set in such scary expressions. Their massive muscles strain the seams of their matching black suits as they stride toward me, gun holsters clearly visible beneath their jackets.

Call me crazy, but I don't think they're here for core aerobics.

"Uh, hi there," I say, striving for a calm tone as I take in their intimidating expressions. "If you're looking for the law firm, it's actually in the building just around the corner... sometimes the GPS mixes up the addresses and people get confused..."

There's no answer. No sound at all except for four black shoes rapping like gunshots across the hardwood floor as the men come to a stop in the middle of the room. Well, *that* and the steady thumping of my own heartbeat between my ears, growing louder as the giants level me with those icy, thousand-yard stares.

I fight the urge to backpedal, abruptly aware of the fact that I am alone here in this soundproofed studio, wearing nothing but a hot pink sports bra and a pair of ultra-thin leggings, with two very large men who, it must be said, are the scariest dudes I've ever seen in my life.

Chill, Shelby, I chastise myself, squaring my shoulders with a confidence I don't feel. *You don't even know what they want.*

"Can I help you with something?" I force myself to ask, glancing from one giant to the next, my eyebrows arched in speculation. They must be brothers. They're so similar looking, I can't tell them apart.

"We're looking for someone," Righty says in a flat, faintly accented voice that sounds vaguely Slavic.

"Shelby Hunt," Lefty jumps in, narrowing his eyes on me. "Wife of Paul Hunt. Ring a bell?"

My mouth goes dry. Out of nowhere, I feel like a fifteen-year-old girl again, caught in the act of breaking curfew. "Um..."

Two sets of dark eyes burn into mine, searingly cold, and I try not to shiver.

Lie, an inner voice whispers out of nowhere, irrationally afraid to admit my identity to two men who make the gargantuan casino bouncers I encountered in Las Vegas a few years back seem chill in comparison. *Lie your perfectly-toned ass off.*

"Well?" Lefty prompts impatiently. "You Shelby?"

"Sorry — afraid not." I swallow hard. "Shelby called me this morning and said she wasn't feeling well. Asked me to step in and cover her class."

They don't react, so I keep going.

"I mean, yoga isn't really my specialty — I'm more of a barre gal, myself — but she covered for me this summer when I had a seriously intense case of food poisoning and couldn't lift my head from the toilet bowl, let alone lead a class of bored housewives through rigorous choreography, so I figured I owed her one."

The men glance at each other dubiously.

Are they buying this bullshit?

"Uh. So. What is it you want from her?" I ask, dragging their attention back to me. "I'd be happy to pass along a message from you..."

For a long, suspended moment they both just stare at me. I worry they've seen straight through my little white lies — *okay, so they aren't all that little, sue me* — until Righty finally opens his thin-lipped mouth and grunts.

"Tell her we're looking for her husband."

"And that we'll be back," Lefty adds, still eyeing me suspiciously.

Hoping my face hasn't gone pale, I give a small nod.

The men turn in tandem and head for the exit. It's not until the door swings shut behind them, leaving me alone in the small, silent studio, that I realize my hand is curled tight around a five-pound free weight, every knuckle pale with tension.

I blow out a long, shuddering breath.

Namaste, indeed.

YOU'RE PROBABLY WONDERING why I'm not exactly *shocked* by the sudden appearance of two armed gunman looking for my ex-husband. Err... *soon-to-be* ex-husband. Once the jerk agrees to sign the damn divorce papers I served him, that is.

The answer to your question — and, perhaps not so coincidentally, the answer to every *other* question concerning strange encounters with scary dudes in bad suits that have cropped up over the course of my life — is just another four-letter word.

Paul.

When I met him, I was an eighteen-year-old graphic design student at a small liberal arts college just outside the city, instantly infatuated with the TA of her mandatory Economics 101 class. Well-mannered and well-dressed, Paul was a few years older — and a few lightyears more confident — than any of the unrequited crushes I'd set my teenage sights on back in high school.

So, imagine my surprise when he made a point to talk to me after class one day. When he requested to meet privately to discuss my end-of-semester project. When he laughed at my jokes and smiled like I was the most adorable thing he'd ever set eyes on. When he asked me out on a real, actual date with real, actual candlelight and a real, actual kiss at my dormitory door when the night came to an end.

Me.

The awkward freshman, still attempting to shed her last layer of baby fat, whose love life until that point was about as passion-filled as a documentary on three-toed sloths. I was, in so many ways, just a girl. I didn't know how to dress properly or highlight my hair to flatter my skin-tone or apply eye makeup that didn't resemble a music video from the early '90s. (Hello, turquoise eyeshadow.) I didn't understand what falling for a man like Paul would mean for my future.

And yet... I didn't stand a snow cone's chance in hell at resisting him.

We were living together off-campus by the time I was a sophomore, married the month I graduated, and settled firmly in the house Paul bought for us before my first student loan payment came due. And, for a while, things were good. Or, at least to me — a girl with exactly *zero* other relationship experience to compare it to — things *seemed* good.

Good enough.

Paul was making great money as a financial consultant at a big Boston firm. I kept myself busy with freelance graphic design projects, despite my new husband's insistence that I didn't need to work.

Just take care of the house, baby.

Be home waiting every night, baby.

Have dinner ready on the table, baby.

I don't want you too busy for me, baby.

His gentle suggestions became increasingly demanding — and increasingly stifling — as the first years of our marriage passed us by. Slowly, at first. Then, so fast it was like I'd blinked my eyes and missed a whole half-decade of existence.

The blushing twenty-two-year-old bride was long gone, and with her the majority of my twenties. By the time I snapped out of my stupor and recognized what had become not just of my marriage, but of me, *Shelby*, a woman with dreams and aspirations outside the shackles of matrimony... I was twenty-eight years old and essentially a stranger to myself.

So, I resolved to get out.

To walk away.

To make a change before I lost one more single second of my life to a man who couldn't even be bothered to make it home for dinner most nights, or ask about my day on the rare evenings he did, or summon the effort to give me an occasional orgasm during our increasingly infrequent encounters between the sheets.

Did I say infrequent?

I meant nonexistent.

Seriously, when you're binge-watching *Mad Men* and start relating on a fundamental level to repressed 1950s housewives like Betty Draper... you know things aren't exactly going well.

Hence: the divorce papers.

Christmas Eve, while Paul was busy working — because *of course* he didn't take the holiday off, don't be absurd! — I left them under the tree with a big red bow on top and tucked myself in bed with an exceptionally good bottle of Syrah that Paul's parents gave us as an engagement gift.

To drink on your ten-year anniversary.

I drained that bottle, every damn sip, having a solo celebration to mark an altogether different sort of juncture — ten years wasted on a man who never cared about me as anything but a possession. Just another antique piece of furniture in his immaculate home. An article of clothing in his pristine closet. An object to stake ownership over, not to cherish until death did us part.

When I awoke on Christmas morning — my head spinning from a hangover rivaling the one I experienced following my friend Phoebe's bachelorette party last month — I fully expected to find the papers signed, dated, and waiting for me on the gleaming granite kitchen countertops we had specially imported from Morocco.

They weren't.

Instead, I found something else waiting for me. *Paul.* And the pure rage contorting his handsome features as his feet slowly closed the space between us and his hands not-so-slowly tore my papers clean in half... well, that was as surprising as it was terrifying.

Suffice to say, it never once crossed my mind that Paul

wouldn't be quite so keen on the idea of divorce. I thought he'd be relieved to be rid of me. After all, *I* wasn't the one who avoided coming home every night. *I* wasn't the one who walked through the door on more than one occasion with ill-concealed lipstick stains on his collar. *I* wasn't the one who gave up trying to make anything resembling an effort starting shortly after our second wedding anniversary and worsening with each progressive year.

And yet, when it finally came down to it, Paul was surprisingly resistant. So resistant, in fact, he shattered a $300 lamp against a wall, put his fist through the foyer mirror, and screamed loud enough that the next door neighbors called the police.

Let me tell you: nothing says Christmas quite like watching your enraged husband being tasered, cuffed, and loaded into the back of a squad car while the entire block watches from their front windows, hot cocoa in hand.

Bring on the carolers!

In the months since, Paul has stayed away. Physically, at least. (The restraining order I filed ensures that small detail.) Unfortunately, a legal document does very little to block him from contacting me via phone, email, voicemail... candy gram, flower delivery, edible arrangement...

You name it, he's tried it.

Despite the fact that I changed both my phone number and my locks... that I have thrown out so many flowers Mother Nature has put me on some kind of hit list... that I have chucked so many chocolates in the garbage Godiva has issued a warrant for my arrest... that I have an entire box of jewelry I'll never wear, including a gaudy Byzantine bracelet and a bejeweled golden egg, the exact purpose of which I've never been able to figure out...

He refuses to see reason.

He won't even entertain the *idea* of a divorce — no matter how many times I have served him with papers via courier. No matter that we're no longer living under the same roof or sharing any facet of each other's lives. (Besides, of course, a last name.)

Short of taking him to court for a messy public trial and forcing a judge to grant my freedom, I'm not exactly sure how to proceed from this point. So, for the time being, I've been letting things simmer on the back burner. Hoping he'll eventually come to his senses and change his mind about this whole '*marriage is forever, I'll never let you go, you're mine until the last breath leaves my body*' crap he started spouting on Christmas.

Don't worry — I'm not living under any sort of delusion that he's trying to win me back because he's desperately in love with me. For Paul, this is merely a point of pride.

I am his perfect wife, who lives in his perfect house, on the perfect street in the perfect suburb. I host posh dinner parties for his co-workers. I mix a flawless gin martini. I attend business functions on his arm wearing gorgeous dresses he buys for me. I am the most important chess piece on the carefully calculated board that is his life.

Giving me up might mean *losing* that game. Losing face in his business circles. Losing the respect of his family and friends. And if there's one thing the man I married can't stand...

It's losing.

I don't know where he's been staying or what he's been up to since I cut off communication. Frankly, it's not my concern anymore. Or... it wasn't until today, when two large thugs showed up at my yoga studio looking for Mrs. Paul Hunt.

I'm not sure what, exactly, he's gotten himself into that

brought those men to my doorstep. All I do know is... I'm wishing like hell he'd signed those damn papers. If he had, *no one* would be looking for Mrs. Shelby Hunt.

They couldn't.

She'd no longer exist.

CHAPTER 2

GHOSTED

I CAN'T QUITE SHAKE the creeping sensation that I'm being watched as I tug an open-weave white sweater over my sports bra, lock the studio doors behind me, and walk to my car. There's an odd tingling at the nape of my neck as my eyes scan the half-empty parking lot, seeking evident signs of danger.

There are none.

What are you expecting, Shelby? A man in a black trench-coat, twirling his mustache and cackling maniacally as he plots your demise?

After this morning's strange encounter, I'm inclined to head straight home and hide behind the safety of a locked oak door... but I don't want to give those thugs the satisfaction of ruining my day. Plus, knowing my refrigerator is currently as empty as one of Paul's promises is enough incentive to turn my wheel in the direction of the Union Square Farmers Market.

It's still early but the crowds are already thick with those out enjoying a quintessential summer Saturday morning. I move from stall to stall, selecting a week's worth of fresh fruit and veggies from vendors I've come to recognize after my many visits, smiling as I barter for a bouquet of hydrangeas and a bottle of wine, plum tomatoes and fresh baked bread, summer squash and a ball of burrata cheese.

Live music drifts in the air, a fiddler playing for tips. Families stroll past on all sides, their squawking toddlers in tow. Couples lick ice cream cones and laugh as they purchase mulled cider from the carts. I watch a clumsy golden retriever puppy tripping over his own paws and contemplate, for the thousandth time, whether I should get a pet to keep me company.

Shelby, you don't need a pet, a snarky inner voice chides. *What you need is a life.*

Sighing, I stow my produce away in a reusable cloth bag — really trying to regain some of my karma points with Mother Nature after the flower debacle — then grab a cup of coffee to sip as I wander around.

I love it here.

If I'm being entirely honest, that wasn't always the case. Somerville wasn't my first choice of living locations. I didn't get a say in the matter; Paul purchased our home without so much as a conversation and told me I should be grateful my name was even listed on the deed of the fixer-upper Victorian he found in an up-and-coming area on the Cambridge border.

We are the new wave of gentrification, the eager millennial homeowners who have rapidly transformed a suburb once known as "Slumerville" into "The Brooklyn of Boston." It may not be as bustling as Downtown Crossing or as hip as the ever-evolving Seaport... but it's close enough to enjoy everything the city has to offer while quiet enough to lead a relatively private life.

The perfect place to raise a family.

Not that I'd know anything about that.

I'm winding my way through the dense crowd toward an impressive display of fresh herbs and spices when something slams into my legs with the strength of a small rhinoceros. I glance down to find a tow-headed toddler tugging at the thin fabric of my yoga pants to steady herself. There's a pink bow in her corn-husk blonde hair and a tiny pair of red sneakers on her feet. My gaze gets stuck on her hands, splayed out like little starfish just above my knees, and I feel something pierce every chamber of my heart.

"Oh! Watch where you're going, sweetie!" The mother apologizes profusely as the father scoops his small daughter into his arms. Both beam at me sheepishly. "So sorry about that..."

I smile politely and try to pretend I'm not struggling to breathe properly. Suddenly, I'm desperate to get home. To get out of this crowd, away from these picture-perfect families that remind me of everything my life was supposed to be. To shut myself inside my car before I start weeping in full view of the artisanal maple syrup stand.

Pathetic, much?

I race for the street as fast as my legs can carry me, flip flops smacking the pavement with each hurried stride, grocery bag swinging by my side. The throng falls away and with it the high-pitched sound of children's laughter as I round the corner onto a blessedly empty stretch of sidewalk. When my low-slung, two-seater convertible comes into view, I breathe a sigh of undeniable relief and beeline for it.

I'm so intent on getting home, I don't even glance around the street as I load my groceries into the trunk. The feeling creeps over me so slowly, at first I don't even register it. Not until the hair on the back of my neck begins to stand on-end. Not until my body begins to hum with that odd, prickly sensation, zipping along my skin like an electric current.

I know, without turning to look, that there are eyes on me.

Someone's watching.

Heart hammering faster, mind whirling with dreadful possibilities, I slam the trunk closed and try not to let my sudden tension show as I take slow steps toward the driver's side door. I cast a surreptitious glance around the quiet street for signs of danger.

Unfortunately if anyone is, in fact, stalking me, they don't make their presence known. Errr, *that*, or I'm simply not astute enough to pick them out amid the collection of nondescript sedans and SUVs parked on this block. To my eyes, things look cheerful as ever in the summer sunshine — exploding flower boxes, quaint brick, outdoor cafes, tree-lined sidewalks. Nothing remotely ominous.

You're just rattled from this morning, I tell myself, dismissing my own overzealous imagination as I climb into my car and grip the wheel with tense fingers. *Calm down, crazy pants.*

By the time I turn onto Merriweather Street and pull into my driveway ten minutes later, I've nearly managed to convince myself that the strange sensation was nothing but a fleeting paranoid delusion. A momentary lapse in sanity. A temporary breach in my otherwise calm, cool, collected mentality.

These assurances would, of course, be far more effective if not for the fact that I make it halfway up my front walkway only to watch as a large, hulking figure detaches from the shadows of my wraparound porch and steps into my path.

"Well, if it isn't Shelby Hunt," Lefty says, eyes glittering victoriously.

My grocery bag falls to the ground, exploding on impact. Avocados and tomatoes roll in all directions like tumbleweeds in a windy Western movie as I backpedal away — right into something rock solid. Something that feels a lot like a man's chest.

Righty.

The scream building in my throat never makes it past my lips; a large hand slaps itself over my mouth before a single squeak can escape. I feel my body go airborne as a beefy arm winds around my waist like I weigh no more than a damn football and starts hauling me up my front steps.

Shit.

"THIS REALLY ISN'T NECESSARY!"

My protests fall on deaf ears. They aren't listening to me — not now, to my plaintive appeals. Not ten minutes ago, when they forced me into my own home against my will as I screamed bloody murder into the palm of Righty's hand, praying someone on my dead-end street would notice me being abducted and call the police.

Of course the one time I'm actually in need of nosy neighbors, they're nowhere to be found...

Righty adds another loop of duct tape around my arm, securing it tighter to the sturdy maple chair at the head of the massive dining room table Paul and I picked out seven years ago and have never once eaten an actual meal at. I suppose I should be happy it's finally getting some use — if only for what I assume will be a session of interrogation.

Or torture.

I flex my muscles against the tape, testing its strength. It doesn't budge. I'm officially stuck until they decide to cut me loose.

"You lied to us, earlier." Lefty doesn't sound pleased with me. Actually, he sounds decidedly *displeased* as he bends down to look into my face. His dark brown eyes are terrifying. "Not a fan of liars."

"And I'm not particularly a fan of being kidnapped. We all make sacrifices.."

"You've got a smart mouth." He leans closer and I flinch back in my seat. I try to, anyway. I can barely move with my wrists and ankles strapped so tightly to the chair. "If you're not inclined to use that mouth to cooperate, there are some other uses I'm sure we could explore..."

My face goes pale.

"I can see from your expression you don't like the sound of that alternative. If you tell us what we want to know, we won't touch you..." He strokes a finger down the exposed column of my neck, his eyes dropping to my cleavage. "*Much.*"

"Get your hands off me or I'm not telling you shit," I hiss, struggling to escape his creeping fingers.

Smirking as though this is all some big game, he steps back and leans against the wall near his partner, who's sprawled on the plush cushions of my window seat like we're about to sit down for tea. For a long while, they both stare at me in silence, arms crossed over their chests, expressions unreadable. Simple enough, as intimidation tactics go, but effective as hell; my heart picks up speed and I feel my palms going clammy as the silence drags on, waiting for the other shoe to drop.

"What is it you want from me?" I finally force myself to ask. I'm surprised my voice comes out so steady.

"Like we said before — we're looking for Paul."

"I told you already, I don't know where he is."

Lefty looks doubtful. "He's your husband."

"We're separated. We have been for months." My chin jerks higher. "I have nothing to do with— with— *whatever* it is he's done to piss you off."

"The thing is..." There's a flash of rage in the depths of Lefty's dark eyes — the first emotion I've ever seen from him. Frankly, I think I prefer his icy indifference. "Your husband took something that belongs to our boss. We want it back. And he hasn't exactly been what you'd call..."

"Cooperative," Righty finishes.

"Right. *Cooperative.*" Lefty smirks, but it's colder than a glacier. "We think he might need a bit of cajoling. Just to help him make the right choice."

Okay. I'm not liking the sound of this.

Not *at all*.

"Look, I already told you I don't know where Paul is. I don't have anything to do with him anymore, so whatever you're planning to do to me..."

"We aren't doing anything to you. We just need you to deliver a little message for us."

Relief sluices through me. "Fine! I'll tell him whatever you want, just let me go and—"

"Can't do that." Righty's head shakes.

"Why not? I already agreed to deliver your damn message!"

Lefty smirks. "*You* are the message."

"*What?*"

There's a ripping sound as Righty tears a large piece of duct tape off the roll and steps forward. "When your husband comes home and finds you, he'll know just how serious we are about getting our product back."

"But— you don't understand! He *won't* find me!" I yell, eyes widening as I watch that piece of duct tape coming closer, closer, closer, like a poisonous snake about to strike. I jerk my head to the side, trying to evade him, but he grabs my chin with bruising fingers and holds me still. "I told you — he doesn't live here anymore! If you leave me like this I'm — *Mmmmm! MMMMM!*"

My protests cut off into muffled, indistinct cries as he shoves the swathe of tape across the bottom half of my face. My lips move frantically against the sticky backing, trying like hell to make them understand that their plan won't work, that Paul won't ever get their stupid message because he no longer has a key to this house or a place in my life... but it's no use. My screams are in vain. Useless and unintelligible.

Lefty leans in, meeting my furious gaze, and smiles stiffly. "You tell Paul he has one week to return what he took from Alexei," he murmurs, stroking one finger slowly down my cheek. He's so near, I can feel each of his breaths puffing hot against my face. "If he doesn't... we'll be back to pay you another visit. And next time, we won't be quite so *polite* when it comes to his pretty wife."

Snapping my head forward, I try to head-butt him, but he pulls away before I can make contact.

"Nice try." His eyes gleam with dark amusement. "I must say, part of me hopes your husband doesn't cooperate. You and I could have a lot of fun together, *malishka...*"

I glare up at him. My blood is boiling with fury and, much as I hate to acknowledge it, fear. Because I know, if they walk away and leave me here, tied to a damn antique dining chair with my very existence contingent upon my shit-head husband's decisions...

I'm a dead woman.

I try desperately to convey this message with my eyes.

You can't leave me like this!

Paul doesn't even live here!

No one is going to check on me!

Unfortunately, neither of them seems even remotely inclined to decipher the distress in my eyes. Without another word to me, they turn and walk out of the dining room, their heavy boots sounding sharply against the glossy hardwood floors I refinished this spring, just so I had something to keep my endless days occupied.

"Mmmm! *Mmmm!*" I yell against the tape. "*MMMMM!*"

But the only answer is the click of my front door, followed by thick, pervasive silence.

For a moment I just sit there, stunned into submission, wondering how the hell this has happened. Wishing I could close my eyes and re-do this entire day, preferably not getting out of bed at all. Praying that it's all a terrible dream from which I'll jolt awake at any moment, only to find myself tangled in sweat-drenched sheets.

The bite of duct tape against my bare wrists and ankles pointedly assures me that this is no dream. I'm awake. This is happening.

I'm totally screwed.

My purse mocks me from the center of the table where Lefty dropped it after forcing me into this chair. It's far out of reach — as is the cellphone I know is sitting at the bottom beside my wallet and keys. I glance around the room, looking for anything that might possibly help get me out of this situation, but there's nothing except antique furniture and gold foil art-deco wallpaper. No convenient letter openers or sharp-edged knickknacks I could use to cut myself out of this mess.

Damn my aversion to clutter.

The bright light streaming through the sheer curtains tells me it's probably close to noon. I spend at least an hour thrashing, attempting to get free, trying like hell to scoot the heavy chair from its spot. My bonds don't loosen. I barely budge more than an inch, and succeed only in frustrating myself to the point of tears.

If my life were a movie, I suppose I'd be the sort of heroine who knocked the chair over, splintering it into pieces and freeing herself in the process. As we've already established, my life is *not* a movie. Even if I could topple my chair (which, for the record, I can't; trust me, I tried) I doubt the impact would break its joints.

Say what you will about American Colonial pieces... they're sturdy as hell.

When my muscles are exhausted and aching, I try screaming for help, hoping a neighbor might hear me through the open bay window on the other side of the room. My morose, muffled wails barely permeate the tape, let alone reach the street.

No one can hear me. Or, if they can, they don't care enough to come investigate. (I'm not sure which alternative is more upsetting.)

The sunlight morphs from bright white to mellow yellow as the hours pass by and afternoon yields to early evening. I watch the shadows change, lengthening and growing as twilight approaches, and shiver at the thought of spending an entire night sitting here alone in the darkness.

My captors said they'll be back in a week, if Paul fails to return whatever it is he took from their boss. *One week.* Might as well be a lifetime. I've read enough books about wilderness survival to remember the Rule of Threes.

Three minutes without air, three days without water, three weeks without food.

Good news? I might not starve to death.

Bad news? I'm still going to die — either from dehydration or mortification. Because the fact that I'm here, asscheeks going numb from sitting so long, stomach rumbling with hunger, about to pee my yoga pants because *oh my freaking god* it's been hours since I last encountered a bathroom, all due to my asshole husband getting himself into trouble with some seriously scary dudes...

That's just pathetic.

I hear a beep from the bowels of my bag: my phone is dying. Not that it matters — I can't reach it with my hands bound, anyway. For a while, as I listen to the rhythmic beeps of the depleting battery, I entertain the deluded thought that someone will call and check in on me. That, when I fail to answer my phone, they'll get in their car and come over to make sure everything is A-OK at the Hunt household.

After all, a gal can't just fall of the face of the earth without anyone bothering to notice...

Right?

The reassurances sound thin to my own ears. The truth is, the few family members still in my life reside three states away and don't keep in touch if it's not a major holiday — sometimes, not even then. As a freelance graphic designer, I don't have any co-workers to notice my absence in an office cubicle come Monday morning. And my friends are all far too busy with their own lives to realize mine might be in jeopardy.

Phoebe's off on her honeymoon with her new husband. Gemma is due to have her baby any time now, confined strictly to bed rest until she goes into labor. Chrissy has two toddlers that keep her occupied every minute of the day. Lila is working full-time as a nanny while balancing her brand new relationship. And Zoe is halfway around the world by now, sailing off into the sunset with her fiancé. It's safe to say, "Check in on Shelby!" isn't the most important item on their packed to-do lists.

I'm officially on my own, here.

Night falls, and with it the temperature. I shiver in the dark, wishing I could summon the strength even to cry about my own miserable luck, but I'm too tired. Every bone in my body aches like I've been thrown down a flight of stairs. Ten straight hours of stress have sapped my energy levels completely. To make matters worse, when all is said and done, I'll probably have a UTI from holding my pee for this long... if I manage to survive, that is.

Straining my ears, I listen to sounds from the street as my neighbors return home for the night — slamming car doors, muffled laughter. I imagine them eating dinner, watching tv, climbing the stairs to go to sleep. Eventually, the whole block falls silent as lights are doused and eyes slip closed.

All my life, I've felt invisible. As though no one sees the real Shelby Hunt — merely the illusion I've put forth for so many years, desperate to show the world a brave face instead of a tear-stained one.

The perfect woman in the perfect house with the perfect marriage.

As the hours trickle by, silent and unyielding, I realize my well-crafted facade of perfection will be my own undoing.

No one is looking for me.

No one is coming for me.

I am alone in a prison of my own making.

I have built my walls so high, isolated myself so thoroughly, that even my closest friends and family will not seek me out when a day, or a week, or a month goes by without contact.

I will slip out of existence as easily as a ring off the finger of a cheating husband at a seedy bar whose wife waits at home with dinner on the table.

I am Shelby Hunt.

The perfect woman.

The perfect ghost.

CHAPTER 3

AVOCA-DON'T

I'M NOT sure what wakes me.

Perhaps the stirring of the curtains as wind blows through the half-closed bay window. Perhaps some distant sound — the jiggling of a doorknob, the thudding of foot-steps on a wood porch. Perhaps nothing remotely so dramatic — merely the dull ache in my bones from being stuck in the same upright position for such a long time.

It doesn't matter.

All I know is, my eyes crack open and I'm abruptly awake, heart pounding, senses on high alert. Ignoring the stiffness of my neck, I glance around the dark room. It's the middle of the night. There's no sound from the street, no light except the pale moonbeams shining through the skylights in the vaulted ceiling overhead.

I give my chafed wrists a halfhearted tug and find — *shocker!* — they haven't magically loosened while I slept. I'm surprised I managed to fall asleep in the first place, propped up like this; I typically have a hard enough time dozing off each night in my plush king-sized bed.

A loud creak from outside makes my mind go blank. My

head whips around toward the sound, eyes widening as they study the large bay window where a set of gauzy white curtains flutter gently in the breeze. I tell myself it was just the house settling. Or maybe a raccoon in search of some dinner in the neighbors trash bins.

Don't panic over one squeaky floorboard, Shelby.

My attempts at mollification go up in smoke when I hear the porch creak again, louder this time. This is no nocturnal critter. Someone's on my porch, just beyond the view of that window. My heart lurches into overdrive as I hear yet another groan — another *footstep*, I realize belatedly.

I can't move, can't run. Can't even scream. All I can do is wait for my own worst nightmares to be confirmed.

It doesn't take long.

He steps into view a few seconds later — a large, man-shaped silhouette, clear as day through the thin curtains. There's no doubt in my mind it's a man; one well-trained in stealth, judging by the way he moves. Even from here, I recognize the coiled power of his muscles, the utter alertness of his body, the broadness of his shoulders.

That's not Paul, I think, picturing my husband's lean stature. *And it's definitely not Righty or Lefty. They wouldn't be back already. So... who the hell is this guy?*

My heart is pounding so hard, I fear it heart might explode as the man hesitates just outside the open window. A thousand possibilities about burglars and rapists and murderers spin through my mind as I watch his large hand extend outward to the frame. As he slowly pushes the opening wider, thoughts clang around inside my skull like a pingpong balls of panic.

If he's a burglar, he's in for the surprise of his life...

His leg straddles the sill, his head ducks down, he

scrambles nimbly across the cushions of my pretty window seat...

And then, he's in my house.

Ten freaking feet from me.

Big and scary and, let's face it, more than likely up to no good. (In my experience, people rarely climb through windows in the dead of the night without nefarious intentions.)

Breaths coming in short bursts through my nose, I struggle to hold off a panic attack as my eyes move over the shadowed stranger. He's tall. *Very* tall. So far over six feet, he makes me look petite at five foot seven. And he's muscular. Not in the steroid-induced manner of my earlier assailants; in a way that tells me he knows his way around a weight room and probably doesn't have a single ounce of extra body fat lurking beneath that black, fitted t-shirt he's wearing.

It's too dark to make out his facial features, but I notice he's got one hand resting on what seems to be a gun holster as his head sweeps from left to right, scanning the room. He jolts visibly when he spots me.

"*Christ.*"

His tone low and smooth as velvet. Just that one word sends a not-altogether-unpleasant shiver down my spine.

Shelby! He's probably here to murder you! Now is not the time to be turned on!

Before I can blink, he's across the room — kneeling before me, his face a half-foot from mine. He reaches out and I barely have time to brace myself for imminent death, let alone attempt to struggle away when he peels the tape off my lips in a sharp tug that makes my skin sting like a bitch.

"*Ow!*"

Cursing like a sailor, I blink back tears as I haul desperate gulps of air into my lungs. Hours of breathing through my nose have left me oxygen-deprived. It takes a long moment before the light-headedness abates and I'm able to breathe normally again.

"Are you all right?"

At the sound of his voice, I glance up sharply — straight into a set of the darkest eyes I've ever seen. I suck in an unsteady breath when they lock on mine. They're like two bottomless pits inside his face. A face which, now that it's so close, appears remarkably familiar.

And remarkably handsome.

Mind reeling with adrenaline and shock and something else I can't quite name, I squint at my savior in the dim light, trying to place him in my memories. Try as I might, I can't recall where, exactly, I've seen that chiseled jawline or that aristocratic nose or that lush mouth surrounded by that seriously sexy scruff he's got going on... but I'd swear on my life I've seen this man somewhere before.

Maybe in a fashion magazine because, hot damn, *those are some serious cheekbones...*

His jaw is clenched tight as his gaze moves over my features, scanning for visible signs of trauma. I realize his large hands are still cupping my face, stroking my chapped skin with callused fingertips as if to erase the pain caused by the tape. That sensation — gentleness in the wake of violence — is enough to make the breath catch inside my throat.

"Are you all right?" he asks again, after a long moment.

"Assuming you're not here to kill, rob, or rape me? I'm just *peachy*," I whisper, my voice cracking on the lie. I'm so far from *all right*, I don't even have words to convey it.

I think I see a flare of humor in his eyes before they drop

away from mine. His hands leave my face and he reaches down to slide a knife from inside his boot. I can't help flinching when he flicks it open, the lethal blade catching the moonlight like a mirror. My muscles tense up, momentarily petrified by the prospect of my apparent savior carving me into pieces.

"Don't!" I squeak out mortifyingly.

He registers my sudden panic and goes totally still. Knife held aloft, his eyes find mine in the dark again. When he speaks, his velvet voice is grave. "I'm not here to hurt you, Ms. Hunt."

My eyes widen. *He knows me?*

I wait for him to explain, but he doesn't. He merely pauses for a long moment, holding my stare, then says, "You can trust me."

I don't know how to explain it — whether it's that look on his face or the sincerity in his tone that sways my opinion — but I do. I trust him. Possibly because I don't have any other choice, seeing as I'm stuck in this chair, entirely at his mercy... but mostly because there's something about his presence that tells me he means it when he says he's here to help. I look into his dark eyes and for once, my internal bullshit alarm is silent.

If he was going to hurt you, he would've done it by now, a small voice whispers at the back of my mind. *Why bother removing the duct tape or making small talk if he's merely here to kill you or rob you blind?*

The panic bleeds out of me and I give a small nod of affirmation. With a neat jerk of his blade, he slices through the bonds at my wrists, then bends down to do the same for my ankles. The tape falls away and, eager for freedom after so long in captivity, I immediately rise from my seat... only to sway off balance when blood floods my head in a woozy rush. The room around me is spinning and I'm far too light-headed to find my feet again.

Shit! Is that the floor, hurling high-speed at my face?

I brace myself for impact, but it never comes. Instead, two arms go around me, catching me midair. Before I can fathom what's happening, I've been swept off my feet and find myself cradled against a broad chest like a child. Head spinning — this time for entirely different reasons — I'm too stunned even to struggle as he carries me out of the dining room, toward the dove gray sectional in the adjacent parlor.

It's strange but... his arms feel terrifyingly good around me. Safe and solid and entirely unexpected — like stumbling upon a storm cellar in the midst of an emotional tornado. Everything in my life appears to be coming apart at the seams... but he's holding me. And for just one moment, his arms offer temporary reprieve from the fear and shock and anger swirling inside me in an uncontrollable vortex.

Under normal circumstances, I'd never allow a stranger to carry me like this. To comfort me like some... some... *weakling* in need of coddling. Surely, on any other day, I wouldn't find myself so affected by the feeling of his strong arms looped beneath my knees and back, his broad chest bracing my head like a cushion each time he takes a step.

Even if it has been years since anyone held me this close...

But these circumstances are anything but normal and this day is not any other day. As he carries me, I have to fight the urge to let my eyes slide closed. To absorb his strength, his heat. To set my breaths by his rhythm. To use the steady thrumming of his pulse as a metronome for my own racing heart.

It makes no sense at all, but every inclination inside me

is screaming out for me to take comfort in the circle of this stranger's arms.

This is just transference, the sensible part of my brain chides. *You're redirecting your own feelings of fear and adrenaline into gratitude for this guy, since he saved you. It'll fade, once you calm down. You'll see.*

If I could, I'd roll my eyes at myself.

How dare I lecture me? Who do I think I am, some kind of adult?

He sets me down on the sofa like I weigh no more than one of the down-stuffed cushions. He's not even winded. I keep my eyes on his as he steps away, creating a careful distance between us. The feeling of his arms around me still tingles through my bloodstream like whiskey.

"Who are y—" I start to ask, but the question dies in my throat as the stranger abruptly straightens to full height and pulls his gun from its holster.

"I'm going to sweep the house."

My mouth parts. "But—"

"Keep quiet. And don't move."

Though he speaks no louder than a whisper, there's no denying it's an order. Clearly, this is a man unaccustomed to being disobeyed. My eyes strain to make out his shape in the darkness as he walks out of the room, his footsteps inaudible. For such a large man, he moves with a catlike grace that speaks to years of training. Everything from his posture to the way he holds his gun — arms extended, barrel pointed to the floor — practically screams law enforcement.

Who the hell is this guy?!

An undercover cop?

A rogue P.I.?

In either case, I suppose I should feel marginally better that the cavalry has arrived to rescue me. In fact, I should be thrilled to discover I won't die duct taped to a chair in my dining room, only to be found after days or weeks or months by a concerned letter carrier who notices the Hunts haven't emptied their mailbox in quite some time...

Unfortunately, it's hard to be thrilled about much of anything when every square inch of your body aches, you've got a killer headache from a full day of dehydration, and there's an excruciating pressure in your bladder after nearly twelve hours of holding it.

Alone in the dark parlor, my eyes dart to the bathroom door located off the hallway to my left. I consider making a break for it — I'm not exaggerating when I tell you I have to pee worse than the time I got trapped in a hotel elevator for five straight hours and nearly used my purse as a urinal in front of several unwitting strangers — but before I have a chance, Mr. Macho strides back into the room, holstering his gun.

"All clear."

My brows lift. "*Obviously*. They left as soon as they tied me up. If you'd given me a chance, I could've told you that. Would've saved you a walking tour of my house."

He stares at me blankly, saying nothing.

I prattle on. "I mean, not that I'm an expert or anything... but I'm pretty positive bad guys generally don't hang around after breaking and entering." My head tilts. "Breaking and entering followed by abducting and duct taping, if we're being specific."

I expect him to laugh. Chuckle, even.

He doesn't.

"Jeeze, tough crowd," I mutter, rolling my eyes.

He sighs, as though I'm profoundly annoying. "Ms. Hunt, I need you to tell me exactly what happened that led to your..." He pauses. "Abducting and duct taping, as it were."

"Well, buster, first I need *you* to tell *me* exactly what led to *you* climbing through *my* window and rescuing me." I cross my arms over my chest and level him with a look. I wish I could make out his features clearly, but it's still so dark in here. "I mean... Who the heck are you? How did you know I was here? Furthermore, how do I know you aren't some psycho working with Righty and Lefty? Huh?"

"Righty and Lefty?" he mutters quizzically.

"Yep. I'd give you a pithy nickname too, but frankly I've run out of directions. Oh! I suppose you could be North or South... though I'm pretty sure the Kardashian clan has laid claimed to all of those. *East? West?* I can never remember. Pop culture isn't my forte."

His dark brows furrow. "Did you hit your head?"

"No!" Heat rushes to my cheeks as I realize I may, in fact, be rambling. I blame it on the sleep deprivation. That, or an impending anxiety attack. It's hard to say for certain. "Look, bucko, all I know is, one minute I'm walking up my front steps with a bag of groceries, the next I'm grabbed by two giant thugs and dragged into my own house kicking and screaming. Don't believe me? Check the front walk. I'm sure it's a shrine to my Farmers Market haul still scattered across the front stoop." I shake my head. "Honestly, what a waste of perfectly good burrata cheese."

"Ms. Hunt—"

"And do you know how long it takes to find six *perfectly ripe* avocados? Those babies have an optimal shelf life of about thirty-six seconds before they turn to rotten brown mush!" I scowl. "There goes the neighborhood! Along with my plans for avocado toast."

"Ms. Hunt—"

"If you ask me, they could've at least picked up my groceries after kidnapping me. Set them on the counter or something, like gentlemen. But *nooo*. Apparently that would be far too much to ask."

"How... inconsiderate," he says haltingly, looking at me like I'm nuts.

Which, let's face it, I totally am.

"Tell me about it!" I'm breathing hard now, my tone rising with anger and something else. It might be shock, but I decide not to examine it too closely. "I mean, kidnapping is one thing. But *avocado abandonment*? That's a capital offense!"

"Hunt—"

"You can call me Shelby. You know, since you've just saved my life and all." I throw my hands up in the air. "I guess it's true what they say — there's no honor amongst thieves. *Especially* when it comes to produce. Chivalry really is dead... as are the hydrangeas I bought at an obscene markup. Because the Farmers Market is cute and all, but *boy oh boy* do they price gouge like nobody's busin—"

"*Hey.*"

I blink. Hard.

The nonsensical words I've been spouting evaporate on my tongue because, quite suddenly, he's *there*. On the floor crouching before me. His big hands cup my face, so gently it steals my breath, and his eyes lock on mine. They're so dark, I'm instantly transfixed — sucked into his orbit like an untethered planet falling into a black hole. I don't even try to look away; his gravity is too strong to escape.

"You're all right," he says lowly, his strong fingers flexing against my cheeks. "You're safe, now. Just breathe."

My mouth opens, but there are no words. Just a slow-dawning horror filling the vacuum left behind as my panic ebbs away.

I was kidnapped, I realize, feeling strangely numb. *Manhandled and mistreated. In my own home. In the place where I sleep. In the place I'm supposed to be safest.*

I feel tears pricking at my eyes. It takes all my remaining strength not to let them fall.

"Breathe," he orders again.

And I do.

In and out.

Nose and mouth.

Timing my breaths with his.

I'm not sure how long we stay like that — his hands on my cheeks, our eyes locked together. Long enough for my heart to stop thundering inside my chest. Long enough for my semi-hysterical rambles to fade and reason to return. Long enough for my cheeks to heat with embarrassment over the scene I've just caused in front of this stranger who's done nothing but rescue my crazy ass. And, as a thank you, I let him witness a full-fledged panic attack. About produce, of all things.

Way to go, Shelby.

"I'm sorry," I whisper, mortified.

He just stares at me.

"I..." I avert my eyes from his and pull back, out of his hold. "I..."

"It's fine," he says gruffly, as though he's not quite sure how to be gentle but is trying his damndest. He rises to his feet and shoves his hands in his pockets, blowing out a sharp breath. "Why don't you just start at the beginning."

My eyes flicker up to his for a brief second. "I..."

In the dark, his eyebrows are two black slashes. They lift in question, waiting for me to speak.

"I... I have to pee!" I blurt.

Before he can say another word, I hop to my feet and race for the bathroom. Slamming the door closed behind me, I collapse back against it, breathing hard. After *that* humiliating experience, I think I'd prefer slowly starving to death in my dining room chair to ever again facing a man who's witnessed the true depths of my insanity.

Congrats, looney tunes. Of all the embarrassing shit you've ever done... this truly takes the cake.

I drop my face into my hands and groan softly.

The true irony of it all?

I don't even have to pee, anymore.

CHAPTER 4

GLUTEUS MAXIMUS

IT TAKES me a while to muster the courage to leave the bathroom. But after fifteen minutes — during which I've peed, washed my face, combed my hair, brushed my teeth, and seriously contemplated the use of thirty-minute whitening strips because what can I say, stalling is my varsity sport — I officially run out of bathroom-related activities. I also realize no matter how long I stall, Mr. Macho is still going to be out there, all brooding and bossy, waiting for me.

Sigh.

When I finally open the door and step into the hallway, I find he's turned on the lights. Blinking at the sudden brightness, I walk slowly back into the parlor, rubbing self-consciously at my chafed wrists. He's standing with his back to me, peering out the front window at the street from behind a curtain. He speaks without turning around.

"We should get going."

I flinch to a stop. "What?"

He turns to look at me, arms crossed over his chest, messy black hair falling into his eyes. My gaze drags from

SO WRONG IT'S RIGHT   43

the badass motorcycle boots on his feet up two muscular legs encased in fitted black jeans, past the gun holstered at his belt, over a seriously sculpted chest, and, finally, to his face. My mouth falls open when I see it in the full light for the first time.

"*You!*" I say, recognition blazing through me. "I know you!"

He doesn't move a muscle, but his eyes cut to mine. I see now that they aren't black or brown, like I originally thought, but the darkest shade of indigo. Like a spill of navy ink, piercing and intense as they pin me to the spot.

"You were at Phoebe and Nate's wedding last month!" I exclaim.

My mind spins in circles as I try to reconcile the fact that this stranger is not such a stranger after all.

Dear lord.

I don't know whether to be relieved, confused, or even *more* embarrassed than I was before to learn that the man who's come to my rescue isn't some altruistic law enforcement official or chivalrous crime-fighting good samaritan intent on keeping Somerville's streets safe...

Nope.

He's a man I've met before.

A man whose path I crossed mere weeks ago.

He was the freaking mystery guest I spotted at the wedding! The one whose dark blue eyes I kept trying to catch during slow songs, when all my friends were paired off with their men. The one I couldn't seem to tear my stare away from, even after he almost caught me looking.

Twice.

(Thankfully, he seemed totally oblivious to my attention.)

True, I was drunk on champagne at the time... but I

distinctly remember him standing by the bar, sipping a low-ball glass of whiskey and chatting with several of the badasses who work for Nate at Knox Investigations. No amount of alcohol would be enough to forget those blue-black eyes.

The same eyes that are now fixed on me, unblinking and rife with intensity.

"You're Nate's friend," I say, still staring at him. I have a feeling my cheeks are the color of the doomed tomatoes I bought yesterday morning. "The cop."

He doesn't confirm or deny my words. He just stares at me, jaw working with tension, muscles straining against his black v-neck. It's a bit unnerving.

"Well?" I ask, brows raised. "I'm right, aren't I?"

"Whether or not we occasionally run in the same social circles doesn't concern me," he mutters, shoving a hand through his messy black hair. "We're leaving."

"We?"

"You. Me. *We*." His brows lift. "If I talk any slower, we'll be going backwards here, Hunt."

"If you think I'm going anywhere with you, you are sorely mistaken, mister!"

He blinks at me.

"I mean... Officer. Constable. Deputy. All due respect intended. Obviously." I bite my lip in the vain hope it might shut me up.

He's doing that empty-eyed stare again — the one that simultaneously says so much and so little.

"Please don't cuff me. Uncontrollable rambling is a plague, not a punishable offense," I joke lamely, trying to lighten the mood.

I think I see a flash of humor in his eyes, but they cut away from me too fast to be certain — straight out the window, toward the street. His posture is still tense, as though he's on high alert for the arrival of an impending threat.

"Look..." I haul in a breath and strive for civility. "I don't know you. Generally, I'd be inclined to give you the benefit of the doubt despite that fact, seeing as you're a friend of a friend... and you just so happen to have saved my ass from certain death by duct tape. But you're not giving me a lot to go on, here. You do realize that, right?"

His only response is the slight shift of his shoulder muscles beneath the fabric of his t-shirt.

I swallow a frustrated scream. "All I'm saying is, a little insight would be nice. You know, seeing as my whole world has flipped upside down in the past twelve hours and I'm not even remotely sure how or why you're connected to all of this. But clearly you know more than you're saying — which, for the record, is *nothing* — so it would be really freaking great if you could fill me in. If you do, I promise I'll stop rambling and leave you alone. Possibly forever. Because I'll likely be dead at the hands of two enormous thugs when they inevitably track me down again."

He glances back at me. "If I thought you'd actually shut up for more than thirty seconds, I might just take you up on that trade, Hunt."

"You're an ass."

"Duly noted." His tone is flat. "You ready to leave?"

"You can't be serious."

"As a heart attack, Hunt."

"And where do you plan on taking me, officer?" I snort. "Let me guess! *Down to the station!?*"

His eyes narrow a shade. "You have five minutes. After that, I'm putting you over my shoulder and carrying you out

of here, whether or not your shit is in a bag and your shoes
are on your feet."

I blink at him, mouth agape. "Am I on some sort of
hidden camera reality show? Did Phoebe and Nate put you
up to this? Or Gemma and Chase? Is it some elaborate
prank? An early thirtieth birthday gift, perhaps?" My nose
scrunches up at the thought. "Though, frankly, why anyone
would want to *celebrate* turning thirty is beyond my abilities
to fathom..."

He doesn't dignify my questions with a response.

"Please tell me this is a prank," I plead weakly.

"I could, but I don't make a habit of saying shit that isn't
true." His brows pull in. "Speaking of shit I've said —
could've sworn I told you to start packing."

My spine stiffens. "Do you even *hear* yourself?! Are you
seriously *ordering* me to leave my house with you? Without
giving me even the slightest explanation as to why?"

"I'll explain later."

"No, you'll explain *now*," I counter hotly. "I want to
know why you're here, how you knew to come looking for
me, and where the hell you plan on taking me in the middle
of the night that requires me to break out my freaking duffle
bag!"

"Look, Hunt, the men you encountered earlier will be
back. We can't be here when that happens." His eyes flicker
to the window again before returning to settle on my face.
There's no warmth in his expression. "So walk your stubborn little ass upstairs and pack your damn bag. *Now*."

I tense up at his bossy tone. *Aren't saviors supposed to
be gentleman?* He's certainly not one. It figures, my knight-
in-shining-armor is more of a jackass-in-faded-denim.

Story of my freaking life.

My arms cross over my chest but, otherwise, I don't

move a muscle. Call it pig-headedness, call it stubbornness...
I have a tendency to dig my heels in when I'm feeling
backed into a corner. It's not my best trait but, like I've just
said, I'm nearly thirty so...

Too late to change my dastardly ways, now.

"You wouldn't actually dare carry me out of my own
house against my will." I scoff as though the very idea is
ludicrous.

His eyes gleam with a scary intensity. "Oh, Hunt.
Try me."

I go pale.

He takes a small step toward me and I fight the urge to
shuffle backward. "By my count, you've got just under four
minutes left. Waste any more fighting, you're gonna end up
with nothing but the clothes on your back. Don't cry to me
when you spend the next few days in a hot pink sports bra
and bare feet."

I glower at him to hide the fact that I'm getting a little
nervous. Because this doesn't feel like a prank. And he
doesn't really seem like he's joking. Not at all. In fact... he
seems pretty damn serious about this whole *pack a bag,
we're leaving* crap.

But he can't *possibly* be serious.

Right?

"Three minutes, Hunt."

"My name is *Shelby*," I snap automatically. "Don't act
like you don't know exactly who I am."

A muscle jumps in his cheek. He's pissed.

Good. That makes two of us.

I take a step toward him, eyes narrowing. "And I know
you, even if you won't admit it. You're Colin Something-or-
Other."

"Conor."

"Right, that's what I said. Conor Something-or-Other."

His jaw clenches tightly. "Gallagher."

"Conor Gallagher." I smirk. "Could you *be* more Irish?"

"Christ. We don't have time for this." Scowling, he pushes away from the window, grabs me by the hand, and starts dragging me along behind him as he walks from the room.

Oh...

Did I say *walks*?

More like *strides*.

Those long-ass legs of his cross the room so fast, I'm practically running to keep up as we pass through the foyer and head up the grand staircase, taking the steps two at a time.

"Hey!" I hiss, tugging at my hand. It's no use — his grip is unshakeable. "Let me go, asshole!"

He leads me straight into the master bedroom — apparently he took detailed notes during his brief tour, earlier, because he seems freakishly familiar with the layout of my house — and practically drags me into my walk-in closet.

"Two minutes," he growls, tossing my brown leather duffle bag at my feet. "*Pack.*"

"And how the hell am I supposed to do that with you holding onto me like a caveman?" I yank on my arm again. My already-sore wrist is smarting so fiercely, I'm stunned to find tears suddenly glossing over my eyes.

Dammit. Don't cry, Shelby. Your street cred is hanging by a thread already.

I try to turn away to hide the tears, but it's too late. Conor notices my wet eyes — I get the distinct impression there's not much he *doesn't* notice — and drops my damaged wrist so fast, you'd think I had leprosy. Cursing lowly under his breath, he takes a hasty step away and props his large frame against a nearby rack of shoes.

From the corner of my eye I watch him running a hand through his messy hair and, for the briefest instant, think I spot a flare of remorse in those unreadable indigo eyes. It's gone so fast, I convince myself it was never there at all.

Conor Gallagher isn't the remorseful type.

I bet he's never apologized for a damn thing in his whole damn life. The air of alpha male arrogance surrounding him is so thick, I doubt he can even see his own faults, let alone own up to them.

His voice jerks me back to earth. "I feel obligated to remind you you've got exactly one minute left before we're out the door. You gonna keep staring at me like you're wondering about my star sign or are you gonna pack your damn suitcase?"

"Don't flatter yourself. I was merely trying to see up close and personal whether there is, in fact, a 666 engraved on your skull." I lean in, squinting intently. "I *think* I see it... then again, it could just be a frown line... seeing as you have an Olympic Gold Medal in Scowling."

"Cute," he says in a flat tone that suggests I'm the farthest thing from *cute* on the whole planet. "*Pack.*"

"You're relentless, you know that?"

"And you're a pain in the damn ass."

"Only when I'm teaching a barre class. What can I say? I really like to work the glutes."

I think he actually might throttle me, if the steam leaking from his ears is any indication And the feeling is *definitely* mutual. For a long moment, we're both silent — glaring at each other in mutual dislike, neither prepared to cave to the other's demands.

"Thirty seconds," he warns softly. Funny — I never knew *soft* could be *scary* until right this second.

"If you're describing your average stamina time between the sheets, I can't say I'm surprised," I inform him sweetly.

He doesn't take the bait, but his eyes flicker to the duffle at my feet, then drag slowly up my body — taking in every detail from the bare feet with pastel-painted toes to the fitted yoga pants to the slice of tan skin at my hipbones to the pink sports bra peeking through my open-weave white sweater to the long brown hair cascading around my shoulders. By the time they finally return to lock on mine, I'm having a hard time breathing and there's an intent gleam in his eyes I've never seen before.

"Hunt." His voice is full of gravel. *"Time's up."*

My mouth opens, but all my witty retorts fly out of my head as I watch Conor push off the wall. The closet feels remarkably small as he begins to advance on me.

"What are you doing?" I squeak, backpedaling a step.

"Don't say I didn't warn you."

Holding out my hands like a shield, I back away from him. He keeps coming, pursuing me across the enclosed space like a freaking jaguar — all lithe muscle and dark predatory grace. I scurry around the center island where I store my jewelry, as though having a buffer between us might somehow keep him at bay.

"Stop!" I cry, recalling his threat about putting me over his shoulder and carrying me out of the house, whether or not I'm finished packing or even wearing shoes. "Stop right there, you psycho!"

He keeps coming.

"Don't you lay a hand on me, Gallagher!"

Still coming.

"You. Wouldn't. Dare."

His lips twist into a dark grin — actually it's more of a grimace — and my mouth goes dry at the sight.

He totally would *dare.*

We do a full circle around the jewelry island, like we're playing some absurd game of tag. When he comes back to the empty duffle bag, he pauses momentarily and bends to pick it up off the floor.

"I'm in a generous mood," he informs me.

I snort in disbelief.

He ignores the sound, extending the duffle out to me across the island. "One last chance."

My heart is thudding. "You... I... Oh, for fuck's sake. *Fine!*"

Snarling, I snatch the duffle from his grip and start shoving clothing inside. Not that I honestly believe this crazed gun-toting stranger is about to toss me over his shoulder like a sack of flour and haul me out of my house...

Right?

He's obviously exaggerating, the reckless part of my brain says smugly. *Let's see what'll happen if you disobey. It's good to be bad!*

Hey! Don't test him! the sensible part of my brain warns. *We've already been manhandled enough in the past twenty-four hours. Let's quit while we're behind.*

I shove both voices out of my head and focus on the task at hand. Namely, grabbing an equal distribution of tops and pants and underwear for my unexpected vacation with Conor Asshole Gallagher. It would help if I knew where I was going or what occasion I was packing for...

Light layers?

Sweater weather?

Summer sunshine?

Arctic tundra?

A location would be great. Hell, I'd settle for a continent to narrow things down somewhat. But seeing as my new companion has already been *oh so receptive* to my previous questions, I highly doubt he'll be forthcoming on the subject of attire.

In the end, I wind up with a messy hodgepodge — a handful of sundresses and sweaters, two pairs of sandals, my favorite jeans, a floppy sunhat, and all the underwear I can manage to fit without bursting the zipper of my bag. By the time I'm done, the duffle is so full I have to sit on it to get it closed. And believe you me, is *not* easy to maintain your dignity in front of a cocky, condescending man you despise with every fiber of your being while you're sitting on the floor of your walk-in closet, straddling a leather duffle bag like it's a mechanical bull, jerking the treads closed inch by inch and praying like hell you don't have to start removing lacey undergarments by the handful.

Please, someone hire a sniper to assassinate me.

Right here, right now. Put me out of my misery.

The zipper closes with a final *zzzzzp!* and I slowly dismount. Scrambling to my feet, I know my cheeks are burning. I can't bring myself to glance Conor's way. It's far too mortifying.

"Finally ready?" he asks in a choked voice.

"Finally going to tell me where the hell we're headed?" I retort in a pissy tone.

I bend to grab the strap of my bag, but he beats me to it in a surprising show of chivalry. His face is solemn as ever as he slings it over one shoulder, but I notice there's a slight twitching at the left corner of his mouth — as though he's fighting off a smile — when he turns for the door.

"Don't you dare laugh," I mutter darkly.

"Wouldn't dream of it, Hunt."

I glower at his back all the way downstairs.

FROM THE PASSENGER side mirror of Conor's jacked-up black Jeep Wrangler, I watch the navy blue Victorian I've called home for nearly a decade disappear as we turn off my dead end street, headed god only knows where. My savior (and by *savior* I mean *monosyllabic jackass who rescued me*) hasn't yet deigned to tell me our destination, and I'm feeling too stubborn to ask. Mostly because I highly doubt he'll share that information.

The small message on the reflective mirror surface reads, "WARNING: OBJECTS ARE CLOSER THAN THEY APPEAR." After the past twenty-four hours, I'm beginning to think I should walk around wearing a similar disclaimer. "CAUTION: LIFE IS CRAZIER THAN IT INITIALLY APPEARS." Because somehow, in the span of a single day, my seemingly perfect existence has fallen to pieces.

Seriously. If things get any wackier, I'm going to buy a one-way ticket to Bali and leave Boston behind for good.

I'll teach yoga on the beach by day, sell puka-shell necklaces by night.

I'll become someone else. Someone better than Shelby Hunt: stilted housewife.

I sigh heavily and settle back against the leather seat. It's surprisingly comfortable, for such a souped-up, masculine monstrosity. When I first spotted the Jeep Wrangler in my driveway — four forty-inch tires and no roof — I flat-out laughed at the sight of it parked beside my low-slung coup convertible. No two cars could be more different.

A metaphor that extends easily to their owners, it would seem, judging by the way Conor and I butt heads...

He hasn't said a word to me since we left my house. I try to pay attention to the road, taking note of landmarks as we head southeast toward the city limits, but waves of exhaustion are crashing through me relentlessly. It's nearly dawn now, and with each passing minute it's increasingly difficult to keep my eyes open. With the exception of a few scant hours of rest in a stiff-backed dining room chair, I haven't slept at all... and something tells me I won't be getting much rest when we arrive wherever it is he's taking me.

Was it only yesterday I was opening my eyes to a new day, throwing on workout clothes and preparing for sunrise yoga at the studio?

It feels like a decade has passed since then. An eternity since I've done anything normal — like *eat*, for instance — and my body has definitely taken notice, given the hunger pangs I'm currently experiencing. My stomach gives an embarrassing gurgle, audible even over the rushing of the wind.

Conor glances at me but I stare pointedly out the window, wishing I could evaporate into thin air. Or possibly teleport to Life Alive, my favorite local vegetarian restaurant, for a smoothie and an açaí bowl. My stomach groans again at just the thought.

The crisp air whipping against my face helps keep me conscious as we zoom through neighborhood after neighborhood — for once not gridlocked with commuter traffic or bus-loads of visiting tourists. It's odd to see everything so abandoned. No street performers doing dance routines, no musicians playing acoustic sets for tips in the public parks, no yellow duck boats chugging toward the harbor. In a few hours, all of Boston will be abuzz with life... but right now,

Conor and I feel like the only two people alive in the whole world.

What a strangely terrifying thought.

My brows lift when, instead of heading downtown, we merge onto the Tobin Bridge — taking us over the water, away from the city. I turn my head to look at the receding downtown skyline and see the horizon is going pale with the first hints of a pink sunrise between the towering skyscrapers in the distance.

Hauling a deep breath in through my nose, I steady my shoulders and rally my remaining dregs of inner strength. I'm going to need it — I have a distinct feeling it's going to be a long freaking day.

And it hasn't even started yet.

CHAPTER 5

RUSSIAN ROULETTE

MY PREDICTIONS ARE NOT WRONG.

The day from hell has only gotten more hellish — which is really saying something, since it started with me duct taped to a chair in my own damn house.

Now, I'm in a *different* chair, sans duct tape, but no more comfortable. My ass has officially gone numb after forty-five minutes of waiting for Conor to come back to this ugly, fluorescent-lit holding cell where he left me without any explanation whatsoever.

Crossing my arms over my chest, I glare at the wall on the other side of the room. "Are you trying to bore me to death?" I ask the two-way mirror, certain someone is standing on the other side. Someone with messy black hair and dark blue eyes, if I had to put money on it. "What, is your water-boarding kit occupied? Or is this some new FBI interrogation tactic I'm being subjected to?"

Oh.

That's right.

I said *FBI*.

Turns out, Conor Gallagher the Boston Cop is *actually*

Special Agent Conor Gallagher of the FBI — a fact I learned after he drove us into Chelsea, pulled up to an armored security gate complete with gun-toting guards, flashed his freaking *badge,* and proceeded to park in front of an impressive, blocky building with a black stone sign declaring FEDERAL BUREAU OF INVESTIGA-TIONS: BOSTON DIVISION in neat, chiseled lettering.

Yeah.

That happened.

You said you were a cop! I squawked as he yanked me from the car, marched me inside, and dragged me none-too-gently toward this lovely cross-examination chamber I now call home.

No, he retorted flatly. *You said I was a cop. I simply failed to correct you.*

Before I could do anything — like, say, beam him over the head with my flip flop and make a break for it — he closed the door and disappeared, leaving me locked in here like a common criminal.

Yes, *locked.*

I tried the knob.

Multiple times.

With colorful language — including, but not limited to, all the dirty Russian phrases Paul's parents taught me, back in the days we used to spend the holidays with them — I expressed to both the overhead cameras and the mirror wall just how unhappy I was to be detained as a special guest of the FBI without cause.

Yebat-kopat!

Pizda rulyu!

Yoptel-mopsel!

Yobannoe dno!

By this point, they're lucky I haven't picked up the chair

and attempted to shatter the glass. (Though, I'm pretty sure that would land me behind bars for real.) I'm about ready to risk it — a life of crime has got to be better than dying of boredom in here — when the door finally swings open and Conor walks in.

"You motherfu— *Oh.*"

My mouth snaps shut when I see he's not alone. A female agent slips inside behind him before the door clicks closed. She's annoyingly pretty despite the rather androgynous outfit she's got on — not a hair out of place in her low blonde chignon, not a wrinkle on her pressed black pants.

I suddenly feel extremely underdressed in my hot pink sports bra ensemble. Sitting up straighter in my seat, I resist the urge to smooth my messy hair.

"So. This is the infamous Shelby Hunt."

Infamous?

The woman's voice is a perfect match for her personality — cool, haughty, a bit condescending. I meet her dispassionate ice-blue eyes as she takes a seat across from me at the stainless steel table.

Conor doesn't sit. He leans against the wall instead, his posture totally casual. Still, I can't help noticing there's an edge of alertness in his eyes as they watch his colleague taking my measure.

"Finally, I put a face to the name," the woman says, smiling without teeth. Her fingers drum an absentminded pattern on the thick file in her hands. "It's nice to meet you."

"I'd say the same, but you've yet to introduce yourself."

Her smile vanishes. She pulls a badge from inside her blazer and slides it across the table toward me. "Agent Lucy Sykes, I'm with the Organized Crime Division here at the

Boston Bureau. I believe you've already had the pleasure of meeting my colleague, Agent Gallagher."

I glance fleetingly at her credentials, then push the badge back to her with a rough shove. "Trust me, there was nothing pleasurable about it."

Conor scoffs lowly.

Sykes' jaw clenches tighter. "Mrs. Hunt, do you know why you're here?"

"I'll take a wild guess and say it has something to do with the two men who attacked me, yesterday."

"Right you are." Her head tilts in contemplation. She reminds me of a cat, sizing up a particularly delectable mouse. "We'd love it if you'd talk us through everything that happened. Starting at the beginning, all the way up to the moment Agent Gallagher arrived at your home. Can you do that?"

My eyes move to Conor. He's watching me carefully, that dark stare burning into mine with an intensity that makes me shiver. I can't even begin to decipher that look, so I direct my focus back on his partner, steel my shoulders, and launch into the story with as much detail as I can remember.

The studio encounter after my yoga class.

The feeling I was being watched at the Farmers Market.

The altercation in my driveway with Righty and Lefty.

The threats about Paul returning their stolen property.

Agent Sykes listens intently, interjecting with the occasional question, making small notes on her legal pad. When I finish speaking, the room is totally silent.

"That's it," I say dumbly, when no one else speaks. "That's everything I remember."

Sykes is peering at me with a peculiar expression, her

slender brows arched. "This *boss* they mentioned — Alexei?"

I nod.

"Have you ever heard that name before?"

"No."

"And they didn't say what your husband stole from him?"

"Ex-husband."

"Oh?" Sykes looks down at her file. "I see here that you filed for divorce last December. According to our records, it was never finalized."

"Only because Paul refuses to sign the papers."

"Then you are, in fact, still married."

"On paper," I fire back, taking offense at her tone. "But our marriage has been effectively over for months. Years, really."

"So you say. Unfortunately, Mrs. Hunt, the things *on paper* are all that count, when it comes to an investigation." Her fingertips drum the folder. "Files don't lie."

I tense at the implication.

Files don't lie... but you might.

My eyes narrow on hers. "I don't suppose your precious *file* reflects the restraining order I took out against Paul? And the reasons for it?"

Sykes has the good grace to look slightly embarrassed. "I do see there was an... altercation of sorts on Christmas Day at your residence. Police responded to the scene and filed a report."

The air goes suddenly tense. I have a feeling, if I look at Conor right now, there'll be a scary expression on his face, so I keep my eyes on the icy blonde instead. "Yes. An *altercation* that resulted in Paul being arrested — not to mention me kicking his ass out of the house for good." I lean forward in my seat. "Perhaps that sheds a little light on why I've had some difficulty getting my husband to agree to a divorce. Last time I tried, he broke my favorite lamp. I'd prefer not to give him an opportunity to break anything else."

A low sound comes from Conor's direction. It's almost a growl.

Sykes shoots him a speculative look before pinning me with her stare once more. "Be that as it may, you are still legally and financially bound to Paul Hunt. Which brings us back to yesterday. Clearly there are certain individuals out there who believe they can send your husband a message by putting you in the crosshairs."

"Look, I don't have the slightest idea what Paul is up to, nor do I want to. He's not my concern anymore."

"Mhmm." Her head tilts again in that predatory way. "And you maintain you have no knowledge of what he took from this *Alexei* character you mentioned earlier?"

"No. I mean yes. I mean— I have no knowledge of it!" Her phrasing is tripping me up. I'm not sure if it's the lack of sleep or merely the fact that I'm here, at freaking FBI Headquarters, but my mind is spinning and my pulse is racing. The longer this goes on, the less it feels like being interviewed... and the more it feels like being *interrogated*.

But that can't be possible.

Right?

I'm the victim here!

Except... Sykes isn't looking at me like I'm a victim. She's looking at me like she's holding a hammer and the final nail for my coffin.

"Agent Sykes, I swear — I've told you everything I remember. I don't know what Paul is up to or what the hell those men are after."

"Noted." Her eyes narrow. "And you claim you'd never seen them before yesterday?"

I tense. "Claim? I don't *claim* anything. That's the truth."

Her thin-lipped smile reappears. "I see."

"I don't think you do *see*," I say, feeling my hackles rise. "Otherwise you wouldn't be treating me like a common criminal. Last I checked, you usually investigate the bad guys who commit crimes, not the victims who suffer them!"

Sykes is suspiciously silent.

"Oh my god," I say, finally putting the pieces together. "You think I have something to do with this."

Her brows lift as if to say, *Well, do you?*

"Wow." I shake my head. "You honestly believe I'm behind this?"

"Mrs. Hunt, we have to explore all avenues," Sykes says placatingly. "Once we rule you out as a suspect—"

A suspect!

I'm actually a suspect!

I'd laugh, if I could summon even the slightest sense of humor about this situation. I find myself glancing at Conor. For what, I'm not sure.

Help? Absolution? Explanation?

His eyes give nothing away — they're dark and shuttered as ever. And his expression is stone cold.

He's not going to jump in and save you, idiot, I remind myself, feeling my heart pang. *He's the one who dragged you in here. He thinks you're guilty, too.*

For some reason, betrayal blazes through me, hot as a wildfire. Realizing my so-called savior isn't actually on my side at all burns more than it should. I tear my eyes from him, ignoring the pain in my chest. Agent Sykes is still watching me guardedly.

"Honestly... Do I look like a criminal mastermind to you?"

Her eyes flicker up and down.

I snort. "I'm a freaking yoga instructor!"

"A yoga instructor who married a man with known ties to the Petrov family."

My brows lift. "The who?"

"The Petrov family." When I continue to stare at her blankly, she elaborates. "The Russian Bratva."

Still drawing a blank.

She sighs. "The mafia, Mrs. Hunt."

"WHAT?"

"I take from your rather overenthusiastic response, you were not aware of your husbands connections."

My heart is pounding twice its normal speed. "Agent Sykes, I don't know where you're getting your intel, but it's way off base. There's no way Paul has ties to the Russian mob."

"I assure you, our intel is quite accurate. Your husband has conducted extensive business on behalf of the Petrovs, from equity trading to reallocating family finances. He's traveled to Russia at least five times in the past year on the Petrov private jet. And the East Boston apartment in which he currently resides is owned by a shell corporation the Petrov family uses for real estate dealings."

"But... No. He works as a portfolio manager for a hedge fund. He trades stocks and bonds. I've met his co-workers. They're all average, boring investment banker types. I promise you, they're not members of the Russian mafia." I force out a strangled laugh. "And Paul may be a total asshole, but he's not a criminal."

"Were you aware your husband is no longer employed by LP Consulting?"

I jolt back in my seat. "N-no. No, I wasn't aware of that."

"According to our records, he was fired almost two years ago for making unauthorized trades and subsequently stripped of his Series 65 license."

"Are you sure we're talking about the same Paul Hunt?"

She nods gravely.

"I'm just..." I shake my head, as if that might somehow lend me clarity in the midst of this chaos. "I'm having a hard time wrapping my mind around this. It's a lot to take in all at once. I knew my husband kept secrets — he was a master at it, trust me. But this is a whole new level..."

She gives me a minute to process before lightly clearing her throat. "Mrs. Hunt—"

"Please. Call me Shelby." I attempt a smile. "You've already accused me of being a criminal. The time for formality has come and gone."

I think I actually see a spark of life in her icy eyes. "Shelby, then."

"So..." My laugh is bitter. "If my darling husband hasn't been trading stocks and bonds for the past two years, what has he been doing — besides his secretary, of course — that keeps him at the office until three in the morning most nights? Does he even *have* an office, anymore?"

"That's what we've spent the past six months trying to piece together."

We?

I dart a glance at Conor. He's still watching me, tense as ever. I try — and fail — to read his expression, wondering just how thoroughly he's embedded in this investigation into my life. Just how much he knows about the inner workings of Shelby Hunt's world.

Probably best not to answer that question. Ever.

I shiver and glance back at his partner.

Sykes' lips flatten into a serious line. "We believe, after he was fired, Paul turned to the Petrovs for help securing work. His faulty trades left him blackballed in the United States, but his Russian connections gave him an opportunity to make money in the international market without the SEC breathing down his neck."

"I had no idea. He never said anything about this to me."

"And you never suspected he was doing something for work beyond his duties at LP Consulting?"

I think back, sorting through my memories with fresh eyes. I didn't see it before. Maybe I didn't *want* to see it. But I think, on some deep level, I knew whatever my husband was doing during business hours wasn't entirely above board. He always tried to keep me as far from his professional practices as possible — to maintain our well-established two party system: his arena the boardroom, mine the homestead.

But keeping his dutiful, apron-wearing wife out of his affairs wasn't always easy; mainly because I don't own an apron and I'm far too obstinate to ever be described as *dutiful* by anyone with more than three functioning brain cells.

Over the years, I've witnessed my fair share of deals happening behind closed doors in Paul's home office — deals with men in dark suits carrying reinforced briefcases who never made eye contact or stopped to make smalltalk on their way in and out in the middle of the night. At the time, I assumed they were colleagues from his firm. But now...

"There were a few times," I murmur, watching Sykes' eyes light up with interest. I tell her everything I can remember about the men who came to the house — never the same one twice, never there for longer than twenty minutes.

"Did you ever hear him talk about offshore accounts?" she asks.

"No."

"What about the Cayman Islands?"

"No."

"And he never mentioned the name Petrov to you?"

"Never."

She caps her pen with a frustrated click.

"I'm sorry I can't be more helpful," I tell her. "But if Paul has a business connection to this... Petrov family... it's one he kept secret from me."

"It's more a blood tie than a business connection, I'm afraid."

My brows lift. "What?"

"Paul doesn't just work for the Petrovs. He *is* a Petrov."

"That's... that's not possible. Paul's family is from Colorado. He was born and raised on the cattle ranch his great, great grandfather purchased for cheap back at the turn of the century."

"I'm afraid that's just another lie your husband told you, Shelby." She pulls out a sheet of paper. "Paul Hunt, born Paul Sergei Usenko, to Dmitry and Ekaterina Usenko. The family legally changed their surname to Hunt upon their immigration to the United States in 1992, just after the collapse of the Soviet Union."

I suck in a gulp of air, feeling like my whole world is spiraling out of control. "You're mistaken."

"I assure you, I'm not. If you'd like to see the documentation, it's all right here in this folder." She pushes the file across the table at me.

My hands shake as I reach out and take it. For the next few minutes, I'm consumed by the documents before my eyes. Birth certificates, copies of their immigration papers, photographs of my in-laws from nearly thirty years ago, taken the day they entered the country, a brown-haired toddler boy bundled in their arms.

Paul.

"Your in-laws are merely renters on that ranch, who receive room and board in exchange for maintenance of the land." Agent Sykes' voice has thawed — *damn*, even the ice queen feels bad for me right now. "As for Paul, he grew up in government-subsidized housing just outside of Denver from age three to eighteen, at which point he made his way to the East Coast for college. Looks like he got a free ride to—"

"Stone Hill University," I finish for her, feeling like the floor has fallen out beneath me. "Where... where he met me."

Sykes nods.

I look down at my left hand. At the bare fourth finger where my wedding ring used to rest. I curl it into a tight fist and tuck it away beneath the table before I can do something stupid, like punch the wall.

God, I'm such a fool.

Such an utter idiot for spending a decade of my life swallowing pretty lies from a man I thought I could trust. For failing to ask the pertinent questions, to push back when he forced me to keep my nose out of the financial affairs of our household.

I glance up at Sykes. "I understand the name change — my great grandfather came through Ellis Island in the 1920s and went from Pasquale Alfonsi to Patrick Alberts in an attempt to assimilate to American culture." I blow out a sharp breath. "What I *don't* understand is why Paul would keep it a secret... why he'd lie about his entire background..."

"We believe, in leaving Russia, your in-laws were hoping to cut ties to the Petrov family and get a fresh start." Sykes reaches for the folder again and locates a faded photograph. "Here. The woman in this photo is—"

"My mother-in-law," I say, staring at a much younger version of the woman whose son I married. "Katrina."

"Katrina Hunt. Also known as Ekaterina Usenko. And before that... Ekaterina Petrov. "

My eyes lift to hers. "She's a Petrov?"

"That photograph was taken in Moscow in the early 1980s. See the man standing next to her?"

I nod, my gaze following Sykes finger as she points out the blurry figure beside Katrina. His features are hardly recognizable due to the poor picture quality. All I can make out is dark hair and dark eyes and a full beard.

"That's her brother, Alexei, beside her."

I glance up at the name. "*Alexei.* As in...?"

"Alexei Petrov. The same Alexei your attackers mentioned yesterday." Sykes sits back and folds her hands together on the table. "He's the leader of the Petrov crime syndicate. The boss, if you will."

"Oh," I say weakly. I'm suddenly having trouble breathing. "But... why would he come after Paul?"

"We believe your husband has bridged the gap his mother created when she ran from Russia — and her older brother — all those years ago. Our surveillance suggests he's been doing business with his uncle for some time, now."

"Paul..." I shake my head. "You're saying Paul is in business with a Russian crime lord."

"Well..." Sykes sighs. "Yes. He was. For a time."

"I don't understand."

"We believe your husband attempted to extract himself from the business dealings he conducted for the Petrovs — money laundering and tax evasion, mainly — when he got a good look at the extent of their criminal activities." She pauses. "As I said earlier, the Petrovs aren't just any family. They're embedded in every illegal operation on the planet, from dirty bombs to black tar heroin to off-market weapons to sex slaves. There aren't many pies the Petrov family won't stick a finger or two in, if it means turning a profit. We're talking extortion, arson, assassinations—"

"Sykes," Conor says sharply, breaking his silence for the first time. "That's *enough*."

His partner shoots him a look. "I'm just trying to give her the facts, Gallagher."

If he says something else, I don't hear it.

I've gone pale. My stomach has turned to lead. Everything I thought I knew about my husband, my marriage, my life has turned to ash inside my mouth.

This is far, far worse than anything I could've imagined. Worse than the prospect of a torrid affair with a secretary. Worse than a violent outburst that leads to locked doors and leaking eyes. Worse than torn up divorce papers and a bruised cheekbone and police sirens sounding in the distance on a bright Christmas morning.

When I manage to find my voice, it's shaky at best. "So... let me get this straight." My hands clench so hard, I worry my fingernails are going to break the skin. "My no-good, dirty-rotten, lying, cheating bastard of a soon-to-be ex-husband actually turns out to not *just* be a no-good, dirty-rotten, lying, cheating bastard... but also the nephew of a Russian mobster."

After a hesitant beat, Sykes nods.

"And, after aiding and abetting in his uncle's criminal activities, my gem of a soon-to-be-ex has somehow managed to royally piss off said mob boss."

She nods again. "Judging by the visit Petrov's hitmen payed you yesterday, we're guessing his uncle is less than thrilled about Paul's decision to walk away from the family business," Sykes explains. "And the language they used when making their demands — *tell Paul he has one week to return what he took from Alexei* — suggests he has some sort of leverage to ensure his freedom. Leverage his uncle wants back pretty desperately, if he's willing to send two of his top assets across an ocean to retrieve it."

"What the hell did Paul possibly steal that warrants sending large, scary hitmen to his wife's yoga studio in retribution?"

"It could be money, it could be proof of criminal activity... Incriminating photographs or documents... Anything, really. We're still trying to find out. The problem is..."

"What?"

"No one has seen or heard from your husband in weeks. He's hiding out. Probably trying to formulate a plan that'll keep his uncle from killing him long enough to return whatever he unwisely stole. But the longer he's off the grid, the less patient Petrov is becoming."

"Well, I guess that explains why they came after me. They're trying to draw him out. Thinking he'll step up and protect me." I laugh bitterly. "Clearly they don't know him very well."

"Or..." Sykes bites her lip.

"Or what? Don't leave me hanging."

"They're under the impression that you either know where Paul is hiding... or you know where he hid Alexei's property."

"I don't."

"Right. But *they* don't know that, Shelby." Her eyes are intent. "And they aren't the type to take your word on it."

"Wait just a second." My throat feels tight. There's a lump of something — I think it's panic — blocking my airway. "If Alexei and his cronies think *I* have something to do with whatever Paul is hiding... that means..." I trail off, feeling the blood drain from my face.

"It means," Conor says, breaking his strained silence as he walks over to the table and braces his hands against it in an intimidating pose that makes every muscle in his forearms flex tightly. His dark blue eyes find mine, and I see they're brimming over with intensity. "You are in a shitload of danger, Hunt."

CHAPTER 6

JAIL BAIT

A COFFEE CUP hits the table in front of me.

I jolt out of my dark reverie — a montage of distorted memories from a marriage I no longer recognize — and jerk my eyes up in time to see Conor take the seat across from mine. Agent Sykes is nowhere to be found. She bolted soon after our earlier conversation under the pretense of 'giving me time to process' but I'd put money on the fact that she's got her pert nose pressed up against that two-way glass at this exact moment, jotting down every word I say in her orderly notebook of clues.

I stare at the styrofoam cup like it contains a cluster of garden snakes. "What's this?"

"Some call it coffee." Conor leans back in his seat, arms crossed over his broad chest. "Fair warning, it's pretty shitty."

"I meant what's *this*—" I gesture across the table, indicating his general presence. "The whole *good-cop-bad-cop* routine is pretty stale, don't you think? Let me guess... she blows my whole world to pieces, then you swoop in — bearing coffee — to cherry-pick intel from the wreckage?"

"Hunt, I hate to break it to you... If anyone here is good cop, it's Sykes."

"Is that a threat, Gallagher?"

"That's a fact. Though I understand you not recognizing one, seeing as you've spent the past ten years of your life swallowing lies."

I flinch visibly. That might be the meanest thing anyone's ever said to me... but it's also the most honest. Which is probably why it stings so damn much.

"Forgive me if I'm hesitant to trust *facts* from a man who dragged me in here like a common criminal when he led me to believe he was helping me."

"Not a *common* criminal." He shrugs. "White collar. Much classier."

I glower. "Was that supposed to be funny?"

He doesn't answer. "Hunt, you can hate me all you want, glare at me till your face turns blue... you're not going anywhere until we get some shit sorted."

"Am I under arrest? Because last I checked, it's illegal to hold a civilian in custody without charging them with a crime. Not to mention interrogate them without reading them their rights or allowing them to contact an attorney."

He whistles. "Yoga instructors are really up on their law, these days."

"Not that it's any of your business, but I've watched every episode of *Law and Order: SVU* ever made." My eyes narrow. "You know, in my spare time, when I'm not helping launder money on behalf of Russian mobsters."

His lips twist. "Can I consider that your full confession?"

I start clapping. "Bravo! Case closed! Someone give this man a gold star and a promotion!"

Conor stares at me, attempting to keep a straight face,

but I can tell he's at least slightly amused. "You aren't under arrest. That doesn't mean you're safe."

"Safe?" I snort. "Safe is the least of my worries. I'm hangry. I'm sleep deprived. My contact lenses are starting to chafe my eyeballs. I want to go home."

His expression flattens into that familiar blank mask. "You can't go home."

"And why not?"

"Firstly, because we still need you to go through the books and try to identify the men who attacked you from a group of Petrov's known affiliates."

"I'm guessing there's a *secondly*?"

"It's not secure. Plain and simple."

"I have a state-of-the-art security system."

"That did you a hell of a lot of good yesterday. Or have you forgotten what happened already?"

"The system wasn't armed yesterday," I admit in a small voice.

"What?" he growls.

"I forgot to activate it when I left for yoga! So... when Righty and Lefty forced their way inside... they just used the keys in my purse."

His face contorts with rage and disbelief. "*Hunt.*"

I wince in anticipation of the coming lecture.

"You're a woman who lives alone in a modern metropolitan area with half the damn Bratva out for her blood — not to mention all the everyday psychos who live on your particular block — and you're telling me you don't bother to arm your fucking security system when you leave the house?" Conor looks like his head is about to explode. "*Christ.* You're smarter than that."

My attention snags on a minor detail. "Wait. What psychos live on my block?"

"Not my point."

"Come on, Gallagher. You can't just drop a juicy tidbit like that and not fill me in."

He hesitates for a long beat then sighs tiredly, as though he's already regretting this. "The old lady in the green house, diagonal from you? She puts arsenic in cans of cat food and leaves them out at night to kill strays."

I gasp.

So much for sweet old Susanna...

"Couple two doors down, in the yellow house? They have BDSM swinger parties twice a month. Whips, chains, leather, the whole shebang."

I gasp again, louder.

Looking at those two, you'd never guess their sex life resembled a Rihanna song...

"And the family that lives around the corner, the ones who look like something out of a catalog? That house is triple-mortgaged and the husband spends most nights gambling away his paycheck while his wife works two jobs."

Really giving new meaning to the term 'spousal privilege'...

My jaw is practically on the table. "How do you know all that?"

"I've been working this case for six months."

My eyes widen. "Translation... you've been *watching me* for six months."

"Your husband, actually. You were just collateral damage."

"Oh, that makes me feel so much better!" I snort. "I suppose I should be flattered you spent day after day monitoring my every move."

"Not every move," he mutters.

"Just most of them?"

His jaw clenches, but he doesn't refute me.

"God, Gallagher! That's such an utter violation of privacy, I don't even know where to start!"

"It's not a violation of privacy," he grits out. "Surveillance is part of my job."

"Whatever you say, stalker." I roll my eyes. "What else have you learned in these six months? Hmm? I think I have a right to know. It is my life you've been spying on, after all."

He runs a hand through his hair, sighing deeply. "The man in the house on the corner was charged with murder twice in his home state before moving to Massachusetts — due to the disappearance of his ex-girlfriends. *Plural.* Only reason he got off was a lack of physical evidence. The police never found the bodies."

"*What?!* Not the guy with the gorgeous petunias!?"

He nods tightly.

"Wow. What a shame." I pause. "Honestly, his garden is unparalleled."

"Hunt. The man is an accused killer."

"And an exquisitely talented gardener!"

He shakes his head at me in disapproval.

"You don't think..." I trail off.

His brows lift.

"Never mind."

"Spit it out, Hunt."

"No."

"Been watching you six months, never seen you blush before. Call me intrigued."

"They never found the bodies!" I blurt before I can talk myself out of it. "You don't think his gardens are so gorgeous because... he's using some extra special... fertilizer..." I wince. "Gives a whole new dimension to the concept of *community farming*, doesn't it?"

"You really have watched every episode of *Law and Order*, haven't you?" He shakes his head at me, eyes glittering with humor. "That's dark, Hunt. Seriously dark."

"I am not dark!" I scoff. "I'm a rainbow of kittens and unicorns!"

"And I'm the fucking Tooth Fairy," he says flatly. "Now, can we get back to the important shit? Namely, the fact that your neighborhood — cat killers and sex addicts aside — is no longer a viable option for you to return to."

I bite my lip. Honestly, after everything he's just told me, I'm in no race to get back home.

Who knew my neighbors were such freaks?!

Still, the thought of staying here — in a holding cell, at the mercy of federal government officials who may or may not have my best interests at heart, seeing as they suspect I may be an accomplice in my husband's unsavory activities — isn't one I'm eager to entertain.

You have to understand — normally, in a situation like this, I'd call my friend Phoebe. Her husband Nate runs Knox Investigations, the best private security firm in Boston. Nate's boys have helped out in the past whenever any of my friends have run into trouble, whether it's a scheming cousin, dangerous car chase, school of loan sharks, or hostage situation. There's no doubt in my mind they'd be able to keep me safe from anyone on this earth — even Russian mafia members intent on revenge.

Regrettably, Nate and Phoebe are currently off on their honeymoon, soaking up the sunshine on a beach in the South Pacific. And I'm not about to call them and ruin their happily ever after. No freaking way.

Which means... I'm on my own.

Well... except for a blue-eyed special agent who seems to enjoy pissing me off to no end.

"You know I'm right," Conor interjects on my thoughts with impeccable timing. "You can't walk out of here and go back to living your life like nothing has changed."

"Well if you think I'm staying *here*, you're insane."

"Not here. We'll set you up in a safe house. Somewhere off the grid where you can hide out until we track down your husband."

"If I trusted you — which, for the record, I don't — I might consider that offer. As it stands, I think I'd rather take my chances with the Russian mobsters."

"Hunt, don't be pigheaded."

"Are federal agents supposed to insult civilians?"

"Technically, you're still a person of interest."

"Oh, give me a break. We all know I don't have jack-shit to do with Paul's foreign interludes. If I did, I wouldn't have wound up tied to my damn dining room furniture yesterday and I sure as hell wouldn't be here right now, chatting with you."

"In all this debriefing, did you somehow miss the part about bad men being after you?"

"Did *you* miss the part about me not trusting you?"

We glare at each other across the table. My blood is boiling over with rage. Rage and something else. Something I've decided not to acknowledge, for the time being, because the thought that I might be feeling anything other than pure, absolute loathing for Conor Asshole Gallagher is too absurd to contemplate.

You hate him, my inner voice reminds me as our gazes clash like swords on a battlefield. *He's gruff and grumpy. And bossy. And not at all hot when he pins you to the spot with those mega-blue eyes, like he's looking straight down into your soul.*

We're so tangled up in each other, neither of us notices

Sykes has entered the room again until she clears her throat gently. Our heads both snap in her direction. The look on her face is a mix of speculation and amusement as she sets a thick binder on the table.

"If you two are finished bickering... I have the books for Shelby to look through. And I also have an idea that might work for everyone..."

———————

"ABSOLUTELY NOT."

"Gallagher."

"Sorry, did you not hear me?" Conor growls. "I said absolutely *fucking* not."

Sykes sighs. "You aren't seeing the big picture."

"I'm seeing the big picture, Lucy. It looks a lot like our primary asset getting herself killed."

I try to ignore them as I flip through the book of mugshots. I'm on page fifty and their argument is still going strong. On the one hand we've got Agent Sykes, who wants to send me home with an invisible net of protection, hoping my presence might draw Paul or Petrov out of the woodwork long enough for them to make an arrest.

On the other hand, Conor is vehemently opposed to any plan that involves me walking out the door of FBI Headquarters without an armored vest and a full battalion of guards, en route to a safe house in the middle of nowhere.

"You're too close to this case," Sykes tells him, shaking her head. "You aren't being objective here."

"Oh, piss off, Lucy. You know damn well I'm just protecting my asset. You'd do the same, if you'd put in six months on this case. I'm not about to fuck it up just because you want to take a shortcut. Not when I'm this close to the finish line."

"She'd be fully protected the whole time."

"She'd be *bait*," Conor snarls. "It's not happening."

"Gallagher—"

"She's going to the safe house. That's final."

"You weren't even supposed to bring her *here*! Not until we'd officially cleared her of involvement. Now you want to send her to a safe house when you know as well as I do that she's our only chance at closing this case?" There's a heavy pause. "I know this is your op, Gallagher, but if you refuse to see reason here... I'll have no choice but to go around you."

"To who, Shapiro?" He laughs, but it's cold as ice. "Try it, Sykes. This is my division. I don't answer to Shapiro. And though you seem to have forgotten, *you* answer to *me*. Unless you'd rather find another department to work for."

Conor is in charge of the whole division?!

"Look, I'm sorry, but I wouldn't be of value to you if I didn't speak my mind. Isn't that why you brought me in on this case?" She pauses and her voice grows hesitant. "I'm concerned your personal involvement is becoming a roadblock, here."

I don't look up, but I can practically hear Conor's jaw ticking.

Personal involvement?

I'm not sure I understand what she means by that; I *am* sure it's probably safer to be left in the dark on this subject. Or any subject concerning Conor Gallagher.

The sooner he's out of my life, the better.

"What am I supposed to think?" Sykes asks him, her tone softening. "You show up here, no warning, no paperwork... It's just not like you to break protocol."

"Protocol went out the window the moment my asset was kidnapped."

"Still. Bringing her in was a huge security risk. And in the three years I've known you, you've *never* taken any sort of risk like this for an asset—"

"You do realize I can hear you?" I interject, looking up from the book of mugshots.

Both agents glance at me from the corner of the room, twin looks of surprise on their faces. Clearly, they'd forgotten I was still within earshot.

"Not very stealthy for two badass special agents," I point out.

"Yes. Well." If I didn't know better, I'd say Sykes is blushing. "Have you made any progress with the book?"

I spin the binder around so they can see it and point out the men toward the bottom half of the page. "These two."

Sykes bends forward to read. "Viktor and Vladimir Evanoff."

"The Evanoff brothers?" Conor growls. "Great. That's fucking *great*."

"I'm guessing they aren't known for their winning smiles and charming dispositions?" I ask, wincing.

"Not quite." Sykes looks rattled. "They're two of Petrov's top men. They spend most of their time in Moscow. If they're here..."

"It's serious." Conor's voice is flat. "Which is what I've been reiterating for the past hour."

"This could be huge," Sykes murmurs. "The Evanoffs have been on the Most Wanted list for years, since they set off that car bomb at the American Embassy a decade ago. If we can bring them in..."

"Picture your promotion later, Sykes. We've got more important things to deal with. Namely, getting Hunt to a safe house. Now that you understand the threat, surely you're on board with that plan."

"On the contrary," she retorts. "I'm more certain than ever that we need Shelby to return home — under constant surveillance, of course — to draw these bastards out into the open so we can finally take them down."

"Out of the question," Conor growls.

"It's not just your decision!" she snaps back.

"Like hell it isn't. She's my asset. This is my case."

"This is bigger than one asset! Bigger than one case, even!" Sykes is breathing hard. "Five Americans died in that embassy bombing. Don't we owe it to them to take down their killers when we have a chance?"

"Stay out of this, Sykes."

"We might never get this opportunity again, Gallagher. You know I'm right, even if you don't want to admit it. "

His hands curl into fists.

An ugly silence descends over the small room.

"Um," I chime in, clearing my throat delicately. Both of them whip their furious faces my way, and I gulp. "Yeah. Hi, there. Me again."

They keep glaring.

"So... Are you planning to keep up this verbal sparring session until one of you drops dead of exhaustion? Or would you like to hear my thoughts on the matter? Since your entire plan hinges on whether or not I decide to cooperate?"

"No," Conor says flatly, frowning.

"Yes," Sykes says at the same time.

I take a deep breath. "If these Evanoff brothers are as bad as you say they are, I'm not going to be safe at some remote location. I'm not going to be safe *anywhere*." I pause, ignoring the racing of my pulse. "So... I might as well go home and let you catch them when they come calling again."

"You don't understand what you're risking." Conor takes a step toward me, expression furious. "You don't understand how much danger you'll be in."

"They could've killed me yesterday," I point out. "They didn't. They barely laid a hand on me."

"I doubt they'll be so merciful the second time."

"Like you said, they think I have information about Paul. Even if they get close enough to hurt me, they won't — not before I can tell them what they want to know. That gives you the perfect opportunity to take them down." My eyes move to Sykes. "Right?"

"Exactly." She's actually smiling. "We'll have eyes on the house at all times. They'll never get close enough to touch you."

"Forget it." Conor crosses his arms over his chest. "It's too risky."

I meet his cold stare. "This is Paul's mess. *My* mess. If there's something I can do to help fix it, I'll do it." I sigh. "I just want this over with, so I can finally move on with my life."

"Hunt, you might not *have* a life if you go through with this plan." Conor leans in, trapping me with an intent look. "You're not putting yourself in the crosshairs. I won't allow it."

"You won't *allow* it?" I jerk my chin stubbornly. "Last I checked, you aren't my father or my brother or my husband. You don't make decisions for me. Starting now, the only one who makes decisions for me... is me."

His eyes flash with dark rage. I get the sense he'd like nothing more than to take me by the shoulders and physically shake some sense into me.

"You are making a mistake," he growls. "Trust me on that."

"Didn't you hear me earlier?" I whisper. "That's the problem, Gallagher. I *don't* trust you."

Something flashes in his eyes. Call me crazy, but it looks like hurt. Before I can overanalyze it, I tear my eyes from his and turn in my seat to face Sykes. She looks pleased as punch by this turn of events.

"So..." I take a deep breath. "Tell me how this is going to work."

———————

THE CAR RIDE back to Somerville is quiet.

Did I say *quiet?*

I meant *a deathtrap of awkward silence so thick, it's a struggle to breathe.*

Conor has been seething in silent rage since I agreed to act as bait for the Evanoff brothers. Honestly, I'm not sure why he's so angry. It's not *his* ass on the line, here. He should be thanking me! If things go well, he'll probably end up with a promotion and a pay raise for bringing down two of Alexei Petrov's top henchman.

It's late afternoon now, and I'm so exhausted I can hardly hold my head up. Today's nonstop interrogation has worn me out far more than yesterday's kidnapping. I can't wait to get home, lock my door, set my alarm, and crawl into bed — safe in the knowledge that Conor and an entire SWAT team of trained FBI agents are armed and ready just down the block, should the Evanoffs decide to make an encore appearance.

We're five minutes from my house when we take an unexpected detour. I glance over at Conor, prepared to tell him we're going the wrong way, only to see him turning the wheel into the drive-thru of my favorite healthy(ish) fast food place. The words die on my lips as he pulls to a stop by the speaker and I realize someone up there has heard my prayers.

We're finally getting food!

Praise the lord!

I'm so hungry, I could eat a cow right now — and I've been a strict vegetarian since my freshman year of college. My mouth fills with saliva as I listen to Conor ordering himself a large steak burrito with a side of chips and guac. I wait for him to turn and ask me what I'd like, but he doesn't bother.

He already knows.

"Can I also get the squash blossom quesadilla on a corn tortilla — hold the quick-pickled onions — with a side of the grilled street corn. And a double serving of the blue tortilla chips with the black bean salsa on the side. The mild one, not the spicy." He pauses, lips twisting. "Oh, I'll also need one of those iced pink drinks with the round ball shit on the bottom."

I'm flabbergasted to hear him rattle off my regular to-go order, word for word — down to the spice threshold of my salsa and the hibiscus bubble tea. Either this is some freakish coincidence, or...

Conor looks over at me. His brows lift when he sees my expression. "What?"

"That's... that's what I always get!" I blurt.

"I'm aware," he says like I'm an idiot. "You want something different this time?"

"N-no," I stutter. "I just..."

I just want to know how the hell you memorized my exact favorite meal without ever asking me.

"Spit it out, Hunt."

"How did you know?"

He shrugs. "You come here all the time."

"But— but—"

"Is there a problem? Or can I pull up to the window?" His scowl is back. "We're holding up the line."

My mouth closes and I shake my head. "By all means. Carry on."

He takes his foot off the brake and I stare dead ahead as we roll forward, trying like hell to get my wildly spiraling thoughts under control. But it's no use. Even after we're back on the road to my house, a bag of delicious Mexican food warming my lap, I can't stop myself from stealing small glances at the man in the driver's seat... and wondering what other infinitesimal details of my life he's committed to memory, these past few months.

CHAPTER 7

CONTROL FREAK

"OHMUHGAWD," I say around a massive mouthful. "This is the best meal I've ever had."

Conor shakes his head at me and takes another bite out of his burrito.

I slurp down a large gulp of my iced tea. "What? I mean it."

"You eat this exact meal twice a week."

"So?"

"So how can something you eat two times a week suddenly rank as the best meal you've ever had?"

"Certainly not due to the company." I toss a chip at his head.

"Cute."

Wadding up the empty wrapper from my quesadilla, I shift forward on my stool so I can reach the chips and salsa sitting between us on the kitchen island. "God, someone take these away from me. I could eat an entire bag of them."

"Why do you think I got a double order?"

I sigh and pop another in my mouth, chewing absently.

"I'll pretend it's a cheat day. Calories don't count after FBI interrogations. Right?"

"Relax. I doubt they'll strip you of your Health Freak status based on one day of indulgence."

"Spoken like a man with a super fast metabolism." I tilt my head. "I suppose you, like most cops, subsist on a diet of doughnuts and crappy coffee?"

"Not exclusively." His lips twitch. "Though I will admit, your close proximity to Union Square Donuts has been one silver lining about this surveillance gig. They make a mean Boston Cream."

"Mmm, I can hear your arteries clogging as we speak."

"I'll take my chances."

"It's your funeral."

"My bad." He swallows the last bite of his steak burrito. "I forgot how uptight you get about food."

My mouth falls open at that statement. "I am *not* uptight about food! I'm merely... health conscious."

"You eat all organic, all the time. Never skip a day of working out, so far as I can tell. Not to mention you get all high and mighty when someone has the nerve to consume sugar around you."

He takes a large sip of his soda, just to prove his point. I can't quite hide my wince as I think about the amount of fructose settling in the pit of his stomach.

"See what I mean?" He shakes his head. "You can hardly watch."

Not wanting to fuel the fire of his accusations, I bite my lip to contain the words... but they burst out anyway. "Processed sugar is a death sentence! It's just as dangerous to your health as smoking cigarettes! Ask a doctor if you don't believe me."

"Why would I need a doctor when I've got you here to lecture me for free?"

I pause. "Are you mocking me?"

"Only a little." His mouth tugs up at one side as he contemplates me. "You know, you're kind of cute when you're all fired up, Hunt," he says in a voice that, compared to his regular steely tones, is remarkably warm. So warm, it makes *me* feel warm too. Warm and flushed and fluttery with...

With embarrassment, I tell myself stubbornly. *Nothing more.*

"Perhaps you should get your head examined as well, next time you visit said doctor," I suggest sweetly.

"I'll do that. Soon as you get *yours* checked out for being such a control freak."

"I am not a control freak!

He just stares at me.

"I'm not!" I insist.

He doesn't refute me but his eyes sweep around the kitchen, taking in every surface, every detail in that intense way of his. I know what he's seeing — the lack of clutter. The total organization of every shelf, every drawer, every nook and cranny.

My whole house is this way. More like a beautiful museum of artifacts, than a place to call home.

"Stop looking at me like that," I say, narrowing my eyes.

"Like what, Hunt?"

"Like I'm some kind of freak!"

"Never said you were a freak. Never said anything, actually."

"Oh, whatever. You communicate more with a condescending look than most people can in ten minutes of blabbering."

"Was that a compliment or an insult?" he asks, bemused.

"Guess," I snap caustically.

"I didn't mean to offend you. I was just wondering why you're so fixated on making every facet of your life scheduled and organized."

"What's so wrong with liking things neat?"

"There's neat, then there's... *antiseptic.*" He holds my eyes. "There's no trace of you in this whole house. Nothing personal. No photographs. No mementos. No cheesy collectable keychains from bad vacations or boxes full of ticket stubs. Nothing sentimental at all. It's been scrubbed clean of all signs of life."

The things he's saying are making impact in the left side of my chest, each word another knife wound, cutting me open.

"First time I came in here, I thought I had the wrong house," he murmurs. "Surely someone so full of life couldn't live here, in this glorified mausoleum."

I scowl at him to cover my suddenly racing heartbeat. "So, I'm orderly! Sue me. I happen to like things organized."

"It's not about order or organization. It's about control." His voice has gotten remarkably serious, his eyes unusually intent. "You control every aspect of your life with meticulous precision, whether it's every piece of food you put in your mouth or every piece of furniture in this house." He gestures around at our immaculate surroundings. "Fact is, Hunt, you control every perfect detail of your life. Six months watching you, I've hardly ever seen you with a hair out of place until yesterday — and only then because you were kidnapped."

My temper is rising. "For the record, there's nothing

wrong with control. There's nothing wrong with having a routine and sticking to it."

"Sure," he says simply. "So long as that routine doesn't start controlling *you* — not the other way around."

I bristle and hop off my barstool. "Listen here, bucko... You think just because you watched me from afar and memorized my take-out order, you somehow know me? You don't know anything about me!"

He doesn't reply. He just stares at me for a long beat before asking, "You always this defensive?"

"Are you always this invasive?"

He holds his hands up in a gesture of surrender. "Just trying to get to know you a bit better. See why you're so damned obsessed with appearing flawless to everyone in your life, whether its friends, neighbors, yoga students, or your idiot husband."

"Your psychoanalysis is noted and summarily rejected."

I snatch the wrappers off the counter and toss them in the trash beneath the sink, moving on autopilot to clear away all traces of the mess. With an angry yank, I grab a paper towel from its roll along with a bottle of multipurpose cleaner and begin aggressively spraying the kitchen island. I grit my teeth as I wipe it clean, channeling my anger into each swipe of my arm.

What a jerk! Thinks he knows me... HA! The only thing he knows is how to piss me off in five seconds or less...

When the counter is sparkling, I stow my supplies back beneath the sink and take a deep breath. Feeling marginally calmer, I finally look in Conor's direction... only to find him watching me with undeniable amusement. His eyes are knowing; his lips are twitching. I can practically hear his thoughts as he scans the shining countertop.

What were you just saying about not *being totally obsessed with perfection?*

"Ugh!" I grunt. "Don't even say it!"

"Say what?"

"You know *exactly* what, Gallagher." My eyes narrow. "I am not some science project to be dissected."

His jaw locks. "That's not how I see you at all."

"Oh — but wait!" I slap a hand against the countertop with a loud bang. "That's right! I *am* your little science project, aren't I? A case to be studied? An asset to be analyzed? Thanks so much for reminding me. I almost forgot you're just here doing your job!"

The whole room goes scarily silent. I don't even dare to breathe as I stare at him, wishing I could snatch back the words I've just blurted. Words that, like it or not, offer a bit too much insight into the unfamiliar emotions churning inside me.

I almost forgot you were just here doing your job.

It's true.

I had forgotten.

Conor is watching me carefully. When he speaks, his voice is dangerously soft, but there's nothing gentle about it. "And what else would I possibly be doing here, Hunt?"

My mouth opens. Shuts. Opens again.

I have no retort. No clever comeback.

He climbs to his feet, looming over me as he advances. A lock of messy black hair falls into his eyes. He's so tall, I have to crane my neck back to continue glaring at him when he comes to a stop two feet away.

"We aren't friends," he says in that same scary-soft tone. "I am here to protect you. That's it."

"Obviously," I snap coldly, ignoring the lance of pain through my heart. "You weren't invited into my life, that's for damn sure. I actually have to *like* the people I spend time with."

"My purpose here is not to make you like me."

"Mission accomplished, then! Because *I don't*."

"Let's get something straight." His jaw tightens. "I don't give a shit if you wind up hating me when this is all over, Hunt. So long as you're *alive* and hating me, I'll consider it a success."

"So long as I'm alive and never have to spend another second in your company, I'll consider it a blessing!"

"Glad we're on the same page."

"Same bloody syllable!"

We're both breathing too fast, glaring at each other through narrowed eyes. I'm not sure how it happened, but we're each leaning in — so close, there's only a half-foot of space remaining between our faces. I tell myself to pull back, to walk away, to take some cool-down time alone in my bedroom... but I can't seem to do any of that. The only thing I'm capable of focusing on in this moment is Conor's mouth, alarmingly close to my own.

I stare at the thin top lip, the fuller bottom one, and find myself wondering whether they're soft or hard. Whether he kisses like he talks — with an all-consuming presence that commandeers every ounce of my attention without even trying.

"*Hunt*."

My name is practically a growl on his lips. A warning and a plea all rolled into one. My eyes fly up to his and I see they've gone cold again — closed off from all emotions. Flat and unfathomable as a quarry.

"Go to bed," he orders, visceral tension radiating from every atom in his body. "*Now*."

I flinch back instantly, reeling out of his space like he's

slapped me across the face. Cheeks flaming with indignation — *certainly not embarrassment, what on earth would I be embarrassed about?!* — I turn away from him so I don't have to see that look in his eyes anymore. That cold indifference.

I'm here to protect you, he told me earlier. *That's it.*

Good.

Great.

My shoulders are as stiff as my tone. "I plan on it. As soon as you leave."

"I'm not leaving."

"That wasn't part of the deal," I protest, spinning back around. "You're supposed to sleep in the surveillance van with the rest of your underlings. You know — around the corner, out of sight, so you don't tip off the bad guys with your lurking."

"That was the old deal."

"Oh? And there's a new deal I'm unaware of?"

"Yeah."

"Which is…?"

"I'm not leaving."

My jaw clenches to contain a scream. I can tell from the stubborn set to Conor's shoulders that nothing I say is going to sway him on this decision. And after nearly two full days without any sleep, I'm far too exhausted to fight. Worn far too thin to spend any more time in his presence, trying to decipher the thoughts occurring behind those indigo eyes.

"Fine," I grit out. "You can crash on the couch."

"You have four guest rooms."

"That's right, I do," I murmur sweetly. "For *guests.* Not for prickly FBI agents with boundary issues and an insufferable need to be right all the time."

"Fine." He smirks darkly. "But if you get scared of the

boogeyman in the middle of the night and need someone to save you, you'll have only yourself to blame."

"Don't hold your breath." Huffing, I turn and walk out of the kitchen. "Or do. I couldn't care less."

I'd swear I hear him chuckle as I climb the stairs to the second floor.

CONOR ASSHOLE GALLAGHER.

I curse his name as I slam my bedroom door shut. I curse it again as I strip out of my yoga outfit — which I never want to wear ever again, so long as I live — and hop into the shower in my ensuite bathroom. I curse it a third time as I shampoo, a fourth as I condition, and a fifth as I let the water stream down on my head in a soothing torrent, washing away the grime of the past two days.

He's infuriating, I seethe, brushing out my wet hair in the fogged up bathroom mirror. *A total alpha male with zero regard for anyone's feelings except his own.*

He's annoying, I rant, tugging on my favorite silk night-gown and climbing under my covers. *A bossy, infuriating, ape of a man who cares more about his job prospects than the people he's supposed to protect.*

I toss and turn for hours, unable to sleep despite the anvils pressing down on my eyelids. The thought of Conor in my house, one floor away, stretched out on my gray sectional, is distracting enough to hold sleep at bay.

The nerve of that man!

Barging into my home, my life, my head. Analyzing me like I'm some puzzle to piece together, some intriguing set of clues to figure out. I have half a mind to storm down there and shove him out the front door to sleep on the damn porch swing. (Considering he's two hundred pounds of pure muscle, I decide it's probably best *not* to act on that particular impulse.)

As the hours slip by, sleep eluding me like the fickle bitch she is, my brain keeps wandering to the man on my sofa. He's still such a stranger to me. I know virtually nothing about him — not his favorite sports teams or where he grew up, not where he lives now or his relationship status.

He doesn't wear a wedding ring, so I assume he's not married. But that doesn't necessarily mean he's unattached. The man may be a certifiable asshole but, much as it pains me to admit... he's not entirely unpleasant to look at. Some — *not me!* — might even say he's devastatingly handsome in a roguish, unpolished sort of way.

But who would put up with him? I ask myself, scoffing into the dark. *Any sane girl would run for the hills after a week with his overbearing neanderthal antics.*

Then again... a small voice pipes up from some remote corner of my brain before I can banish it. *There's something sort of nice about a man with a protective streak. Not like Paul, who treated me as a possession to be owned. Just... someone who knows the value of what he has and isn't afraid to protect it.*

Punching my pillow into a more comfortable shape, I roll onto my side and scowl into the darkness. I don't even know why I'm thinking about these things. I can barely stand Conor — it's not like I'm interested in him romantically. I'm not interested in *anyone* romantically.

Not anymore.

Not ever again.

As soon as my divorce is finalized, I'll have no use for entanglements of any kind. Love is lost to me. After all, it's only ever led me astray in the past. The last time I followed my heart for a man, it was Paul. I'd be crazy to ever risk doing it again.

And so... here I am: twenty-nine years old and officially retired from the game.

A spinster.

I feel like that must be some sort of record.

In lieu of a cash prize, I will accept a lifetime supply of cabernet sauvignon. Please send the goods to 29 Merriweather Street, Somerville, MA. (Blue Victorian. You can't miss it — it's the prettiest house on the block. Maybe the prettiest house in the Greater Boston area.)

I wasn't always such a misanthrope. Not that I was ever what you'd call a hopeless romantic, either. I guess I've always been somewhere in the middle, balancing on a tightrope of cynicism and wishful thinking.

The way I see it, when it comes to love people generally fall into one of two categories — they're either scared to be alone or they're scared to be rejected. All those stomach-butterflies and sweaty palms and soul connections boil down to a single, burning question.

What are you more afraid of — abandonment or commitment? Loneliness or love? Never putting yourself out there? Or potentially being blown off when you actually do?

Me? I'm in the first category.

Scared to be alone.

At least, I used to be, when I first met Paul. Now, after a decade of being ignored by the person who was supposed to love me most, I've been alone so often, it feels far scarier to even consider letting someone in again.

My self-imposed seclusion is a shield. A safety net.

Superman and his Fortress of Solitude ain't got nothing on me.

Conor was a jerk, earlier... but he wasn't entirely off base about my need for control. I *do* like order and organization. I like routine. I like perfection — or, at least, the appearance of it. There's a certain comfort in living my life by a set of strictly-monitored rules, in making decisions and sticking to them like clockwork.

Perfect Shelby Hunt, in her perfect house, with her perfect life.

And if I know one thing, it's that falling in love — crazy, dramatic, complicated love — is the exact *opposite* of control. It's a spiral into chaos. A messy tangle of emotion and irrational thinking. Pure pandemonium with a side of heartbreak.

Which is just about the last thing I need in my meticulously-managed little world.

So I guess... maybe somewhere along the way, I switched categories. Maybe being alone isn't the scariest thing in the world, anymore. Because the idea of loving anyone again... of putting myself out there, only to get my heart shattered a second time...

That's the most terrifying thing I can imagine.

I JOLT awake when a hand claps itself over my mouth.

Panic floods my barely-awake brain. My eyes snap open and I begin to thrash against the hands holding me down, a violent scream bursting from my throat before I can stop it.

Nooooo!

It's Righty!

Or Lefty!

Probably both!

They've got me!

I'm dead!

So freaking dead!

"Shhh! Shhh, Shelby! It's me. Chill!"

I go still as I register the voice. It's suspiciously familiar — and suspiciously lacking the faint Russian accent I was expecting to hear. The room is pitch black, but after a few seconds I manage to focus on the face hovering scant inches from mine.

Crooked nose. Pale brown eyes. Chestnut hair.

"Paul!" I exclaim. Only it comes out as *'PUUUHH!'* because his palm is still pressed tight over my mouth.

"Quiet," he pleads, staring into my eyes. "Do you hear me? You have to be quiet."

I sit up sharply, grabbing his hand and ripping it from my lips. The covers go flying, but I barely notice. I'm too busy glaring at my husband.

If looks could kill, he'd be so dead right now...

"What the fuck are you doing here, Paul?"

"Shhh! Keep it down! That cop is still downstairs."

Conor!

"Are you freaking kidding me?!" I whisper-yell, not entirely sure why I'm complying with his demands. "Give me one good reason why I shouldn't start screaming my head off."

"Because if you do, I'm a dead man." There's a desperate sort of conviction in his voice that tells me he's not lying.

"Paul..." I shake my head. "The police can help you—"

"No!" Rocketing away from the bed, he crosses to the front-facing window and peers out at the street with a paranoid look. "If I'm in custody, I'll be a sitting duck. You don't understand. There are some people after me and if I don't give them what they want... things could get bad. Really bad."

"No shit, Sherlock," I hiss. "Who do you think they came after when they couldn't find you?"

He glances back at me and winces. "I worried that might happen."

"Thanks for the warning, jackass!"

"Shh! Not so loud." His eyes are more remorseful than I've ever seen them. "The last thing I wanted was to drag you into this, Shelbs. You have to believe me."

"Sorry, Paul, but your credibility is shot after the shit you've pulled." I scoff in disbelief. "You have some nerve showing up here after everything you've done. Especially given what happened the last time we saw each other. Or did you think a few gifts, some flowers and chocolates, would make me forget about Christmas?" I touch my cheek-bone absently, tracing an invisible wound.

"God, Shelbs." His face has gone stark white. "I'm sorry, okay? About Christmas. About all of it."

"No! It's *not* okay! None of this is okay!" I throw my legs over the side of the mattress and clamor to my feet, planting my hands on my hips to scowl at him properly. "Petrov's men kidnapped me yesterday! They duct taped me to one of our dining room chairs and held me hostage in an attempt to get your attention!"

He pales further. "I'm sorry. God, I'm so sorry..."

"A little late for that, Paul."

"I'm going to fix it, okay? I have a plan." He takes a few strides toward me, but I instantly backpedal away, main-taining a safe distance between us.

He may've forgotten what he did the last time we were in the same room, but I certainly haven't.

Paul pulls up short, his handsome face contorting with

hurt. Once, seeing that sad, puppy-dog look would've sent a dagger through my heart. Now, all I feel is cold indifference as I stare at the man I married.

"Shelbs..." His voice breaks. "I know we're going through a rough patch right now... but don't you trust me anymore?"

"A rough patch?!" I explode, louder than I intended. "I filed for divorce, threw you out, and am now being targeted by the fucking Bratva thanks to your bad decisions... And you honestly think this is just a *rough patch?*"

"Shhh! That cop is still downstairs." Paul's expression contorts from hurt to anger so fast, I have trouble keeping track. "What the fuck is he doing in my house, anyway?"

I stiffen. "It's not your house anymore. It's mine."

He takes a step toward me. "Why did you have to bring the cops into this, Shelby? I told you, I have a plan!"

"Maybe if you'd bothered to share that plan with me, I wouldn't have been blindsided, kidnapped, and hauled in for questioning about your various criminal activities!" I hiss. "You have no right to question anything I do. Not anymore. And definitely not when it comes to this mess you've made."

"I said I was sorry, Shelbs!" He rubs his hands over his face nervously. "God, this has all gotten so out of hand. I thought, since we were separated, it would be safe with you."

"*What* would be safe with me?"

He doesn't answer. "They were never supposed to come after you."

"What aren't you telling me, Paul? What the hell did you steal from Petrov? And what does it have to do with me?"

He sighs. "I'm going to sort it out, okay? I'll tell them

you had nothing to do with this. I'll convince them you don't have it."

It?

His voice is almost manic. "Once they're gone, we'll have enough money to run away. Anywhere you want — spin the globe and pick a spot, Shelby. Sky's the limit." He takes a step toward me, brown eyes shining in the dark. "But first, I need you to tell me where it is. I swear, I've looked everywhere. Searched this house top to bottom."

"Where *what* is?" I ask, genuinely confused.

"Now is not the time to play dumb, Shelby!"

My heart kicks into higher gear as I stare at the man I married. He's not making sense and, to be perfectly honest, he's starting to scare me. "First of all, don't call me dumb. Secondly, I'm not going anywhere with you. And thirdly, I don't have the *slightest fucking clue* what you're talking about."

He unleashes a frustrated groan and runs his hands through his hair. It's longer than I've ever seen it — as though he hasn't had a haircut in quite some time. In fact, now that I'm taking the time to really examine him, I notice he doesn't look so good. Certainly not like the snappy dresser I remember from our years together. His clothes are rumpled, as though he's been wearing them for more than a single day, and there are deep shadows under his eyes.

My sleep-dulled brain finally catches up with my body and several thoughts occur to me in rapid succession.

"How did you even get in here, Paul?" I ask, narrowing my eyes on him. "There are a dozen FBI agents watching the house. Not to mention the one sleeping on the couch downstairs. I highly doubt you slipped in without a single one of them noticing."

"Wait. They're *FBI*?" Paul groans. "God, Shelby, I can't believe you did this."

"I didn't do a damn thing, you monumental jerk!"

"Bringing the feds into this is only going to fuck me over more thoroughly!"

"And whose fault is that?"

He sighs sulkily.

"You didn't answer my question," I prompt, growing impatient. "How the hell did you get in here undetected?"

He suddenly looks a bit embarrassed. "I've... kind of been..."

I arch my brows.

"Crashing in the attic," he finishes, avoiding my eyes.

"*WHAT?!*"

"Keep it down!"

"Keep it down? *KEEP IT DOWN?* You just said you've been sleeping in our attic! Without my knowledge! After I threw you out of the house!"

"Relax, will you? It was only a few nights last month, when these two scary guys started tailing me home from my office... "

"Oh my god! I *knew* I heard scuffling! I thought I had a raccoon living in the chimney!" My eyes shoot daggers at him. "I hired someone to come put a cap on it and everything!"

"Yeah... *surprise,*" he says weakly. "That was me, moving around up there."

I'm too pissed to speak.

"Silver lining? You don't have a raccoon problem."

"That's such a relief," I snap sarcastically. "I'm just tickled pink that my ex-husband has been sneaking into my house at night to evade dangerous Russian mobsters, despite the fact that I had the locks changed to prevent ever seeing him again!"

"Yeah... you should really start using your alarm system."

An angry growl rattles from my throat. "So I've heard."

"Anyway, who needs a key when you know about the basement window?" Paul shrugs lightly. "Remember — the one with the broken lock you were always harping on me to fix?"

Rage floods me in a great tidal wave, setting my blood boiling. I'm suddenly so angry, I'd like nothing more than to wrap my hands around Paul's throat and squeeze the life out of his body.

The dirty-rotten, no-good, lying, cheating, breaking-and-entering bastard! As if everything he's done to me isn't bad enough...

Scheming with mobsters!

Putting me in the crosshairs!

Sneaking into my house!

To top it all off...

He.

Never.

Even.

Fixed.

The.

Damn.

Basement.

Window.

!!!!!!!!!!!!

Paul must recognize that I'm about to blow a gasket, because he holds out his hands in a placating gesture. His tone is soothing. "Shelby, baby, you're making this a bigger deal than it needs to be. I needed a place to crash for a couple nights, after those guys showed up at my apartment. I knew there was an old twin mattress up there. That's all." He pauses. "Plus, no one would ever think I'd be stupid enough to hide out in my own house." He cracks a grin. "I thought it was a pretty genius idea, actually."

"*Genius* wouldn't be the word I'd use, Paul." My syllables are clipped — short staccato bursts of fury. "*Psycho stalker* might be more accurate."

"I was trying to do something good! Checking in every week or so, just to make sure you were safe! But around dawn, when I got here and realized you weren't home... I got worried. Decided to stay, just to make sure nothing had happened to you." His expression darkens. "I didn't expect you'd come home with a fucking Fed in tow."

"I wasn't home because I was being interrogated by the FBI about the very large henchman who attacked me while they were looking for *you*, you idiot!"

"I already said I was sorry for that."

"An apology doesn't exactly make it okay, Paul." I shake my head in disbelief. "And I suppose while sneaking in here you conveniently forgot about the restraining order that prohibits you from coming within two hundred feet of me."

"This is my house. You're my wife. No piece of paper is going to keep me away." His brown eyes narrow on mine. "We made vows. *Till death do us part. In sickness and in health. For richer or poorer.* You promised you'd be by my side, always."

"That was before I knew you were a pathological liar," I say bluntly. "Before you spent a decade womanizing, manipulating, and putting your hands on me without permission."

"I'll admit, I haven't always been the perfect husband. We have some issues to work through..."

I snort. *Understatement of the decade.*

"But Shelbs, I need you by my side. I need you now more than ever!"

"I'm sorry, Paul, but... I really don't give a shit what you need."

"How can you say that?" he asks, an edge of anguish in his tone. "Don't I get any points for checking in on you?"

"No."

"Didn't you get my gifts? My messages? All the flowers? I've been trying to make things right! You just need to give me a chance."

"Don't tell me what I need. I don't need anything from you except for you to leave. *Now.* Before I have a change of heart and call the nice FBI agents in to arrest you."

"You wouldn't."

I cross my arms over my chest. "Oh, I think I would."

"If you do that, I'm as good as dead. These men who are after me aren't screwing around. If I'm in custody, it'll only make it easier for them to get to me."

"That's not my responsibility, Paul. Maybe if you'd told me you'd been fired... or given me a warning about the freaking *Russian mobsters* you've gotten in bed with... I'd be slightly more inclined to help you."

Or not.

But he doesn't need to know that.

"You haven't taken my calls in months! How was I supposed to tell you about this? Huh?"

"Oh, give it a rest." I shake my head. "You've been lying about this for *years*, not months. Long before I cut off communication. Everything you say is a lie, Paul."

"That's not true!"

"Isn't it, though?" I hold up a hand and start ticking off a list on my fingers. "You lied about getting fired from your job. You lied about the fact that you've been working for your uncle. You lied about the fact that you even *have* an uncle. You lied about your family background, your child- hood home, even your given name." I sigh deeply, wondering how I could've been so blind as to trust this char- latan for so many years. "Tell me, Paul — was anything you told me in our decade together actually true? Or was our marriage just another facet of your elaborate fabrications?"

"You've got it all twisted," he says, voice plaintive. "I never meant to drag you into any of this. You, this house, our marriage... it's all I have left. *You* are the one good thing I have left."

"Except you don't have me anymore," I tell him plainly. "You lost me a long time ago."

"Don't say that!" Expression clouding over with anger quicker than a summer storm, he advances on me. I backpedal until I hit the opposite wall, heart pounding in my chest as I watch the distance between us shrinking rapidly.

"It's time for you to leave, Paul. *Now*."

"I'm not going anywhere," he says, coming closer. "I told you, I'm going to make this right with my uncle and then it'll be like it was before. *Better* than before."

"No, Paul—"

"Don't say no! Just listen..." The distance disappears — five, four, three, two, one foot remaining — and then he's right there, reaching for me. Reaching for me like he has so many times before, every time I mouthed off or questioned his authority or challenged him on something. Every time I tried to push back against his controlling behavior and condescension.

I know I should be running, screaming, doing *something* other than merely standing here like a statue. But I'm strangely paralyzed as I watch him closing in. The rage on his face is as familiar as the feel of the back of his hand and I brace for it, already anticipating the sting of his fingers closing around my throat...

It never comes.

There's a sickening thud as Paul falls to the ground, clutching his nose — which is gushing blood in a bright torrent. It happens so fast, I barely see the fist that flies seemingly out of nowhere and clips him squarely in the face. One minute he's standing there, the next he's on the ground moaning.

My wide eyes lift to Conor, who's looming in front of me like a human shield. The knuckles of his right hand are red, even in the darkness. The expression on his face can only be described as wrath.

Pure, undiluted wrath.

"Paul, I presume," he snarls, staring down at the pathetic heap that is my husband. "Please. Don't get up on my account."

CHAPTER 8

NECESSARY ROUGHNESS

I THINK it's safe to say I'm in deep shit.

Conor's arms are crossed over his chest and he's fixed me with such an intense look, I'm about to pee my pants. Which is awkward since I'm not wearing any pants — I'm still in my lacey little negligee, flashing entirely too much thigh and leaving very little to the imagination when it comes to the chest region.

Hello, ladies.

Thankfully, Conor seems too pissed to notice I'm practically naked. He's glaring at me like I've just spoiled the final season of *Game of Thrones* for him.

"What the fuck is wrong with you, Hunt?"

"Like... overall? Or are you just referring to tonight's mishap?"

He is not amused by my cutesy answer. "When were you planning to tell me your husband was in the house?"

My teeth sink into my lip. "Um... right now?"

"Uh huh. Not, say, *ten minutes ago* when I heard the sound of voices and came upstairs to investigate, finding the door to the attic open wide and your ex spewing a whole lot of bullshit about winning you back?"

I gulp.

He was listening to all that?

"Tell me the truth — and keep in mind I'll know if you lie to me." His tone is severe, his jaw clenched tight. "Did you know he was staying here?"

"No!" I exclaim, offended he'd even ask that question. "Of course I didn't know. Do you honestly think, after everything he's done to me, I'd *protect* him? Give me a little credit, Gallagher."

"I just find it hard to believe you didn't notice him periodically coming or going, these past few weeks. On multiple occasions, he was living fifteen feet above your damn head."

"Um, excuse me, but aren't *you* the one highly trained in surveillance?" I counter. "Because last I checked, you didn't seem to pick up on his presence either during your many, many hours spent watching this street."

A muscle in his eye twitches and I know I've scored a point.

"Believe me, Paul is the last person on the planet I'd ever want in my house. Just the thought of him being here while I was sleeping..." I shiver. "It's going to give me nightmares for months."

"And yet, when he snuck down from the attic and woke you up tonight... you somehow thought it was a good idea to confront him on your own, despite me being a single goddamn shout away?" His tone is sharp enough to flay me where I stand.

I shift from one bare foot to the other, digging my toes into the carpet. "He caught me off guard, okay? And then..."

Conor's brows lift.

"I thought he might be more receptive talking to me

than he would be if you charged in here and pummeled him," I say with a roll of my eyes. "Wasn't the whole point of me staying here to draw him out? To find out what he took from Petrov that's worth getting us all killed over?"

Conor grunts in lieu of a response.

Score two for the girl in the peach lace nightie.

My eyes drift through the entryway of my walk-in closet, where we've been talking in hushed whispers for the past few minutes, across the bedroom to the armchair in the corner. Paul is slumped over, wrists restrained behind his back, still whimpering like a baby. The handcuffs, courtesy of Conor, prevent him from wiping his broken nose. Two bloody trails streak down his chin and drip onto his white shirt.

He looks like a Halloween horror experiment gone wrong.

Wincing, I glance back at Conor. "Frankly, given the fact that your greeting consisted of an incapacitating blow to the face, I can't say I'm all that sorry I waited to call you in here. He hasn't said a word since you arrived."

"He was about to put his hands on you." Conor's voice has gone scary again. "The fucker is lucky I left him with the ability to use his limbs."

I gulp. It's no idle threat — I have no doubt Conor would take true pleasure in beating Paul to a bloody pulp. "Be that as it may, I don't think you can actually *throttle* the truth out of someone, Gallagher."

"Might be fun to try," he mutters darkly.

"And here I thought FBI agents were supposed to be beacons of fidelity, bravery, and integrity." My lips twist. "Or is that slogan similar to the Pirate's Code — more of a loose guideline than a hard and fast set of rules?"

He doesn't even crack a smile. He just shakes his head

and sighs, as though I'm testing his patience again. "You trying to be cute doesn't change the fact that you should've called for me right away, Hunt. What if I hadn't woken up? What if I hadn't gotten to you in time?"

My lips flatten into a frown. I glance down at my feet, studying the pink polish on my toes so I don't have to meet his gaze. The fact of the matter is, I've been mulling over that same question for the past few minutes... and I'm not sure I like the answer. Because if Conor hadn't showed up when he did...

Paul's angry face flashes in my mind and I shiver.

"Hey."

My eyes flicker up at the sound of Conor's voice. He looks conflicted, almost wary, as he reaches out and sets one large, callused hand on my shoulder. I suck in a breath at the contact.

Oh boy.

His light squeeze is meant to be comforting... but the feeling of his touch on my bare skin does nothing to settle my nerves. If anything, it sends them fluttering into hyperdrive. Every cell in my body is suddenly on fire as I stare up into his indigo eyes.

"Look, Hunt... I know you think I'm this monumental asshole who's barged into your life, who's bossing you around nonstop, disrupting everything in your orderly little world..." Conor's voice is grave. "But the bottom line is, I can't protect you if you don't trust me. *You have to start trusting me.*"

"I know. I... I'm sorry."

"I don't need an apology. I need a promise that you're going to stop thinking you have to handle this situation entirely on your own. That might be how things went in the past... but this time, things are different."

"How?" I whisper.

"Because this time you aren't standing on your own. This time, you have me." His fingers flex against my skin, squeezing tighter. It takes all my resolve not to go weak at the knees. "I'm in this with you, every step of the way... Got it?"

"Got it." I pull in a shaky breath. "I promise next time, I'll call for backup."

"There better not be a next time." He shoots Paul a deadly look.

"What's going to happen to him now?"

"I already radioed the surveillance team parked outside. Two of my men are on their way in. They'll take him into custody and bring him back to a holding cell at headquarters, until we have a chance to question him about his involvement in all of this. At the very least, he should be able to give us some new intel on Petrov before he's arraigned for fraud, money laundering, and embezzlement."

As if on cue, a few seconds later two federal agents in tactical gear step into the bedroom. Conor and I walk out of the closet to greet them.

"Van's waiting in the driveway," the first agent says while his partner hauls Paul to his feet. "We're good to go."

"Did you radio in to let Sykes know you're inbound?" Conor asks.

"Yes, sir."

"Good. Tell her I'll be in touch soon."

We make our way down the staircase single-file. The silence is thick, punctuated only by Paul's small moans of pain as the agents drag him into the foyer. He keeps his head down and there's a defeated slump to his shoulders — the fight has definitely gone out of him. He's resigned to his fate.

Conor and I trail behind as the agents prod Paul toward the front door. I feel strangely unsettled, watching him go. Like it or not, he was a big part of my life for a long time. It's strange to see the man I married being led away in handcuffs. Stranger still to think about him going to trial, or wearing an orange jumpsuit, or being locked up behind bars.

What's this? Sympathy for the devil? That's weak, Shelby. Even for you.

The unforgiving voice whispers from a dark place inside me — a place that's undeniably glad Paul is about to be out of my life. For good, this time. It's the same place that holds all my darkest fears and insecurities. A lockbox of my deepest shame, embedded in my psyche.

But you've always been weak, haven't you? So weak, you didn't even fight back when he hurt you. A pathetic little girl, trapped in her own delusions of perfection.

I try to shut the voice out, but it mocks me all the way to the door.

Look how that turned out.

Look at your perfect life, now.

Heart pounding hard, I blink back hot tears. Conor's looking at me strangely, but I avoid his eyes. I'm not about to explain my own humiliation — not to him. And certainly not now, in front of two federal agents and my no-good, dirty-rotten, lying, cheating, bastard of a husband.

We reach the front door. The agents are pushing Paul outside when he suddenly seems to snap out of his stupor. Struggling against their hold, his head whips around to find me.

"Shelby!" His wild eyes lock on mine as the agents attempt to subdue him. "Shelbs, listen — if I don't make it out of this..." He groans as they yank his arms back roughly, nearly pulling the joints from their sockets. "You have to *run*. They won't stop looking for it. No matter what. It's too valuable."

It?

"What?" My brow furrows. "What are you talking about?"

"If I'm locked up, they'll come after you again, Shelby!" he calls back to me as he's shoved roughly through the door, onto the porch. He's straining to maintain eye contact, now. His tone turns desperate. "Alexei wants it too badly to let it go. Even if you try to give it back, he'll probably have you killed as retribution for hiding it from him."

Killed?!

Retribution?!

I've gone white as a sheet. My words come out shaking. "Paul, I don't understand. You're not making any sense!"

"Your only chance is to run. You hear me? You have to take it and *run*."

"*It?* What do you mean, *it?*"

"Nécessaire, Shelby! *Nécessaire!*"

I tilt my head to the side, more than a little baffled by his sudden switch to appeals in French. Last I checked, Paul doesn't speak any other languages besides English and the small smattering of Russian he picked up from his parents.

Or maybe that's just another lie he told you. For all you know, he's a freaking expert linguist.

"Paul—"

"YOU'RE NOT SAFE AS LONG AS YOU HAVE IT!" His voice has gone ragged, piercing the dark night air. "I'M SORRY, SHELBS! I'M SO SOR—"

"That's enough!" One of the agents throws out an elbow, catching Paul across the nose. I flinch when I hear his howl of pain. He crumples to the porch, bleeding anew.

"Let's go," the agent barks. "Get up! On your feet, right now!"

When Paul makes no effort to rise, they haul him into a vertical position, then strong-arm his limp form down the front porch steps. Shock and horror simmering inside me, all I can do is watch as they drag him across the grass toward the waiting van. He's still mumbling incoherently, but I can't make out all his words from this distance. Merely snippets.

Run!

Take it and run!

I'm sorry, Shelby!

Nécessaire!

Nécessaire!

Half of me wants to block my ears, to shut him out before any more of his poisonous lies have a chance to take root in my mind.

This is just some last-ditch effort to sway you to his side, I tell myself. *Probably so you won't testify against him in federal court.*

Yet, as I watch him being led across the lawn, I'm uncomfortably conflicted.

He doesn't *seem* like he's lying or playing any sort of trick. He seems...

Scared.

Genuinely scared.

Not for his own fate — for mine.

A chill moves down my spine as I play back his words. He's given me more questions than answers, during his brief reappearance in my life.

What is this mysterious 'it' he keeps referring to?

Why does he think I, of all people, have it?

And, while I understand he thinks it's 'necessary' that I run for my life... what the fuck is with the French?

I stand beside Conor on the porch, leaning heavily against the wood railing as the agents lead Paul slowly toward the waiting van. Hearing my deep sigh, he glances over at me, brows raised.

"That was... interesting."

"I was going to say *unhinged*, but sure." I shrug. "Interesting works."

"Don't worry. We'll get him in an interrogation room, calm him down, and sort out the truth. Sykes can be very... *persuasive*... when she wants something."

My brows lift and, before I can shut down the thought, I find myself wondering about Conor's relationship with the pretty blonde agent.

Has she used her powers of persuasion on him in a non-professional capacity?

I don't have a chance to wonder for more than a second. The inappropriate notion flies out of my mind entirely when an unfamiliar whizzing sound splits the midnight sky.

Before I've managed to so much as turn my head to look, I'm tackled to the porch. The wind is snatched from my lungs as Conor's body comes down hard on top of mine. He's crushing my ribs — I can hardly draw a breath — but I don't care about that in the slightest, because my mind has finally processed what that strange whirring is, peppering the air with increasing frequency.

Shots.

From a silencer.

On a gun.

A freaking gun.

A gun someone is firing at us.

My blood runs cold as I hear the sharp metallic zing of bullets striking the van, lodging in the aluminum door panels. We're painfully exposed out here on the porch. Even with Conor lying on top of me, sheltering my body with his own, I don't feel remotely safe. He shifts, reaching down to extract the gun from the holster strapped to his thigh.

"Don't move," he barks, rolling off me into a crouch and taking shelter behind a narrow balustrade column. "Stay low."

I nod, but he's no longer looking at me. His eyes are scanning the dark street, searching for the source of the gunfire. Through the narrow railings, I squint to make out the black van in the driveway. It looks like a slice of Swiss cheese, it's so full of holes. Both FBI agents are crouched behind the hood, returning fire. If Paul is with them, I don't see him anywhere.

Plink!

Plink!

Plink!

More shots, firing faster with each passing moment. I gasp and duck my head when a bullet lodges itself in the gabled porch roof ten feet overhead, sending down a shower of sawdust. Another strikes the ornate lamp fixture mounted beside my front door, shattering it into unrecognizable shards that spill across the stoop.

I fear the next round might hit something far less replaceable.

Namely, one of us.

"We have to move," Conor says, grabbing me by the hand and dragging me along behind him. I'm on my hands and knees, half-crawling, half-crouching as we make our way along the front section of the porch, then take a sharp left around the side of the house. Momentarily safe, we press our backs tight to the shingled wall and haul in deep gulps of air.

We're out of direct range.

For now.

I can't say the same for Paul or the other agents, though. My quiet neighborhood has turned into a war zone. The night sky is still a flurry of flying bullets — and there's no doubt in my mind about who's pulling the triggers.

The Evanoffs.

They're here.

To kill us.

I'm breathing hard and my pulse is roaring so loud between my ears, it's downing out everything else. Conor repeats my name three times before he manages to break through the thick fog of panic.

"Hunt! Hunt, look at me."

My eyes, wide with fear, slide to his.

"Listen. The other agents are pinned down behind the van. I have to lay down covering fire so they can get out of there. You understand?"

Don't leave me! I want to scream as terror spikes in a deadly fever pitch. *Don't you dare leave me alone!*

I bite my lip to contain the selfish words and nod, not trusting myself to speak.

"I need you to do something for me," he says, adjusting his grip on his gun as he sidles along the side of the house, peering around the corner with shrewd eyes.

"Okay," I whisper, steeling myself for whatever task he's about to give me.

I'll run to the back door.

Get inside.

Find the phone.

Call the police.

"You see that bench? On your left?" Conor's chin jerks toward the oak seating nook built out from the side of the house. There's a narrow gap underneath it — barely big enough for a child to squeeze into. "I need you to crawl under there and stay put until I come back."

I don't budge. "You want me to *hide*?"

"Hunt, this is not up for discussion," Conor snaps without looking at me. "For once in your fucking life, just do as you're told without comment."

I'm frozen in place, watching as he steps out from the shelter of the house and takes up a new position behind a column. The hail of gunfire never seems to cease — the Evanoffs must have some serious artillery at their disposal.

And Conor only has one gun.

I find myself unable to move, unable to tear my eyes away from him as he braces his Glock against the railing and begins to return fire with a calm proficiency that tells me it's not the first time he's used his service weapon.

Bang!
Bang!
Bang!
Bang!
Bang!

I jolt with each discharge, the rapport ringing in my ears as the acidic smell of gunpowder hits me in a cloud. When Conor pauses to reload, he spares a brief glance in my direction. He scowls darkly when he sees I've yet to worm my way into hiding.

"Hunt! Get under the damn bench!"

I hesitate.

"Shelby," he says pleadingly, snapping the clip into place. His eyes pin me to the spot. "*Please.*"

Watching his lips form those words, my resistance evaporates. I nod tremulously. "Okay! Okay, I'm going."

He returns my nod and, without another beat of hesitation, turns and runs out from behind the column.

Headlong into danger.

Straight into the firefight.

Out of my line of vision.

I hear the sound of his gun letting off rounds and try my best not to count how many he has left in the chamber, not to consider how many more ammo clips he has at his disposal before he's rendered defenseless. Closing my eyes to keep from imagining the scene unfolding on my front lawn, I wedge myself beneath the bench. It's a tight squeeze. I feel several splinters pierce my bare legs. A rusty nail snags on my nightgown, tearing a hole through the thin fabric by my ribcage. I yank myself loose and keep going, until my whole body is concealed beneath the wood frame.

As I lay there in the dark, hiding like a damn coward, listening to the sound of bullets and wondering whether Conor Asshole Gallagher — who, it must be said, might not actually be such an asshole after all — is going to make it out of this alive... I replay the look in his eyes just before he left me. And I hear his voice in my head, saying my name for the first time ever.

Shelby.

Please.

A tear trickles down my cheek as I pray the first time isn't also the last.

I THOUGHT the sound of gunfire was the scariest thing I'd hear tonight. Turns out I was wrong. The silence that falls in its wake is far more terrifying.

Beneath the bench, I'm a statue — waiting for Conor to come back for me, to tell me it's all clear.

Unless... it's not...

An eternity passes before I finally hear the sound of footsteps ringing out across the wood porch, closer and closer. They stop just beside the bench and I swallow a bleat of terror. I'm half-convinced it's one of the Evanoff brothers, come to kill me... until a familiar head of messy black hair ducks down to my level.

"Hey."

His voice is gruff, stripped of anything resembling warmth, but he extends a hand out to me. I slide my palm into his and suck in a breath when he twines our fingers together before pulling me slowly from beneath the bench. I emerge covered in dust, short of breath, and full of more splinters than a pincushion...

But I'm alive.

I'm breathing.

"Is it over?" I ask when I'm finally back on my feet. I tell myself to drop Conor's hand, to pull away from his touch, but I can't seem to make my fingers comply.

Then again, he hasn't pulled away yet either...

He blows out a terse breath. "They're gone, if that's what you mean. But it won't be over until the fuckers are in custody."

"They got away?!"

He nods, but he's not looking at me. His eyes are fixed on my legs with concern. I glance down and see I'm covered in small cuts and bruises. There's a long laceration running up my right shin, the pretty pink polish is missing from several of my toes, and the skin of both knees appears to have lost a battle with a cheese grater.

It looks far worse than it feels. Not that I can feel much of *anything*, with this much adrenaline pumping through my veins.

His brow is furrowed. "Are you okay?"

"Fit as a fiddle." I try out a smile but it soon turns to a yelp of pain when Conor pokes me in the side with his free hand. "*Ow!* What was that for?"

"You've got a cut here," he murmurs, his fingers exploring the sensitive skin of my ribs through the ripped fabric of my nightgown.

"Right. *That.*" I shrug. "I got snagged on a nail when I was wedging my body under the bench. It doesn't even hurt."

"It will later," he assures me, still prodding the wound.

"Oh, goodie. Something to look forward to."

"The paramedics will treat it when they arrive."

"That seems like overkill," I protest.

"Know what's overkill? Winding up with lockjaw because you're too stubborn to get a tetanus shot and some antibiotics."

I roll my eyes, but decide it's best not to fight with him.

Much.

"You know, you're unnecessarily bossy. One of these da — *Oh my god!*"

His brows lift calmly. "Yes?"

"You're bleeding!" I exclaim, eyes locked on the bloom of red near his bicep. "Christ, Gallagher, you have the nerve to lecture me about a tiny *scrape* when you've been freaking *shot?!*"

"Relax. It's just a graze."

My eyes are still bugging out. "Just a... Are you... *Ugh!* You are the most infuriating, stubborn, hypocritical man!"

His lips twitch. "Noted."

"Are the other agents okay?"

"One took a bullet to the leg, but it was a through and through — he'll be fine."

My stomach clenches. "Is there anything I can do for him? There's a first aid kit inside..."

"We put a field dressing on it. His partner is waiting by the van with him now. The ambulance should be here shortly."

I nod, my ears picking up the faint sound of sirens in the distance. "And... and Paul?"

Conor's grip tightens reflexively on mine. His eyes are suddenly unreadable. "I lost track of him when they started shooting. I think he was trying to run for cover, but..."

"But what?" I breathe, heart pounding.

"The Evanoffs grabbed him." He shakes his head. "We tried to chase them down, but they must've had a car stashed a few blocks over. By the time we got there, they were gone. And so was your husband."

The blood drains out of my face. "Oh my god."

"I'm sorry, Hunt." He's watching me carefully. "We'll do everything we can to get him back."

"I... I..." My mouth snaps shut.

I'm not sure what I'm trying to say. There are no words to describe what I'm feeling right now, seconds after learning that my no-good, dirty-rotten, lying, cheating bastard of a husband has been taken by a duo of men who want his existence wiped from the face of the earth... and that, in all likelihood, they will get their wish.

Fear.

Guilt.

Sorrow.

And, inexplicably, undeniably, unforgivably...

Relief.

That's the one that kills me. The one that damn near brings me to my knees, that breaks my heart into a thousand awful fragments inside my chest. Because as horrible as it is, as unconscionable as it sounds... if the Evanoffs have Paul...

They won't come after me, anymore.

He can't come after me anymore.

Which means... I'm finally free.

Of them.

Of him.

Of this clusterfuck.

Of this whole life.

I stumble backward into the side of the house, needing something solid to prop me up as my mind spins in circles. I'm horrified by my own thoughts — by the deliverance I'm experiencing in my husband's most desperate hour.

No doubt about it: you are going to Hell, Shelby Hunt.

My eyes lift to Conor and I see he's watching me, something like resignation etched all over his features. His hand tightens on mine, just once more.

"I will get him back for you," he says in an oddly thick voice.

And if this were any other time, I'd probably notice the strain in his shoulders when he makes that strange vow. The tension in his face when he forces out the words. The flash of unguarded emotion that moves through his eyes when he takes a deep breath and finally releases my hand.

Any other time, I'd notice the moment he lets me go.

But right now, I'm far too caught up inside my own head to wonder what's going on in Conor's.

Paul is gone.

I am free.

My hand falls limply to my side. My eyes stare unseeing at the street as two ambulances slam to a stop by my front curb, followed closely by a fleet of police cars, lights strobing a medley of blue and red that draws all my curious neighbors from their beds to their front windows.

Jaw ticking with tension, Conor turns on a heel and walks away to greet the arriving officers, not once pausing to look back at the woman leaning against the side of her house, her stricken face flashing blue-red, blue-red, blue-red as the whole world shifts beneath her feet.

Free.

CHAPTER 9

HOTEL MOTEL HOLIDAY INN

I SCOWL at the locked door for an hour or so, willing it to open.

It doesn't.

Desperate for a change of scenery, I shove to my feet and stride to the front window. Flicking back the corner of the curtain, I peer out at the parking lot.

Steam is rising off the pavement in the midday sunshine. It's one of those muggy July afternoons, when the air is so thick you practically need gills to breathe properly.

The air-conditioning unit gives an ominous rattle, struggling to beat the heat. It's on its last legs. I can only hope it doesn't stop working while I'm still a guest here at the lovely Budget Inn.

Oh. Did I say guest?

I meant *prisoner*.

The black SUV is still parked directly across from my door. Even from here, I can make out the two federal agents watching me through the windshield, their faces show clear disapproval as soon as they spot me. With a sigh, I let the curtain fall back into place and step away from the dust-streaked window.

Stay out of sight, they barked when they shoved me in here ten — or was it twelve? — hours ago. *Gallagher's orders.*

I begin to pace angrily back and forth across the small motel room, a ping pong ball of rage scoring treads into the carpet. I glower at my surroundings as if that might somehow make them more appealing.

The rusty red sofa. The orange and purple bedspread. The tacky watercolor wall paintings of Dutch windmills and winding rivers. The stained puce carpet, clashing horribly with the striped yellow wallpaper.

I'm not sure which ring of hell this is, but it seems to have been specifically designed to assault the senses with as many contrary patterns and color schemes as possible. I eye the bed, wondering what it would look like under a blacklight.

Probably best you never find out.

Honestly, after today, I'm considering writing to the Vatican to apply for sainthood, because I have given new meaning to the phrase *patience of a saint* after spending twelve long hours sitting in this tiny ass room, going out of my mind with worry. So bored I considered gouging out my own eyeballs just so I'd have something to do besides stress and panic and pace.

Wait.

Actually...

I take it all back.

I don't have the patience of a saint. *Oh, no.* I have the patience of a fangirl waiting for the next installment in her favorite book series. Because, seriously, no one does the whole *suffer-in-silence-for-years-on-end-without-any-hope-of-a-sequel* quite like bookworms. (Also, there's the small fact that I don't think I'd make a particularly good saint... what with my short temper and propensity for colorful curse words and, oh yeah, the one way ticket to Hell I've probably earned myself after practically celebrating my husband's impending doom last night.)

With a groan, I collapse on top of the grody bedspread and close my eyes. They spring open again almost instantly when I hear the beep of a keycard followed by the sound of the door swinging inward. I sit up just in time to see Agent Lucy Sykes step inside the crappy motel room.

"*Finally*! An intelligent life form on this desolate planet!"

"Hello to you too, Shelby." Her lips tug up in a smile. It wavers a little as she eyes the questionably clean armchair across from my bed. Nonetheless, she sinks into it with a sigh and crosses her long legs. "Sorry it took me so long to get here. Turns out, shootouts involving the Russian mob require an exceptional amount of paperwork."

"Ah."

"How are you holding up?"

I heave a mighty shrug. The FBI sweatshirt — courtesy of one of the agents who locked me in here wearing nothing but my freaking peach nightie — hikes higher on my thighs. I tug it down with annoyance.

Sykes eyes my scraped-up legs. "Gallagher told me you got pretty banged up, last night. If you're in pain I can get you some Advil."

At the mention of his name, I have to bite my tongue to keep from asking the question that's been nagging at me since I was loaded into a black SUV last night and carted from my house to this crappy motel just off Route 1 without so much as an explanation.

Where the hell is Conor?

Why isn't he here?

"I realize this isn't exactly the Ritz," Sykes says, pulling my attention back to her. "But it's close to the Bureau, which means we can keep a revolving shift of guards staked out. Plus it's nondescript enough to keep you safe until we're sure the Evanoffs are no longer a threat."

"And how long do you expect that'll take?"

"Unclear. We searched your attic and found some of your husbands belongings stashed there... but nothing of any value. Certainly nothing worthy of Alexei Petrov's wrath."

"So you still have no idea what Paul took from him?"

"Unfortunately not." She blows out a breath. "Nor do we know why Petrov's men seem to believe you're the one in possession of it."

"They aren't the only ones. Paul seems to think I have it, as well. Which makes *no freaking sense* considering he's the one who stole it in the first place."

"Shelby, I need you to think. Is there anything you can remember — anything at all — that your husband said last night that might help us sort this mess out?"

"He kept saying I had to run away. That I wasn't safe so long as I had '*it*' and that they'd never stop looking." My eyes narrow in concentration. "But I don't know what '*it*' is. It makes no sense. How could I have something that's supposedly *this* valuable and not even realize it?"

"It's my personal belief that '*it*' isn't an object at all. It's money. A lot of money, siphoned from Petrov's private accounts into Paul's pockets. Only... he probably put it in *your* name to cover his tracks, hoping his uncle wouldn't connect the dots until it was too late."

"Oh." I blink as I digest this news. "But wouldn't I know

if there was a Cayman Island out there with a designated Shelby Hunt vault of cash?"

"Not necessarily. As your husband, Paul could've made deposits on your behalf without your knowledge. But... by putting your name on the account, he needs your authorization to access the stolen funds. Which is likely why he's been so fixated on recapturing your affections, these past few months." She pauses. "It also explains why Alexei Petrov sent his thugs after you in the first place."

I have to admit, her theory does sound plausible. Far more plausible than the idea that I have in my unwitting possession some mythical object that Petrov is desperate to recover.

"I guess that makes sense," I murmur. "I should've known Paul wasn't actually interested in winning me back out of some twisted sense of love or husbandly duty."

Sykes pauses tactfully. "Right. Well. As of now, this remains a theory. We haven't found any sort of paper trail yet."

"But you will?"

"If it exists, our analysts will find it. They're the best in the world."

My head tilts as something occurs to me. "I thought, when they took Paul, my part in all of this would be over. But if you're right about this — if they can't access the funds without my authorization... they're going to keep coming after me, aren't they?"

"It's unlikely they'll pursue you now that they know the FBI is involved. As soon as we locate the accounts, we'll freeze whatever funds they contain. Their only shot would be to grab you before we have a chance." Her eyes narrow. "And we don't plan to let that happen."

I pull in a shaky breath, suddenly feeling a bit light-headed. "What does that mean for me, exactly?"

"For the time being, it means you're stuck here where we can keep an eye on you."

"Great." I grimace.

"It shouldn't be too much longer. We've got every available agent trying to track down the stolen money, running your name through every database known to man. If that account exists, we'll know about it soon. That's the beauty of a paper trail — follow it to the end, you always find your treasure."

My lips twist. "Files don't lie?"

"Precisely." Her eyes crinkle up. "Oh — before I forget — I have something for you," Sykes says, reaching into her bag. "Your phone. I grabbed it from your purse when we were doing a search of the house. I hope you don't mind the intrusion — I just figured there might be someone you'd like to call..."

"Thanks. That's really nice of you." I take the phone and charger cable from her. The battery is dead, so I plug it into a nearby outlet.

Sykes is watching me carefully. "Have you talked to your family at all since..."

"Since my life exploded? No. My parents and I are on more of a HEB schedule."

"HEB?"

"Holidays, emergencies, birthdays." My smile is weak. "We're not all that close."

"I'm sorry."

"Don't be. It's nothing new. They never approved of me getting married so young. They pretty much cut me off as soon as I told them about Paul." I laugh, but it's joyless. "Ironically, I think that's one of the reasons I tried to make it work with him for so long, even after things went cold between us. A part of me thought if he turned out to be a shithead, it meant my parents were right about him. Right about *me*."

"Ah. And you're afraid, if you call them now..."

"It will just validate what they did — cutting off their daughter because they didn't approve of her choices."

"I'd tell you they'll come around eventually, realize the error of their ways, and apologize, but..." She shoots me an empathetic look that says she understands my struggles all too well. "Parents have a unique ability to constantly point out their children's mistakes without ever taking account-ability for their own."

"Truer words never spoken."

"What about your friends? Can you talk to them?"

I wince. "I don't want to burden them."

"I doubt they'd see it that way."

"One of my friends is pregnant — about to pop, no exag-geration — so she definitely doesn't need this stress in her life, trust me. Another has two toddlers under the age of three, so every day is already a catastrophe without me adding drama to the mix... One is on her honeymoon... Another is sailing around the world..." I trail off. "So, it's just me. On my own. Again."

Sykes is staring at me with sad eyes.

"Oh, don't look at me like that, Sykes! I'll start to think you actually have a heart."

"Dear god, we can't have that." She laughs and rises to her feet. "I should probably get going, anyway. Someone will be by later to drop off dinner for you. Any requests?"

"I'm a vegetarian. Anything green is generally a safe bet, though I never turn my nose up at some chips and guac."

"Got it." She scribbles a note on the small pad she seems to carry everywhere. "I'll be back in touch when we have an update on the Petrov situation. In the meantime, just sit tight and try not to go too stir crazy."

"No promises."

"Here's my card." She slips a small white rectangle from her purse and sets it on the end table. "If you need anything, you can call me."

"Thanks, Agent Sykes."

"It's Lucy."

I smile softly. "Oh. Well, then... goodbye, Lucy."

She walks to the door. "See you soon, Shelby."

I manage to keep the smile on my face until it clicks closed at her back, leaving me alone once more in the dingy motel room.

I WAKE to the sound of a keycard beeping.

Sitting straight up in bed, my covers go flying as I watch the door swing inward. A large man's silhouette fills the frame, massive enough to send my heart lurching into my throat. Before he can take a single stride into the room, I'm out of bed — leaping off the mattress, grabbing the lamp off the bedside table, holding it aloft like a baseball player stepping up to home plate.

Just try me, bucko!

The overhead light flickers on. I blink my eyes as they struggle to adjust to the brightness. When the room comes into focus, I feel my cheeks flame the same color red as the gaudy motel sofa.

Conor is standing in the threshold, his hand still poised

on the light switch, his lips twitching like he's about to burst into laughter.

"Hey, batter batter."

With as much dignity as I can muster, I lower the lamp and set it on the table.

I hear a low chuckle a few seconds before the door swings closed. Avoiding his eyes, I tug my sweatshirt down so it covers my underwear a bit more thoroughly and smooth a hand through my sleep-mussed brown waves.

"What are you doing here, Gallagher?"

"Bringing you this." He sets my duffle bag on the sofa — the one I packed the first day we met. It feels like years have passed since then. "I didn't mean to wake you."

"I'm a light sleeper."

"Clearly."

I finally look up. He's leaning against the wall across from me, his dark eyes totally alert as they sweep me from head to toe. They linger on my bare legs for a second longer than strictly necessary.

My chin jerks upward in a stubborn move. I wait for him to say something, but he's silent as a freaking grave. After a long moment of frigid silence, during which my hands curl into frustrated fists and my teeth begin to gnash together with rage, I finally realize he's not going to speak at all.

"Well. If that's everything you came for..." I look pointedly at the door. "I've got some vital beauty rest to get back to."

He doesn't move a muscle. "You angry at me about something, Hunt?"

"Why would I be angry?" I snap.

"I don't know, that's why I asked." His eyes narrow on

mine, hard as lapis and twice as blue. "You're not acting like yourself, that's for damn sure."

"And how am I acting?"

"Bitchy, for starters."

"When you wake someone up in the middle of the night, it's called *cranky* not *bitchy*. Not my fault you caught me during a bad REM cycle."

"No. That's not it."

I lock my jaw tight, refusing to say another word.

The truth is, I *am* angry with him. I'm so angry I could spit. So angry, my hands are itching to pick up that lamp and chuck it at his head — for real this time. And the strangest part is, I'm not even sure why I'm so mad. I don't have a good reason to be so full of rage. I don't even have a *bad* reason for it.

I'm perfectly aware that I should be grateful for everything he's done for me. After all, he's been there every step of the way since this insanity started — a constant, annoying, reassuring, infuriating presence in my life, keeping me out of harm's way and well stocked in Mexican take-out, shielding me from gunfire and saving me from scary bad guys. (On more than one occasion.)

Hell, he's barely let me out of his damn sight for three straight days.

At least... until last night.

After the shootout at my house, not only did he allow me to drive off with two strange agents I'd never met before... he didn't even bother to check in on me when I finished getting my ribs bandaged by the paramedics. In fact, he never spoke to me again after pulling me out from beneath that porch bench and telling me about Paul's capture.

Not at the scene. Not all day yesterday, as I sat alone in

this shitty room, wondering what the hell was happening out there... whether he'd caught up to the Evanoff brothers and engaged in another shootout... whether he'd had another close encounter with a bullet...

Whether he was alive or dead.

When he finally did decide I merited some intel, he sent Sykes to do his dirty work. I'm not sure why that stings so much; it's not like he answers to me. He has no obligation to tell me anything. As he's reiterated *multiple times* over the past few days... this is just a job for him. I'm nothing more than an asset. Something to be managed. One more task on a checklist before he gets to clock out at night.

"That's a new look," he murmurs.

I flinch. "What?"

"The look on your face right now. Can't decide if you're preparing to kill me or..."

"Or what?"

He shrugs and pushes off from the wall. I go tense, watching as he closes some of the distance between us. Every muscle in my body is poised to either bolt or...

Or what, Shelby?

Throw yourself into his arms?

And what, exactly, would you do when you got there?

Hit him or hug him?

Kill him or kiss him?

I shake myself to clear the absurd thoughts. "What do you want, Gallagher? It's late and I'm tired."

"I'm not leaving until you tell me what's got you so riled up."

"I am *not* riled up!"

He just stares at me.

A scoff flies from my mouth. "Fine. I'm riled up. But only because it's three in the damn morning."

"Not buying it, Hunt."

I throw out my hands. "I don't know what you want to hear."

"How about the truth for once, instead of an evasion or a dodge or a cutesy comment designed to distract me from what you're actually feeling," he says lowly.

Oh boy.

My stomach drops to my feet.

Conor takes a step nearer. "Or, if you're not inclined to share why you're so pissed off at my general presence tonight, how 'bout you tell me something else instead." His voice is soft, cajoling. "Why don't you let me in on one of those other secrets you're determined to keep so close to the vest? The ones you hide from everyone — whether it's your neighbors or your family or your friends. The ones you're afraid to admit out loud, 'cause they terrify you too much."

"I don't know what secrets you're referring to," I lie, heart pounding too fast, thinking about bruised cheekbones and cold bedsheets and Christmas mornings and my uncontrollable need for control.

"No?"

"Nope."

He leans in. "*Bullshit.*"

I suck in a gulp of air and try to look away from him, but my eyes seem to be stuck in a dark blue tractor beam. There's no escape. No avoiding that deeply perceptive stare, that sees straight through every wall I put up.

He is the one person who's never been fooled by my smoke and mirrors. Who's ever called me out on my need for perfection. Who's ever pushed me to talk about all the not-so-picturesque parts of my marriage to Paul.

Judging by the pointed direction of his questions, he already knows all my secrets. Or... suspects, in any case. But if he thinks I'm going to admit them out loud, to share them with him of all people... he'd better get accustomed to disappointment.

Why would I ever confide in someone I can't stand?

Conor's eyes never shift from mine, nor does he back away a single inch. Knowing him, he'll be more than happy to stand here until the sun rises, waiting for me to speak. He may call *me* stubborn, but he takes the freaking cake when it comes to digging in his heels.

Until tonight. Because I am absolutely not breaking the silence first.

Nope.

No way.

Not happening.

"Tick tock," he murmurs, egging me on. "I've got all night, Hunt. And I'm not leaving without an explanation. So you can either tell me why you're pissed... or you can tell me something else. Something real. Something that matters."

"Why do you even care?" I hiss.

"Call it... professional curiosity."

"I can think of a few other names for it. And for *you*."

We glare at each other as the silence drags on, as the air grows heavy with unspoken thoughts. The narrow foot of space between our faces seems to simmer with tension the longer we go without speaking. I grit my teeth to keep the words inside, determined not to cave to the pressure, determined not to let him win, determined not to—

"Where were you?" I blurt before I can stop myself.

His brows skyrocket to his hairline. "Sorry?"

"*Where were you?* And where have you been? Last night, after the shootout, you just... you disappeared on me." I swallow hard, hoping it might unravel the fragile thread of vulnerability running through my voice, woven between thick cords of anger. "I didn't know what was going on. I didn't know where you were."

He's silent, watching me through narrowed eyes.

"Not that I even care," I tack on hastily. "It just would've been nice to know, seeing as there are insane twin mobsters wandering the streets of Boston, out for our blood and armed to the teeth, if last night was any indication."

His loaded pause is legendary. It makes all previous pauses seem utterly insignificant, by comparison. "You worried about me, Hunt?"

"No," I snap. "Don't be ridiculous."

"Wasn't aware I was."

"It's just inconsiderate to banish me to a sleazy motel for an entire day with nothing to do except watch soapy shows on a static-prone television and wonder what the hell was happening with Paul and Petrov and the Evanoffs, before falling onto a lumpy mattress to get some rest and most likely catching a severe infestation of bed bugs in the process because, *dear lord,* did I mention how sleazy this place is?" I plant my hands on my hips. "I know our government is cash-strapped but *come on.* Spring for a Hilton, for the love of god. There are *prisons* more pleasant than this motel."

I finally run out of breath... and out of words. In the silence that follows, a fierce blush slowly steals its way up my neck and over my cheeks as I realize Conor is watching me with unmistakable amusement.

Why can't you ever just keep your mouth shut, Shelby?

Conor's lips are twitching and his eyes have turned ultra warm. Up close, the effect is dizzying. It's like staring into two melty blue galaxies, swimming with stars.

"If I didn't know better, I'd say you missed me, Hunt."

I snort. "Did the paramedics check you for brain damage?"

He takes a step closer, forcing me backward, crowding my body up against the wall beside the bed. I feel my spine hit the hard plaster and lock my knees to keep them from going weak when those constellation eyes come within six inches of mine. Before I can bolt, Conor's hands come up to rest on either side of my head, effectively caging me in.

"You're pissed I locked you up here alone, instead of staying with you."

My jaw clenches tightly to contain my comeback.

"You're pissed I sent Sykes here today instead of coming myself."

My chin jerks up but I don't refute his words.

"Hunt." He blows out a breath. "I'm the head of my division. Do you know what that means?"

"I'm sure you're simply *dying* to tell me."

"It means," he says tiredly. "I'm in charge of all the organized crime cases that come through the Boston Bureau. I'm at the top of the chain of command. I have a lot of people who report to me. And though this case is our top priority right now, there's more than one file on my desk at the moment that requires attention."

"I understand that!"

"Then why the fuck are you so pissed off about it?"

"That's not what I'm pissed about!" I retort, breathing hard. "I'm pissed because—"

Because I let myself believe this was more than just a job for you. That I was more than just another file on your desk to be dealt with. That what we were doing here...

Mattered.

I bite down on the words before they escape.

God, I'm such an idiot.

"Waiting on pins and needles here, Hunt."

"I... I'm..."

My lips press together as I search for something to say. For *anything* to say, except the scary truth that's suddenly staring me straight in the face:

This is not Conor Gallagher's life.

His life is what happens when he walks away from me at the end of the day. His life is outside this conversation, outside this crappy motel room, outside anything having to do with me. And I'm not sure when I started to care, or why it bothers me so much. I'm not sure of anything at all, anymore.

"Let it go," I whisper, voice stripped of all anger. "Please... just let it go."

A fissure of concern appears between his eyes. "Now you're really freaking me the fuck out, Hunt."

"It doesn't matter."

His jaw clenches. "Like hell it doesn't."

"Just go home, Gallagher."

His fist bangs the wall beside my head, hard enough to make me flinch. "No. I won't fucking go home. I'm not about to leave you here when you're clearly upset and refuse to tell me how I can fix it."

"It's not your responsibility to fix it!" I yell back at him, anger returning in a flash. "You're not my keeper or my savior or my knight-in-shining armor. *We aren't friends.* You're the one who told me that. Or did you already forget?"

"Hunt—"

"Don't *Hunt* me!" I shake my head and, for some baffling reason, I'm suddenly fighting tears. "You know, when you climbed through my window and rescued me that night, right when this first started, I thought you were on my side. I thought you cared. But now I see nothing you've done is out of loyalty or anything resembling actual human emotion. I'm just an obligation to you. And you're just a robot, going through the motions, handling me like you handle every other case that comes across your desk."

His teeth grit. "Glad to know you think so highly of me."

"What else am I supposed to think? Huh? Three days ago, you dragged me into an interrogation room like a criminal and set your blonde attack dog on me. Two days ago you accused me of harboring my asshole ex in the attic. And one day ago you left me all alone, had me locked up in here without so much as a word, while you went off to deal with... with... whatever issues you deemed more *vital* on your freaking to-do list!"

"You want to know what I was doing yesterday? I was *looking for your idiot husband,*" he roars back at me, anger contorting his handsome features. "I was out doing my damn job. And I'm sorry to disappoint you, but I'm not your fucking fairy tale hero. Real life doesn't always have a happy ending. It's not all sunsets and roses and carriage rides with some asshat princeling in tights who swoops in to save the day with a glass slipper!"

"You think I don't know that?" I try to laugh but it comes out as a sob. "You think I don't know how very fucked up life can be? You think I don't know that Prince Charming sometimes turns out to be the villain? You think I don't know that sometimes the princess winds up getting totally screwed over?" I shake my head. "What story have *you* been reading that has a happy ending? Or a happy beginning and middle, for that matter? Because it's not mine. If you think it is, you haven't been paying attention."

"Except I *have* been paying attention — for six long

months, in fact! Which is why I'm not about to let this case fall to pieces just because you might get your goddamned feelings hurt in the process!"

My spine snaps straight. "Thanks *so much* for clearing that up!"

"Anytime!"

"Perfect!"

We both fall silent, too angry to say another word. The only sound in the room is our equally ragged breathing. Conor's mouth is so close to mine, I can feel each puff of air on my lips. The animosity is so thick between us, you could cut it with a knife.

My eyes narrow. "I'm *so glad* we're in agreement, then."

"That'd be a first," he mutters. "What are we supposedly in agreement on here, Hunt?"

"That there's no need for us to interact anymore."

"Woman, what are you—"

I cut him off. "Seeing as we aren't anything to each other besides agent and asset... surely it doesn't matter who debriefs me. So, I'd prefer to deal with Sykes from this point forward."

"Too fucking bad."

"Excuse me?"

"You heard me," he spits. "You don't get to push me away just because you're pissed at me."

"Push you away?" I scoff. "This has nothing to do with you."

"I think has everything to do with me."

"Oh, you are more full of yourself than a damn Russian matryoshka doll!"

"Nice dodge."

"I'm not dodging *anything*, you jerk. I don't need to. Sykes told me your analysts are tacking down that bank

SO WRONG IT'S RIGHT   145

account as we speak. And once they do... the case is just about closed. Filed, finished. *Over.*" My voice drops to a low, angry whisper. "Which means so is this god awful chapter of my life. And *so are we.*"

Conor is glaring at me like he's never hated anyone on the planet as much as he hates me. His mouth opens and I brace myself for his reply, knowing it'll be something truly terrible. Something that'll hammer the final nail in the coffin of this antagonistic work arrangement we're both so desperate to escape.

It's almost funny — after everything we've already screamed and shouted and sneered at each other, I think I'm well prepared for whatever he might say to me in this moment. Yet, when he finally retorts...

I'm thrown for a loop.

Because he does something far worse than anything I ever could've imagined. Something that brings my whole world crashing to a stop. Something that makes those words I uttered to him in anger entirely obsolete.

"We aren't over, Shelby," Conor mutters darkly, eyes burning into mine. "We haven't even begun."

And then he kisses me.

CHAPTER 10

IT'S LIT

CONOR'S MOUTH slams down on mine — hard and hot and possessive.

At first, I'm so stunned I can't do much more than hang on for dear life. It's been so long since I've been kissed, I've almost forgotten how. But as his hands slide into my hair, as his chiseled body presses me into the wall, as his stubble scrapes against my cheeks and his lips move with mine...

A long-forgotten spark inside me flares to life.

It doesn't take long for that spark to become a flame... for that flame to become a blaze... for that blaze to become an unstoppable inferno.

I am combustible, I think as I begin to return his kiss in earnest. *I am burning up, burning out of control.*

Who knew immolation would feel so damn good?

Leaning into Conor, my mouth opens beneath his to grant him access. Our tongues brush and he growls low in his throat, a thready sound of desire. Pent-up passion explodes between us. It's a ravenous flood of lust, a fiery torrent of unleashed need so strong it threatens to drag me under.

If it does, I worry I'll never find my way back to the surface.

I'm not sure how they get there, but suddenly my hands are around his neck, sliding up into his hair. I drag him closer, desperate to hang onto this feeling for as long as it lasts, to hold him in the circle of my arms for every possible second before we inevitably realize this is wrong, that it shouldn't be happening, that we've crossed an unspoken boundary. Before we snap back to our senses and stop this madness and return to hating each other's guts.

Except... the thing is...

It doesn't feel like madness.

It doesn't feel wrong.

It feels *right*. So right, I can't believe it took us this long to get here, to this moment — devouring each other with no regard for the rest of the world, without a single care about the case or the crazed men after us or even the small fact that we can't stand each other.

He pins me harder against the wall, every delicious plane of his muscular chest pressing into mine through the fabric of my sweatshirt as he strokes his way down my body. When his fingers find the bottom hem, they slip beneath it. I can't help the gasp that flies from my mouth when his hands hit the bare skin of my hipbones.

God, it's been so long since I've been touched this way.

With desire and passion and need.

With big hands and rough fingertips.

I feel like I'm coming apart at the seams, like I might explode outward into a thousand pieces, my body unable to contain all the emotions firing through my nerve endings as his hands slide around to the small of my back. He tugs me closer, until we're flush together, his mouth never breaking from mine.

The sensation is sinful. Criminal. So good it should be illegal.

Not that I'd really mind him breaking out the handcuffs, sometime...

Conor's mouth drops to my neck. He's kissing the sensitive hollow beneath my ear and my whole spine is arching with pleasure and things are really starting to get good when...

RIIING.

RIIIIIIG.

RIIIIIIIIIIG.

He groans as he rips his lips from my skin. Fishing his cellphone from his pocket with one hand, he glances at it with such annoyance, I half expect him to hurl it across the room. Before he has a chance, it rings again — flashing SYKES across the screen.

With a low curse, he lifts it to his ear. "Someone better be dying."

He stares into my eyes as he listens to whatever she's saying. We're still pressed tight together. Beneath my hands, his chest rises and falls rapidly as he struggles to regulate his breathing. I'd bet his pulse is racing just as fast as mine.

"You're sure?" he says sharply, eyes going alert.

My brows arch.

Whatever Sykes called to report is not making him happy. In fact, based on that expression, it's making him decidedly *unhappy*. Which shouldn't exactly be a surprise. In my experience, calls that come in after midnight generally aren't conveying good news.

"No. No, you were right to inform me." His body tenses, every muscle tightening as though he's preparing for battle. "I'll handle her extraction personally."

Extraction?

My mouth opens to interject but there's little point. Conor is already stepping away from me, all his attention absorbed by Sykes' words. I swallow down my protests as he walks across the room, ignoring the lance of hurt that shoots through me at the abrupt loss of his touch. Slumped back against the wall, I try to slow my breathing as I watch him sling the strap of my duffle over one shoulder.

I never even got a chance to change.

"Keep me apprised of the situation as it develops, Sykes." He runs a hand through his hair, mussing the dark locks. "I want everyone working on this. Yes. I'm aware of that." He pauses. "I don't care. She's priority number one."

My heart flips.

Conor's eyes meet mine. "I want hourly reports on his movements."

His?

"Yes. I will." He blows out a sharp breath. "See you there."

He disconnects the call.

From opposite sides of the room, we stare at each other. It's clear neither of us wants to break the silence first. It's even clearer that something between us has changed, shifted like a tectonic plate beneath our feet — and I'm not referring to whatever *situation* Sykes just told him about on the phone.

I search for the right words and come up pathetically short. What can I possibly say about our unexpected seven minutes in heaven? Besides, of course, the obvious...

It never should've happened.
We weren't thinking clearly.
Momentary insanity.
Never to be repeated.

The room is so quiet, I can hear the ice machine just outside the door humming in the night.

"So," Conor says finally. I notice his hand is clenched around the phone so tight, his knuckles have gone white. "That was Sykes."

"I gathered as much."

"Right." He shakes his head, as though he's trying to clear a haze from his thoughts. "She had some rather alarming new intel. Intel that concerns you."

Okay, so... I guess we're just going to skip right over the fact that we just made out like two handsy, horny teenagers in the backseat of a car after prom.

Fine by me, Gallagher.

Avoidance is my middle freaking name.

(Actually, my middle name is Quinn. Not that that's vitally important, at this moment. Or at any moment. Ever.)

Moving on!

My brows lift. "More alarming than the Evanoffs taking Paul?"

At the sound of Paul's name, something dark flashes in Conor's eyes. He buries it away so quickly, I'm almost convinced I imagined it... but when he speaks again, his tone is no longer hazy or warm. He's returned to that typical cool indifference I've come to know so well.

"Alexei Petrov was just caught on camera entering the country at Logan Airport. His private jet landed an hour ago."

"What!? You don't mean..."

"Paul's uncle. The head of the Petrov crime family. Yes, *that* Petrov." His expression is grave. "He hasn't been in the USA for years. I very much doubt he decided to take a spontaneous holiday to Boston for no good reason."

"He's here because of Paul."

He nods tightly.

"And the stolen money."

"We still haven't confirmed this is about money. Despite our analysts best efforts, they've uncovered no evidence that Paul was embezzling cash on the side."

My brows lift. "So you don't agree with Sykes' theory?"

"Petrov just flew halfway around the world." Conor's head shakes. "That fact alone leads me to believe this isn't about money. If it were, he would've let his associates handle it without ever stepping foot outside his mansion in Moscow."

"Then what is it about?"

"I don't know. But it's clear whatever your husband stole is not merely valuable. It's also personal. It must mean a great deal to Alexei. So much so, he's determined to reclaim it — in person — from whoever has taken it."

"And... just so we're clear... he thinks that person is *me*."

Conor nods again, jaw clenched.

"So..." My mouth goes dry. I'm afraid to ask, but I force myself to do it anyway. "What does that mean?"

"It means you're not safe out in public. It means we have to get you off the grid. *Now.*"

Taking two strides forward, he grabs my hand, laces our fingers together, and starts tugging me toward the door. Hesitating at the threshold, his eyes meet mine. I think I actually see worry in their depths. But that can't be right.

Conor Asshole Gallagher never gets worried about anything.

"He's coming for me, isn't he?" I ask before I can stop myself. The fear in my voice is potent.

"He will not lay a hand on you," Conor growls menacingly. "That's a vow."

I do my damndest to believe him as we step out into the

night. The two agents in the SUV flash their headlights at us as we bolt toward the Jeep Wrangler — hand in hand, like two fugitives on the run.

Bonnie and Clyde.

I can only hope we don't meet the same grim end those two did.

WE'RE DRIVING SO FAST, the world is nothing but a dark blur.

I'm not sure where we are, exactly. Somewhere on the outskirts of the city, in a neighborhood I don't recognize. I stare out the window, searching for any sort of landmark that might help me narrow it down, but nothing familiar jumps out from the barren urban sprawl.

The endless stream of looming brick warehouses to either side of the street look half-abandoned, their windows either boarded up or bashed in, their adjacent parking areas full of litter, broken-down cars, and off-duty construction vehicles. We speed under a bridge overpass, fly by a row of round petroleum storage tanks, and careen around a huge lot full of dirt, piled higher than the treetops. At least, I *think* it's dirt... until we get a little closer and I see the mound is pure white: a massive mountain of road salt, already being stockpiled in preparation for the brutal Boston winter to come.

It's been twenty minutes since we got the call about Petrov, and Conor hasn't uttered a single word to me since we climbed into his Jeep. His jaw is clenched even tighter than his grip around the steering wheel as he maneuvers expertly around deep potholes and exposed manhole covers, shifting gears so seamlessly I think he must've been a NASCAR driver in a former life.

Thankfully, there aren't too many other cars on the road at this time of night.

Or is it morning, now?

Honestly, I've lost track of the hour.

I'd ask where we're going, but I doubt he'd give me a straight answer even if he could hear me over the roaring of the wind through the Wrangler's open roof. I pull my whipping hair up into a high ponytail, then reach into the duffle bag at my feet and dig around until I locate a pair of jeans. It's past time to ditch the sweatshirt-dress. Comfortable though it may be, it's not exactly conducive to life on the run. Not unless you plan to distract the bad guys by flashing your lady business before making a swift getaway.

Hell, you never know... it might just work...

We drive through the dark, low-rent neighborhood for another few minutes before we turn down a narrow dead-end street and pull into the driveway of a nondescript, single-story house with a very small, overgrown yard. My eyes widen as I take it in. At least, what little I can see of it illuminated in the headlight beams.

Shabby brick facade, peeling paint, rusted mailbox.

I think we must be lost, but Conor shuts off the engine and hops out onto the cracked pavement. Before I can so much as ponder what we're doing at a place that — it must be said — makes me homesick for the glamorous Budget Inn, he's rounded the front of the Jeep and pulled open my door with an aggressive yank.

"Let's go," he mutters, grabbing the duffle by my feet.

I decide it's best not to put up a fuss as I follow him around the side of the dilapidated dwelling, stepping over crushed beer cans and dirty plastic bags. The grass is so long, I don't think it's seen a lawnmower since the Paleozoic Era.

Conor stops at the back door and knocks three times. My eyes widen at the sound of approaching footsteps. Someone's definitely home.

I'm not sure who I expect to open the door — *a crack dealer, perhaps?* — but when it swings inward, I find myself staring at the last person I'd ever presume to encounter in a place like this.

"Sykes?!"

She smiles faintly and throws the door wider. "Get in here, you two."

My teeth sink into my bottom lip as Conor ushers me inside, following close on my heels. Given the state of the yard, my expectations are quite low for the interior design of this ramshackle little hovel. Thus, I'm stunned to step into a lovely, updated kitchen complete with granite countertops, modern appliances, and polished chrome light fixtures.

What the eff?

My eyes widen further as Sykes leads us into the living room, where two men in all black are waiting on the plush black sofa, sipping styrofoam cups of coffee and typing rapidly into heavy duty laptops that appear to be military grade. I recognize them from last night — they're the same agents who drove me to the motel. Evelson and Kaufman. I'm not entirely confident which one is which.

When they spot Conor, they both cease typing long enough to nod and mutter a respectful '*Sir*' before resuming their activities.

What the mother-effing eff?

I feel like I've stepped into an episode of *Black Mirror*. Or a fantasy film. Nothing is as it appears. If they led me into the bedroom down the hall and told me there was a magic wardrobe that opened straight into Narnia, I wouldn't blink twice.

"Where the hell are we?" I ask.

"Safe house," Conor says flatly, dropping my duffle to the floor with a thud. "May not look like a palace from the outside, but it's equipped with all the latest tech, a world class security system, satphone capabilities, and bulletproof windows. Should suit our purposes nicely for the next few days."

I swallow hard. My brain is stuck on the phrase *bullet-proof windows* and I can't seem to move past it.

"*Hey.*" Conor's eyes find mine. "I told you. Petrov will not get to you. Not here. This place was designed to hide in plain sight. Blackout curtains, no tenants in either of the neighboring houses, and a pantry with a steel-enforced door that doubles as a panic room in a pinch. You'll be safe here, Hunt. I promise."

Our gazes lock like magnets, charging the air between us in the length of a heartbeat. I tell myself to look away but I'm completely transfixed. Lost in a deep blue sea, remembering exactly what it felt like to have those indigo eyes three inches away... that body pressed close... that mouth moving against mine with urgency and heat and passion.

It's probably the last thing I should be thinking about, given the circumstances, but I can't seem to force my brain to stop replaying our stolen moment against the motel wall, when we set aside our grudge match and struck a temporary truce. One sealed with an unforgettable kiss.

Look away from him, you idiot!

No good will come of this!

It's all too easy to ignore my own advice.

The moment drags on far longer than it should. I feel

heat rise to my cheeks when Agent Sykes clears her throat gently.

"*Anyway...*"

Conor's eyes cut away to focus on her. "Status report?"

"Evelson and Kaufman are attempting to geo-target Petrov's cellphone to get a beat on where he's headed." She gestures toward the men on the sofa. "We're also actively monitoring traffic cameras and deploying drones all over the city, trying to figure out where he went when he left the airport."

Conor's jaw tightens. "Is a team in place at 29 Merriweather?"

I jolt at the mention of my home address.

"Yes. We've got snipers on a neighbor's roof and SWAT on standby."

He nods tersely. "Where do we stand on the Evanoffs?"

"They've been off the grid since last night. I assume they're lying low, waiting for Petrov to arrive. Now that he's in the country, they'll likely rendezvous with him to deal with—" Sykes' eyes flicker to me. She shifts nervously on her shiny black shoes.

"Paul," I finish for her, filling in the blank. My heart clenches with guilt when I think about him in Righty and Lefty's not-so-gentle hands. "Do you think... is there a chance he's still alive, then?"

"They won't kill him. Not yet, anyway." Conor's lips are a flat line. I notice all the warmth has fled his eyes. "His uncle will want a chance to deliver his own brand of justice to your husband."

A shiver moves through me.

Conor sees it. His frown grows more pronounced. "Don't worry. We'll do our best to get him back to you before any permanent harm comes to him."

Back to me?

"What—" I start, but he's already turned to look at Lucy.

"Any leads on their location?"

She sighs. "Nothing solid yet."

"Sir, if I could interject," one of the agents on the couch chimes in. Kaufman, I think. "We've got a B.O.L.O. out with all local BPD units for the vehicle they used to flee the scene. Think we may have a hit on the license plate. A sedan matching the description was just spotted parked outside an apartment building in Eastie."

"What's the address, Evelson?"

Oops. Not Kaufman.

The agent rattles off a street in Orient Heights.

Conor glances at Sykes with raised brows. "That's the Petrov apartment where Paul Hunt's been staying."

She nods. "Can't be a coincidence."

"We swept that area yesterday. There were no signs of their car," he mutters. "Why go back now? They have to know we're monitoring all known Petrov properties..."

"Maybe they thought it would be safe since we'd already done our sweep?" Sykes shrugs. "No one ever accused the Evanoffs of being particularly bright."

A muscle is ticking in his jaw. "Something feels off about this."

Her blonde brows are by her hairline. "Be that as it may, boss... we're obligated to at least check it out."

"It's too easy."

"Or maybe we just got lucky for once," Sykes retorts. "Either way..."

Conor runs a hand through his hair, then gives a shallow nod. "Do we have vests here?"

"Hallway closet. I'll get them." She walks out of the

room without another word.

He turns to me. "Hunt—"

"You're leaving," I say softly.

"I have to take point on this."

I nod. I'm afraid to open my mouth — afraid, if I do, I'll beg him not to leave again. Not to leave *me* again.

He takes a stride toward me, a conflicted look on his face. "Evelson and Kaufman will stay here with you. We won't be gone long."

I nod again.

He takes another step closer. His voice goes low. "Hunt—"

Whatever he's about to say never makes it out of his mouth, because Sykes walks back into the living room carrying two black kevlar vests. They look heavy, judging by the way her arm muscles are straining as she passes one to Conor and straps herself into the other.

My heart pounds a mad tattoo inside my chest as they prepare for the raid — loading up on ammo from the gun locker hidden inside the kitchen pantry, communicating back and forth with the tactical team at the Bureau. I've never felt more useless. I might as well be a piece of furniture; some decorative fruit bowl, sitting in the corner of the room with no purpose at all.

"SWAT is en route," Sykes tells Conor, double checking the safety of her gun. "Ready to roll?"

"I'll meet you at the car in two."

She nods, waves at me, and disappears outside.

Alone in the kitchen with Conor, I suddenly don't know where to look or what to say. Nothing is settled between us. In fact, after the kiss we shared earlier, things are more confusing than ever.

I'm not sure whether we're friends or enemies, whether

we still hate each other, whether anything from here on out will be different. The only thing I am sure of is... there's an undeniable part of me that's terrified by the prospect of him putting himself in danger.

Despite the heavy protective vest he's wearing, despite the three guns I know he has strapped to various parts of his person...

I'm so unbelievably scared that if he walks out that door, he'll never come back through it.

Inexplicably, I find myself wanting to cross the room to him. To close this frozen distance between us, wrap my arms around his waist, and beg him not to go.

But that would be absurd.

He's a grown man. A badass FBI agent. The head of his division.

He can take care of himself.

He's done this before.

He'll be fine.

Still... no amount of reassurance is enough to stop the next words from popping out of my mouth.

"Tell me you'll be careful."

His Adam's apple bobs up and down. "I'm always careful, Hunt."

My mouth opens. Closes. Opens again. "I just..."

His brows lift. "What?"

"I don't know how I'd handle any of this without you," I admit in a whisper, my voice barely audible. "I... I need you here. I need you with me."

He doesn't move, doesn't speak... but his eyes are suddenly warm. So warm, they're practically burning into mine as he stares at me from the threshold of the open door.

"Plus," I add nervously. "If you don't come back, who's going to boss me around and do that death-glare thing when

I start to ramble and call me by my last name in a very severe tone that would probably be intimidating under different circumstances, but sort of pales in comparison to the bad guys with guns running around, continually threatening my life?"

His lips tug up at one side. "Glad to know my services are appreciated."

I try to smile back at him, but my lips aren't cooperating. "Good luck out there."

Conor turns and starts to walk out the door. At the last second, he pauses with his hand on the knob. He doesn't turn around, but his gruff voice carries back to me.

"*Shelby.*"

Every muscle in my body tenses. "Conor?"

"I'll be back before you know it."

Then, he's gone — the door swinging shut behind him with finality.

For a long, frozen instant, I stand there in the kitchen, hardly able to draw breath. After a minute, I realize it's because something is lodged firmly in my throat.

My heart.

TO DISTRACT myself from thinking about the Eastie raid, I take the longest shower of my life, standing beneath the hot torrent until the entire bathroom is fogged up with steam. When the water finally runs cold, I find a hairdryer in one of the vanity drawers and blow out my long locks into soft, summery waves, taking far more care than I usually would.

I tell myself it's merely a way to pass the time. A stalling tactic to keep my anxiety at bay.

Certainly not because I want to look nice for someone...

The lie would probably be easier to swallow if, afterward, I didn't upend my toiletry bag using all my best products to achieve the perfect sultry red pout and smoky eye combination. I'm not generally a big makeup fan, preferring a fresh, natural look for most day-to-day outings, but this particular morning I find myself going all out.

Mascara, eyeliner, lipstick.

The whole shebang.

To complete the ensemble, I pull a casual white linen sundress out of my duffle and slide on a pair of brown leather sandals. It's the most put-together I've looked — and felt — in days.

Not bad for a neurotic, sleep deprived gal on the run. I smirk, examining the final results in the mirror. *Not bad at all.*

Back in the living room, Evelson and Kaufman are still hard at work on their laptops. Neither of them so much as glances up when I pass through on my way to the kitchen. I can't help but admire that level of concentration.

The clock on the wall informs me it's not even nine in the morning. It feels more like midnight to me — probably because I've had about twelve cumulative seconds of sleep over the past few days. My internal clock is upside-down and backwards. Yawning cavernously, I put on a pot of coffee and settle back against the counter to wait.

Again.

Waiting seems to be my new specialty. It's practically all I've been doing lately, whether waiting for rescue in a dining room chair, waiting to be questioned in an FBI interrogation room, waiting for answers in a crappy motel room...

Waiting for him to come back.

Time is ticking by in achingly slow increments. Despite

my rather elaborate getting-ready routine, not even two hours have passed since Lucy and Conor left. I assure myself they'll be back soon as I pull three mugs from the cabinets and fill them to the brim with coffee.

Balancing a steaming cup in each hand, I make my way slowly into the living room. "Hey, I thought you guys could use some—"

My words dry up.

My feet go still.

Evelson and Kaufman aren't typing. They're on their feet, phones pressed to their ears, both talking rapid-fire into the receivers. There are twin expressions of fear and anger on their faces as they stare across the room at the television screen mounted on the wall. And believe you me, seeing two badass dudes with giant muscles looking *fearful*...

It's enough to make my hands shake so badly, several drops of coffee spill onto the hardwood floor.

Moving in slow motion, I pivot around to look at the television. The sound has been muted but the picture is crystal clear. As is the headline blaring across the bottom of the screen.

EXPLOSION AT EAST BOSTON APARTMENT COMPLEX

There's a field reporter talking into a microphone in the foreground, but I barely see her. My eyes are fixed on the building behind her. The one that's currently consumed by flames, a raging inferno bursting out every window, eating its way through the panels of the roof, devouring wood and stone alike. A living, breathing monster of fire.

A new headline flashes across the screen.

SEVERAL CONFIRMED DEAD AT SCENE

Both coffee cups hit the floor, shattering into pieces on impact.

CHAPTER 11

TAKE IT OFF

I WATCH THE CLOCK.

One more hour.

Still no news.

I'm sitting at the kitchen table, drumming my restless fingertips against the surface. Evelson and Kaufman are long gone. They left me here alone as soon as we saw what happened during the raid. I'm not sure where they went.

I'm not sure I care.

There's no room in my head for anything except a single thought. It's more of a prayer, actually, repeated to the heavens over and over until the words lose all meaning. Until they're nothing but useless syllables strung together with fragile hope and a shaky sense of faith.

Please be alive.

Please be alive.

Please be alive.

I couldn't watch the news coverage anymore. The networks are spinning a bogus story about a gas leak in the condo complex — whether the result of an FBI coverup or sheer journalistic ineptitude, it matters little. They don't have the answers I'm so desperate for.

Before they took off for the scene, Kaufman and Evelson told me there was an ambush at the apartment. They didn't know the details — just that, as soon as the SWAT team stepped through the front door, they unknowingly triggered a special gift left behind by the Evanoffs.

The whole room exploded.

And, with it, several FBI agents.

Please not him.

Please not him.

Please not him.

I drop my face into my hands, struggling to breathe. Struggling to believe this is my new reality. Kidnappings and firefights and explosions. Fraud and blackmail and death.

My life has become an action movie.

But it's so strange... because those onscreen heroines I've spent years watching in films, cheering for in theaters... they're pictured on the front lines, battling it out blow by blow with the bad guys. They lead the charge into every fight, their courage never faltering. And in the end, they always, always, always walk away victorious.

I'm learning the hard way that real life is nothing like the movies.

There are no assured victories. No easy paths to defeating your enemies. No soaring scores to spotlight the importance of a particularly poignant moment.

Sometimes, the heroine isn't perfect.

Sometimes, she's not a born warrior at all.

She's just a normal girl, pulled from the sidelines into the fray.

And maybe she doesn't fight battles against dragons or Vikings or vampire lords. Maybe the biggest battle she ever has to endure is also the hardest one of all — the battle to hold on to the thin thread of hope that things will work out in the end. Even if there's no award-winning script to guide her way. Even when the fortunes appear dire. Even when the odds are stacked against her.

I look up.

I watch the clock.

And I hope.

THERE ARE CERTAIN MOMENTS THAT, even as they're happening, you know you'll remember with perfect clarity for the rest of your life. Fragments of time you'll look back on in fifty, sixty, seventy years and replay in your aging mind with razor-sharp acuity.

Every element. Every facet. Every detail.

The sound of a car door slamming.

The sight of a man stepping into a sun-drenched kitchen.

The smell of smoke and fire and sweat.

The feel of arms coming around you, holding you close.

I fly from my seat. One minute I'm at the kitchen table and the next I'm standing in front of him, staring up into his face. His beautiful goddamned face, still streaked with black from the fire. He reeks of ash and looks like hell.

I don't care.

I don't think.

I don't wait.

I hurl myself against his chest, arms going tight around his waist, head tucking in the hollow where his shoulder meets his neck. Hugging him fiercely, as though I'm afraid that letting go, even for a moment, might make him somehow disappear.

He's alive.

He's breathing.

He's here.

For a minute, he just stands there unmoving. But after a while, I feel his arms lift from his sides — tentatively, like he's not entirely sure whether he's doing it properly — and slide around my back. His soot-stained fingers press against my white dress, tugging me into him. Closer, closer, closer. Until we're pressed so tight together I can barely breathe.

It doesn't matter.

Breath doesn't matter. I don't need air in my lungs. I don't need anything except this. *Him.* Here with me, alive and sturdy and blessedly retaining the full use of all four limbs.

Releasing a shuddering breath, Conor's chin lowers to rest on the crown of my head. I feel the tension go out of him in a gust as he allows himself to sink fully into the embrace. Surrendering to his own need for comfort after a day of flames and fear and uncertainty.

I lose track of how long we stand there, twined together. Taking comfort in a wordless embrace. When we finally pull apart, I don't let go. Not completely. I keep my fingers laced with his as I peer up at him.

For once, his emotions aren't closely guarded; they're brimming over, burning bright at the the surface, exposed for the world to see. His face is etched in sadness, his eyes are red with grief.

It damn near breaks my heart.

"Oh, Conor..."

He sighs when I say his name. "I'm fine."

"You don't look fine."

His jaw clenches as he struggles to find the words. "I was still in the hallway when the bomb went off. Got tossed into a wall. A few bumps and bruises. Nothing serious."

"That doesn't sound like *nothing*," I argue. "Getting thrown—"

"Hunt." He cuts me off sharply. "There's more. You need to prepare yourself."

"What? What is it?"

His eyes hold mine, full of anguish. He hesitates a beat, then murmurs just one word. "Sykes."

"No! *No*." My heart is lead, my stomach stone. "No, she can't be—"

"She's still alive," he assures me immediately. "But it's... it's not good. She's in the ICU. Critical condition. They don't know whether she's going to make it through the night."

I swallow hard, trying to keep myself together for his sake. If anyone in this room deserves to fall apart right now, it's Conor. "Is there anything I can do? Any way I can possibly help?"

"Her boyfriend is there with her, now — along with half the OC division, most likely. I told them to go home and get some shut eye, but..." He shrugs. "Lucy is well-liked. Everyone wants to be there when she wakes up. *If* she wakes up."

"Sykes is strong. She's going to pull through this."

He shakes his head slightly, his face a mask of pain as he pulls his hand from my hold and starts to pace. "She always had to be first. First in her class at the Academy. First one to chime in with ideas on any case. First one into the room on a raid..." His paces pick up speed. "Per usual, she was right on the heels of the SWAT team when they stepped into that apartment. The three guys ahead of her died instantly. Blown to bits." His eyes are full of ghosts. "She was... I guess I could call it *luckier*, but that's open to interpretation given the state I found her in. All I could do was carry her out, away from the fire. I got her to the street, tried to stop the worst of the bleeding. They air-lifted her to Mass General."

"Conor." I reach out, blocking his path. Stilling him with a light hand on his chest, directly over his heart. I can feel it racing double-speed beneath the fabric of his cinder-streaked shirt. Now that I'm looking closer, I see some of the stains are dark red, not black.

Lucy.

I swallow. "You did everything you could. You got her out of there before the whole place went up in flames. You saved her life!"

He laughs — a violent, self-loathing snarl. "I didn't save her life, Hunt. I'm the one who nearly ended it."

"Don't say that. You can't possibly think you're responsible for this."

"But I am. She never should've been there in the first place. The only reason Sykes was in that room was because of me. Because I dragged her into this case. And if she dies... her blood is on my hands."

"I won't pretend to know her well, but it's pretty clear from the few interactions I've had with Lucy Sykes that she loves her job. And she's damn good at it. My guess is, she would've been at that scene whether or not you encouraged her involvement."

A muscle in his jaw is ticking with tension and he can't quite meet my eyes. "You don't understand."

"Then explain it to me," I say softly, wishing I could reach out and take his pain within my hands. Hold it for a while, just to ease his heavy burden.

"I'm the one who pulled her in on this case. She was working on something else, but... I asked her to step in earlier this week. Maybe if I hadn't..."

My brow furrows. "You told me everyone's working the Petrov case now. Even if you hadn't recruited her to help deal with him, she still might've wound up at that apartment today."

His head is shaking, rejecting my words.

"What?" I ask, almost afraid of his answer.

"It wasn't Petrov I asked her for help with." He's staring at me gravely. "It was you."

"*Me?*"

"When I brought you into the Bureau... before we knew whether or not you were complicit in Paul's crimes... I needed someone impartial to conduct your interview. Someone unbiased, who could ask about your involvement and evaluate the truth without..."

My breaths are shallow. "Without what?"

"Without being affected by personal feelings." His eyes meet mine and I nearly gasp at the emotions I see lurking just behind the surface of his irises.

The anger, the anguish, the guilt.

He clears his throat. "Because for the first time in my career... I wasn't sure I could do that. I wasn't sure I could be impartial." He pauses. "Not when it came to you."

IT'S MID-AFTERNOON, but there's no sign of the sun in the pitch-black bedroom; the thick curtains have seen to that. I sit on the bed in the dark, feeling my thoughts spiral outward in a thousand directions. My knees are curled tight to my chest, my spine pressed firmly to the wood head-board. The sound of the shower running is the only noise to drown out my thready pulse.

He's been in there for a long time. So long, I'm about to go check on him, just to make sure he hasn't drowned, when I finally hear the valves shut off. A few seconds later, Conor walks in wearing nothing but a white towel slung low around his hips.

I inhale sharply.

His chest is a gorgeous display of chiseled muscle. Water droplets still cling to his wet skin as he strides to the armchair in the corner of the room and pulls a pair of gray sweatpants from the small black bag he carried in from the Jeep earlier.

I try not to stare — *much* — as he tugs them on beneath his towel. But, hell, I'm only human. And let me tell you, the deep V-lines of his torso are a sight to behold. My eyes track his movements, drinking him in like he's a cold wheat-grass shot after a session of hot yoga. I'd say his body is a temple, but that wouldn't do it justice. His body is a Wonder of the World, right up there next to The Taj Mahal and the Great Pyramid.

He dries his hair with the towel as he walks toward the bed, eyes locking on mine as the space between us shrinks from feet to inches. I hardly dare to breathe as he sinks onto the other side of the mattress.

"Hi," I whisper.

"Hi," he returns gruffly.

I search for something else to say to him, but my mind is one big blank. I'm exhausted, down to the marrow of my bones. Emotionally, physically. I could sleep for a thousand years; it still wouldn't be enough.

Conor must be feeling the same way, because without another word he stretches out on the bed and promptly closes his eyes.

Goodnight to you too, Gallagher.

Leaning back against the headboard, I take the opportunity to study the planes of his face. The noble slope of his nose. The lushness of his lips. The clean-shaven jaw. I've never seen him without a beard or stubble before. The effect of that jawline in all its naked glory is undeniably hot.

"You're staring," he says without opening his eyes.

I flush and glance away. "I was not!"

"Whatever you say, Hunt." His lips actually twitch, the first sign of life from him since he walked through the door earlier. I'm so relieved to see it, I barely care that his amusement is at my expense.

He cracks open one blue eye and peers over at me. "You planning on sleeping sitting up?"

"Maybe," I say, just to be ornery.

He watches me, waiting.

With a resigned sigh, I scoot away from the headboard, stretch out my limbs, and roll onto my side so I'm facing him. "There. Happy?"

His eyes are closed again, but his mouth is curled up at one corner in the hint of an undeniable smile. "Depends. You planning on sleeping in that dress?"

I huff. "If I want."

Another lip twitch. "Suit yourself."

We're silent for a moment, simply lying there in the darkness. My eyes close and I think I might actually fall asleep... when he interrupts me with another query.

"You also planning on sleeping in all that makeup?"

I startle. I'd forgotten about my smoky eye and red lip combo. My mouth opens to fire off another snarky response, but instead I tell the truth. "Actually... no. I hate waking up in the morning wearing day-old makeup. I just forgot I'd put it on this morning."

"Don't know why you bothered."

"Excuse me?" I narrow my eyes at his tone. "What's wrong with my makeup?"

He sighs and shifts his head on the pillow to meet my angry stare. "Nothing wrong with it, per se. I just don't think you need it. Faces like yours... "

My eyebrows arch.

"Let's just say, a priceless work of art doesn't need a filter or an expensive frame to make it invaluable," he murmurs.

I blink hard, not sure how to process that.

Did Conor I-don't-have-a-romantic-bone-in-my-body Gallagher just call my face a work of art?

His hand reaches across the gap between our pillows. I hold my breath as his thumb lands squarely on my bottom lip, not daring to move a single inch. With a gentle swipe, he wipes off the smudge of color using the pad of his finger. The lipstick leaves a red stain on his skin.

"There," he murmurs, staring at my tingling mouth intently. "That's better."

He's still touching my lip and I'm barely breathing. There's a flutter of nerves in the pit of my stomach. They feel almost like butterflies. But that's crazy. I'm a twenty-nine-year-old woman, for god's sake. I couldn't *possibly* be experiencing something akin to a schoolgirl crush.

Right?

That would be insane.

Because I'm done with love.

A dedicated spinster.

Even if I did, just yesterday, experience the hottest kiss of my life against the wall of a dingy motel room.

Call it a farewell tour. A retirement party. A last lap around the old libido track, before hanging up my ovaries, so to speak.

Except... Conor's not looking at me like I'm a spinster. Oh, no. He's looking at me like I'm a midnight snack. One meant to be consumed in the dark, without any restraint or semblance of self-control.

"I'll just go take this off, then," I blurt, sitting up abruptly.

His brows lift.

"The makeup!" A blush steals over my cheeks. "I'll take off the *makeup*."

Not my dress.

Definitely not.

Not that I'd necessarily object to someone *else* removing it...

Shelby Quinn Hunt, you little slut! Get it together!

Cursing myself for even allowing such a thought to enter my warped brain, I practically vault off the bed and race for the sanctuary of the bathroom. I just need a little space. A little time away from those intense blue eyes, to sort through my own thoughts. To get my emotions back in check.

Transference, I remind myself. *That's all you're experiencing. That's all this... this... attachment you're feeling for him is. A perfectly reasonable physiological response to stress and adrenaline.*

After I've removed my makeup, brushed my teeth, French braided my hair, and changed into a black silk nightie — *why, oh why, didn't I pack my thick flannel pajamas instead?* — I stall for as long as possible. Which, as it turns out, isn't all that long. Lingering awkwardly in a small bathroom without any reading material or source of entertainment is boring as hell.

Steeling my shoulders, I take a deep breath, crack open the door, and tiptoe into the silent bedroom.

With any luck, Conor is already asleep.

Stopping short at the side of the bed, I survey his slumbering form warily. He's tugged the sheet up to cover his lower half. His eyes are firmly closed. He's totally still, his breaths steady as a drumbeat.

A fissure of relief shoots through me.

Or... I *tell* myself it's relief. If I was being honest, I'd have to admit it feels a bit more like regret. (Thankfully, I have no problem lying to myself for the sake of my sanity.)

Making as little noise as possible, I pull back the sheets and slide beneath them. I settle firmly on my side of the bed, as far from him as possible, feeling unquestionably nervous about our proximity... and the lack of clothing on both our bodies.

The damn FBI couldn't have sprung for a two-bedroom safe house?

It's been ages since I shared a bed with anyone. I've grown so used to my king-sized solitude, it's odd to experience the sound of someone else's small noises.

The brush of bare skin against a pillowcase.

The rhythmic intake of breath in the dark.

Trying to get more comfortable, I roll over onto my back. My eyes spring open when, beneath the sheet, my hand brushes up against something.

A hand.

His hand.

I tell myself to pull away, to yank my arm out of the

dangerous no-man's land in the center of the mattress where it's wandered. But before I can... Conor's fingers twine around mine.

Apparently he's not asleep.

I can't breathe, can't think. Can't do anything at all as our grips lace together, unstoppable as two opposing magnets drawn in by an undetectable charge.

Time seems to freeze.

The air goes still in my lungs.

It's so silent, I can hear the thudding of my own pulse, crashing like thunder between my ears as he holds my hand. And I know it's crazy, feeling like this at the inconsequential tangling of two sets of fingers. I know I shouldn't be affected so acutely. But the longer my palm is pressed against his, the wilder the feelings inside my chest become.

They storm within me, churning and howling in an inescapable vortex, sweeping away every reason in my head telling me this is a terrible idea, obliterating every hesitation in my heart warning me to guard myself against him at any cost...

It's a thousand mile trip from one side of this mattress to another — a terrifying journey into unknown territory. But the winds within me spin faster still, removing all my resistance, wiping out my worries, scouring the sky of everything except the feeling of his hand in mine. Leaving nothing behind in the wreckage besides...

Desire.

Need.

Longing.

I push off the mattress and launch myself at Conor. We collide with a thud, a breath-stealing impact. My thighs straddle his hips, my hands plant against his shoulders, and

I lean down so we're flush together — chest to chest, eye to eye.

For a half-instant, I register surprise in his eyes before my mouth crashes against his. Any sense of shock is over-ridden by lust in a heartbeat. His arms come around me, locking me against his body in a cage of muscle. Not that I need a cage to hold me. I can't imagine ever wanting to escape the fire of his touch, the feeling of his hands on my back, twisting in the thin fabric of my nightie.

As I kiss him, that storm inside me pours outward in a great tempest. With every brush of my lips, every press of my fingers into his skin, I feel myself spiraling faster, further out of control.

He responds to my urgency in equal measure, growling low in his throat when my mouth drops to his neck, his chest, anywhere my lips can reach. His hand shoots out like lightning and tears the band from the base of my braid. The chocolate waves tumble loose, coming undone in an instant thanks to the quick work of his fingers.

Leaning forward, I let my hair spill across his chest in a curtain as I bring our mouths back together and suck lightly on his bottom lip. He nearly bucks up off the bed at the sensation.

"*Christ, Shelby.*"

I laugh lightly, enjoying myself, but the sound quickly turns to a gasp as Conor's hands land on my thighs. Without hesitation, he takes the thin fabric of my nightie between his strong fingers and tears the lacey slit wide open, baring me from hem to neckline in one clean rip. The black fabric falls away in tatters.

"Conor!" I blurt, stunned he's managed to strip me naked in approximately three seconds. "That was my only nightgown!"

I see a flash of teeth — a grin of dark, delicious intent. "Don't worry. You won't be needing your clothes anymore."

My retort never makes it past my lips, because suddenly he takes control, flipping me over onto my back with a sudden thrust of his hips. I gasp as he comes down on top of me, pressing me into the mattress with bone-melting weight. I feel his length, hard against my core through the thin fabric of his sweatpants, and want nothing more than to remove that last barrier keeping us apart.

No more space.

No more excuses.

He touches me everywhere, memorizing every inch of my skin, working his way slowly down my body with his hands and lips. After the not-so-delicate treatment of my nightie, I fear my underwear is about to suffer a similar fate. I'm even more stunned when, instead, he proceeds to use his teeth to drag the lace bottoms — inch by torturous inch — down my thighs, over my knees, past my shins, all the way to my toes.

It's the sexiest thing I've ever experienced, by a mile.

Looming over me like a demon about to inflict the most exquisite destruction, he tosses my panties to the floor with a jerk of his head.

My breath catches in my throat. There's a look in Conor's eyes I've never seen before as he stares down at me, laid completely bare beneath him on twisted sheets.

"You are exquisite," he murmurs in a tone that staggers me. It's something like reverence. Like devotion.

I sit up on the bed, rising to my knees so we're face to face. My hands settle on his sides, tracing the drawstring waistband of his sweatpants with fingers that are shaky from need. As I push the fabric down his hips in a rough jerk, freeing his rock hard length, Conor takes my face between his hands and tilts it upward so he can kiss me again.

He groans into my mouth when I begin to stroke him, clutching me tighter. His hands lace into my hair and the kiss goes wild — a desperate, unyielding dance of tongues and teeth. I'm dizzy with desire, aching for him like I've never ached for anyone else.

"Conor," I murmur as his hands move between my thighs. "Conor, please... I need you."

The lust thrumming through us both has reached a tipping point. It needs a release, an outlet. Surrendering to the fever, we fall backward onto the bed, our mouthes still fused together. He breaks away long enough to look down into my eyes.

"God, Shelby." He groans as he settles between my legs, his massive length brushing up against me in a mere hint of what's to come.

"Please," I beg, nails digging into his back.

His forehead rests on mine, his labored breaths puffing against my kiss-swollen mouth. "Tell me again. Tell me you need me, Shelby."

"I need you." I arch against him, nearly moaning when I feel his cock poised at my entrance. "*Right now.*"

"Tell me you're mine."

My eyes are hazy. My thoughts are scattered. I hardly let myself think about the meaning of the words on my lips as I breathe, "I'm yours, Conor."

His gaze never shifts from mine as he drives his cock inside me, so deep I feel him everywhere. So hard I see stars swimming like constellations across two indigo irises as he begins to move, driving us both toward the brink of something that eclipses mere lust. Something so powerful, my heart is ready to combust along with my body.

I've never felt more alive than this moment, I think, staring up at him in awe as he sends me spiraling into sweet oblivion. *I've never truly been alive at all, until right now.*

Right here.

With him.

I'M LYING in the circle of his arms, half sprawled on his chest. His fingers are tracing lazy patterns on my back. It feels amazing. In fact, every part of me feels amazing, from the crown of my head to the tips of my toes.

Behold, the restorative powers of four mind-blowing orgasms...

My neck arches back so I can meet his eyes. "Conor?"

"Shelby."

"Will you tell me something?"

His fingers go still. "Depends what that something is."

"Earlier... you said you pulled Sykes in on this case to interview me because you were worried you couldn't be impartial."

He tenses at the mention of Sykes name, but gives an affirmative nod.

"I guess... I'm just wondering why."

"She's a proficient profiler, I thought she'd do a good job—"

"No. Not why you picked her." My voice wavers. "Why you felt you needed to."

A fissure of confusion appears between his eyes. "I'm not sure what you're asking me."

"Why did you think you couldn't be impartial with me? What made you think that your feelings would get in the way of doing your job?" I shake my head, undeniably confused. "You barely knew me, then."

"Ah." Understanding creeps across his expression. His fingers begin to move again, sliding up every indentation of my spine. It feels so good, I have to fight off shivers of pleasure.

Then again, I don't know why I'm fighting them... Rround five doesn't sound so bad to me...

He clears his throat lightly, drawing my attention back to the question. "I think you're forgetting... I did know you. You just didn't know me."

"What do you mean?"

"I spent six months watching your life from a distance. I saw you teaching yoga classes and wandering the Farmers Market on Saturday mornings. I saw you volunteering at the dog shelter on Christmas and Easter, days no one else wanted to work. I saw you taking long runs to fill your afternoons, so many miles along the Charles River I knew you were trying to tire out your muscles to the point of exhaustion, to outrun something deep within yourself." His expression softens. "I saw you signing up for classes to keep your weeknights busy — still-life sketching and French cooking and wood sign painting. Workshops for DIY wind-vanes and make-your-own bird feeders. And most of all, I saw the sadness on your face when you'd walk out of those classes clutching whatever new project you'd made and go back home, to that huge, empty house. Alone." He pauses. His voice goes low, rough like I've never heard it before. "*I saw you,* Shelby. I still see you. I think, even if I go blind, I'll see you in my dreams for the rest of my life."

Oh, boy.

My eyes are watering dangerously and my voice, when I can summon the courage to speak, is wavering. "So you mean to tell me... all those times I got tingles on the back of my neck and told myself I was being crazy paranoid, that no one was following me..."

He grins darkly and pinches my sensitive nape in a playful move. "You should really learn to trust your instincts, Hunt."

I smack him on the arm. "Whatever. I may be oblivious to danger, but at least I'm not a creepy stalker."

"For the record, it's not stalking if you're in the FBI."

"Keep telling yourself that." I snort. "I think you need to look up the definition of *stalker* in the dictionary."

Smirking softly, he pulls me closer to his chest and lets his eyes drift shut. "We can argue about it in the morning."

"There won't be any argument. You *have* no argument. I'm right."

"You're stubborn."

"Said the man who makes mules look reasonable."

"Said the woman who makes *me* look reasonable."

I huff.

"Hunt."

"What?"

His lips find mine in the dark, delivering a long lingering kiss that steals my breath and makes my heart pound twice its normal speed.

"What was that for?" I ask dizzily.

"I need a reason for kissing you goodnight?"

"No." I pause. "But if you think you can just kiss me from now on to solve all our arguments—"

"Shelby."

"Yeah?"

"Happy to spend all day tomorrow fighting with you... so long as we can have hot make-up sex after. But right now, I'm dead tired from not sleeping for three straight days and nearly getting my ass blown up. So unless you want me unable to deliver on said promise of hot makeup sex... go the hell to sleep."

My eyes close so fast, I think I set a new Guinness World Record.

CHAPTER 12

STEPFORD WIFE

I TRY my damndest to fall asleep. I really do.

But no matter how many times I toss and turn, I can't seem to shut my mind off. Can't seem to stop replaying all the things Conor told me tonight.

I saw you, Shelby. I still see you. I think, even if I go blind, I'll see you in my dreams for the rest of my life.

Who the hell would be able to sleep, after hearing a speech like that? Not me, that's for damn sure. Which is why, approximately fifteen minutes after Conor has ordered me under penalty of celibacy to stop talking... I sigh dramatically into the dark.

"Hey," I whisper softly. "Are you asleep?"

"Yes."

I elbow him. "You are not."

"But I aspire to be."

Rolling my eyes, I manage to stay silent for another few minutes, holding in the words until I feel like I might actually explode from the strain of trying to keep them contained. "You know, you could've said hello to me."

He cracks open an eye. "*What?*"

"At Phoebe and Nate's wedding last month. You could've said hello instead of ignoring me."

The eye shuts. "I wasn't ignoring you."

"You barely looked my way!"

"Oh, trust me. I saw you doing the electric slide, Hunt. Not a pretty sight."

"Jackass."

His lips twitch.

I glower. "It's just rude, that's all."

"Guess we aren't sleeping," he mutters tiredly.

"I'm just saying, you could've at least acknowledged my existence."

"Couldn't very well do that without blowing my cover."

"It wasn't like you were on duty," I point out. "You can't help it we have friends in common. It was a coincidence."

He's silent.

"Wait... it *was* a coincidence, right?"

He grunts noncommittally.

"Conor Gallagher!" I exclaim, aghast. "Did you crash that wedding just to spy on me?"

His eyes open fully to look into mine. "No."

"Why don't I believe you?"

"Maybe because you enjoy being ornery and questioning every damn thing I ever tell you?"

I stare at him, waiting for the truth.

He sighs. "Nate's a friend. He invited me. But I will admit, I wasn't planning on attending until I found out you were a bridesmaid. Accepting that invitation was a chance to keep a closer eye on you. I took it."

"Ugh! I freaking knew it!"

"Don't get your panties in a twist."

"I'm not wearing panties. You took them off, remember? *With your teeth.*"

"Not likely to forget that. Not ever." His eyes glitter with lazy heat.

"Don't try to distract me with that sexy look. We're having a serious conversation."

"Thought we were trying to sleep."

"No, *you* were trying to sleep. I was contemplating the depths of your stalker-like behavior."

"You know, you should actually be thanking me for attending that wedding — seeing as it ended up getting crashed by those loan sharks who were after your friend Lila." His brows go up. "Who do you think arrested them and kept the whole reception from descending into chaos?"

I blanch. "I... but... you... *wait*, that's..."

"Cat got your tongue, Hunt?"

Yes, actually. I'm quite speechless.

Somehow, in the craziness of the past few days, I never put it together that Conor was the one who stepped in to save Phoebe and Nate's wedding day. It makes sense, now that I think about it... but the knowledge is still hard to wrap my mind around. Perhaps because it stirs scary feelings to life inside my chest. Feelings that terrify me down to my soul.

Conor Gallagher has been saving your ass since before you ever met him.

That particular realization is too complicated to unpack right now, so I push it to the back of my mind and force a light tone.

"Well. Unless you have a death wish, may I suggest *not* sharing this information with the bride — Phoebe will kill you if she learns you crashed her special day just to spy on her friend."

"Relax. I was an exemplary guest. RSVP'd promptly,

ordered the steak, even bought them a damn gift off their registry. A blender. Five-speeds. Very impressive."

I roll my eyes. "Yes, because that's what marriage is about. Small household appliances."

"Suppose I wouldn't know, seeing as I've never been married."

"Consider yourself lucky," I mutter, thinking of Paul.

He's silent for a long time. So long, I think maybe he actually did fall asleep. But then, from the darkness, I hear a quiet, "I used to."

I scrunch up my nose, confused. "Huh?"

"I used to consider myself lucky. Thought I'd dodged a bullet by not settling down. You have to understand... in my line of work, the things I see..." His voice is so soft I can barely make out the words. "It's hard to imagine ever being able to come home at the end of the day and act like a husband. I always figured it was easier just to stay unattached."

"And now?" I ask, almost afraid to hear the answer.

His eyes find mine. "I'm thirty-two years old. I live alone. My parents are out in California, still in the same house where I grew up. No siblings. No pets. No social life to speak of, not counting the occasional after-work function. This career is all I have. I've built my entire life around it." He blows out a sharp breath. "It used to be enough. But maybe it's not anymore. Maybe I want... something more than just the job."

I bite my tongue to prevent myself from asking what changed his mind.

Who changed his mind.

When I speak, I do my damndest to keep my voice steady. "Not that I pretend to be an expert on living the perfect life..."

Eyes closed, he snorts.

"But I have to believe it's about balance."

"Look, Hunt, I'm not doing yoga with you no matter how much you beg."

"Not that kind of balance, asshole. I'm talking about a work-life balance. You should work in order to live, rather than live only to work."

"You get that off a greeting card?"

I throw a pillow at his head. It his him square in the face. Sitting up, he growls as he squishes it in his grip. His eyes are shining with the promise of retaliation. "You sure you want to start a pillow fight with me, Hunt? Guarantee you won't win."

My pulse is thready and my mouth is strangely dry at the prospect of Conor being *playful* with me. Letting loose, laughing. Things I never in a million years thought the two of us would ever do, based on the way we butt heads. But as he sits there looking at me like that... so gorgeous in the dim light...

He really and truly takes my breath away.

"Well?" he prompts, the pillow held aloft.

"No," I breathe. "I surrender."

"Chickenshit."

"Didn't you say something about wanting to sleep?"

"Oh, you want to sleep *now*? After waking me up to ask me about a wedding?"

I blush. "It's not really about the wedding. I was just... curious, I guess. About you. About this job. About..."

"What, Shelby?"

"Why... Why *me*?"

"I don't follow."

"I just... I'm finding it hard to believe. Of all the cases

you've ever worked... *I'm* the one that made you question your ability to do your job properly."

His teasing smile falls away, replaced by a serious look. "You may find it hard to believe, but it's the truth. I didn't lie to you. I won't ever lie to you."

"No, that's not what I meant at all—"

He cuts me off. "I've been doing this job for a long time, first in New York, now here in Boston. It's all I've ever been good at. And, like I told you before, it's all I have. My parents weren't exactly thrilled when I walked away from their plans for me back in California. They cut me off when I told them I was applying for the FBI Academy after my college graduation, instead of helping manage the chain of car washes my father owns."

I blink. "I cannot picture you running a car wash empire."

"Yeah, well, neither could I. That's why I left." His eyes get distant. "I thought New York would feel like home, but it never quite fit. That's why I took the transfer up here. It wasn't about wanting a fresh start in a new city. I simply had nothing tying me there. No unbreakable relationships, no permanent roots. I figured one zip code was as good as another. Simple as filling out a change-of-address card. Because for me, home is just a place to crash. That's it. And when I'm there, I'm usually wishing I could be out in the field instead."

"Your job is your life," I murmur.

He nods. "You talk about a work-life balance... but for the past decade, since I was a twenty-two-year-old kid, this job has been all I've thought about. It's come before every-thing — before family, before relationships, before friend-ships or holidays or vacations. I've put my career first and never blinked an eye about it. Never even come close to questioning the decision." He sucks in a breath. "Until your case came across my desk."

My eyes widen.

"You are the only thing that has ever made me second-guess myself. The only case I've ever gotten so invested in... I couldn't do my job. Couldn't trust myself to make the right call, when it came down to it."

I don't even know what to say. Whether I should apologize for making him doubt his own abilities or do cartwheels around the room because, *holy freaking shit,* if he's saying what I think he's saying...

"You're more than a case, Shelby Hunt. You're more than the job," he murmurs, pressing his lips to the hair at my temple. "You are the exception to every rule I've ever written for myself. And it scares the ever-living shit out of me."

I turn my face into his shoulder to hide the fact that I'm crying.

He's the bravest man I've ever known.

He's not scared of anything.

But he's scared of the way he feels about me.

He doesn't say anything else. He just holds me close as my tears drip onto his skin and strokes my hair until I finally fall asleep.

WHEN I WAKE up the next morning, Conor is no longer in bed with me.

I sit up, looking around for him, but he's nowhere to be found. Throwing off the sheets, I grab the first article of clothing I come across — a large black FBI sweatshirt resting on the armchair — and tug it over my head. My hair feels twice its normal size, bushy and mussed from a night of lovemaking, but I barely care. A smile stretches across my lips as I barrel out into the living room.

"Hey, sexy, where'd you g— *OH!*"

I let out an embarrassed yelp as my eyes catch up to my mouth and I see Conor sitting on the sofa... beside Kaufman and Evelson. My cheeks turn fire-engine red as three male sets of eyes cut to me at once.

I instantly regret my choice of nicknames, though not as much as I regret the fact that I didn't put on pants before rushing out of the bedroom. With as much decorum as I can muster, I reach down and tug the hem of my sweatshirt more firmly over my thighs as I walk toward the sofa.

"Gentleman," I say in a haughty voice.

Kaufman nearly snorts coffee out his nose.

Evelson forces a cough to cover his laugh.

"Hunt. You're awake." Conor's mouth is twitching with amusement. "Tell us... which one of us were you referring to, exactly?"

"Me, obviously." Kaufman smirks. "I'm the sexiest by a landslide. Have you seen these baby blue eyes?"

"Now, now, don't get ahead of yourself," Evelson chimes in, rubbing his buzzed head. "Some chicks dig the bald look."

I will myself to sink into the floorboards and disappear. Unfortunately, my powers of invisibility don't seem to be cooperating at the moment.

"I'll just... grab some coffee..." I mutter weakly, darting into the kitchen and away from their laughter.

Smooth, Shelby. So smooth.

I'm pouring myself a steaming cup when two arms brace against the counter on either side of me. A firm chest hits my back.

"Good morning," Conor rumbles in my ear.

"Is it?"

"Oh, come on. We're required to tease you a little."

I turn around inside the cage of his arms and I kid you not, my knees go weak when I see the amount of warmth in his eyes.

"Hi," I whisper, arching into him.

"Hi," he rasps, leaning down to kiss me.

We lose ourselves for a minute, mouths moving together as unchecked passion blossoms bright between us. It's dangerous — how addicted I've already become to his touch. I crave it like a drug, seek it out with a relentless, limitless drive. After a minute or two, I've forgotten all about my coffee growing cold on the countertop, about the two men sitting in the other room, about the very real danger I'm in...

Conor has a smidge more self control. He pulls back, breaking our lips apart, but his breaths are as ragged as mine.

"This could be a problem." He's staring at my mouth.

"Oh?" I lick my lips innocently. "How so?"

"You are a dangerous distraction."

"Is that right?" I sidle toward him, craning my neck back to maintain eye contact. "I'd apologize, but I'm not really sorry..."

His jaw clenches with restraint. "Keep teasing me, you will be later."

"Is that a threat, Gallagher?"

"A promise, Hunt."

Our gazes hold, full of heat, and I know we're both thinking about that elusive *later*, counting the hours until we're back in bed with nothing to concern us but moans and sighs and bare skin.

"Keep looking at me like that, I won't be held responsible for my actions," he mutters.

"Is that supposed to deter me?"

"Only if you'd like me to actually catch Petrov and his boys before they do more damage to our lives." His brows lift. "If not, by all means, let's tell the world to go to hell and go back to bed."

"*Fine.*" I sigh melodramatically. "I see your point. I suppose I'll let you off the hook so you can go save the world now. But *later...*"

"*Later,*" he echoes.

We both grin like two giddy kids.

First step: save the world.

Next step: all the scorching hot sex we can handle.

I must say, I'm not entirely hating this plan...

"Hey." My head tilts as a thought suddenly occurs to me. "How's Sykes? Any change in her condition?"

He shakes his head, jaw clenched tight.

"I'm sorry."

"So am I." He kisses me on the forehead. "Grab your coffee and come debrief. We'll fill you in on everything that happened while you were sleeping."

"*Psh!* A gal catches six measly hours of shut eye and she misses everything..." I grumble as Conor turns and walks back into the living room. I watch him go, my eyes glued to his ultra-fine ass. Say what you will about the man — he fills out a pair of jeans like nobody's business.

Coffee mug in hand, I follow after him. The men are gathered around the coffee table — laptops open, thick manila folders scattered across every square inch of the glass surface. Catching my eye, Conor jerks his chin toward the open cushion beside him. I sink down onto it, take a large sip of my coffee, and peer at the bevy of documents. There must be thousands of printed pages here.

"What is all this stuff?"

"The Petrov case files," Conor tells me, flipping through the folder on his lap.

"*All* of this is about Petrov?!"

Evelson glances over. "There's more back at the Bureau — this is just what we thought might be important to revisit now that he's in the country. Key intel on his business operations, his past criminal activities, the work your husband did for him..."

I tense up a bit at the mention of Paul.

"Speaking of your husband..." Conor looks at me. His eyes are suddenly remote, unreadable. "That was part of what we wanted to brief you on."

"Is he..." I trail off, bracing myself for bad news.

"Kaufman," Conor prompts. "Show her."

The blond agent leans forward and hits a few buttons on his keyboard. A second later, a series of images pop up onscreen. "These were taken by a traffic camera in Brookline late last night." He hits zoom on one of the photos, and it comes into clearer focus. The quality isn't great, but I manage to make out three figures on the sidewalk, exiting a white van. Two are quite large and almost identical.

The Evanoffs.

As for the third figure... They appear to be carrying him between them, his feet dragging along the ground as though he's unconscious.

Paul.

My stomach twists in an uncomfortable mix of guilt and horror and vindication.

He's merely reaping the seeds he sowed, an unforgiving voice whispers from the back of my mind. *Don't you dare feel sorry for the man who's done you more damage than anyone else on this earth.*

"Here, this one is clearer," Kaufman murmurs, skipping forward a few frames. The next photo he pulls up is far better quality, taken by a different camera. It shows the three men in an alleyway, illuminated by an overhead streetlamp.

I gasp audibly when I see Paul's face. Or... what's left of Paul's face. He's almost unrecognizable — two black eye sockets, a fat lip, his nose broken and swollen to twice it's normal size. It looks more like an eggplant than a facial feature.

Again, the Evanoffs are dragging him between them like a sack of potatoes. I wonder if the extreme damage extends to the rest of his body. If he's unable to walk on his own volition.

"My god," I say, shaking my head vigorously. I'm gripping the coffee cup so tightly, I'm surprised it doesn't shatter in my hands. "Please... don't show me any more."

"Nothing more to show," Kaufman replies. "They entered this building around 3AM and haven't been spotted since. We think there's a good chance they're still inside."

"What's the building?"

"Officially? It's a Russian deli," Evelson informs me. "Unofficially? It's been a mob front for the local Bratva cabal for years."

"And," Kaufman adds, smiling wide. "It's been closed for business all week. Interesting coincidence."

"So you think it's where the Evanoff brothers have been staying? Where they're keeping Paul now?"

"That's definitely a working theory," Evelson says.

I glance at Conor, who's being suspiciously silent on this matter, and find his eyes are locked on my hands. More specifically, on my white-knuckled grip around the coffee mug. When his face lifts to mine, his expression is unreadable.

"Hey." My brows furrow. "Are you okay?"

"I'm fine," he says, but his jaw is so tight I don't believe him for a second. "And Paul will be, too."

Since when does Conor care about Paul's welfare?

Is this the same man who punched him in the face mere days ago?

"Conor—"

"I know the photos looked bad, but it's actually a very good sign he's still alive at this point. If our intel plays out, we'll recover him." He sucks in a breath. "And... you can go back to your life."

"Well, that's a relief," I murmur, thinking of how good it'll be to have all of this behind us. To start living again. *To get to know a certain indigo-eyed FBI agent outside interrogation rooms and cheap motels and safe houses.*

My lips turn up in a small smile at the thought.

Conor's still staring at me with that strange look. When he sees the smile, his face clouds over into a scowl.

I tilt my head. "Are you sure you're okay?"

"Why wouldn't I be, Hunt?"

His tone is sharper than I've heard it in ages. Maybe ever.

My mouth opens to reply, but he's already turned away from me. Rife with confusion, I stare at the back of his messy black head as he questions Evelson about the activity on Petrov's credit cards since he entered the States. I try to pay attention to the answer, but bank statements seem suddenly less vital than the man sitting two inches from me.

And a whole world away.

Something is definitely bothering him. He's acting

strangely. Closed off and cold — like he used to be, the first day I met him. I try to figure out what could've possibly triggered his shift in mood from our playful banter in the kitchen ten minutes ago to this unexpected brooding anger... but I'm drawing a complete blank.

You're just reading into things, I assure myself. *He's under a lot of pressure with this case. But he's still the same man who held you as you fell asleep last night. The man who said you're more important than this job.*

As soon as Petrov and his thugs are off the streets, things will be fine.

Better than fine.

You'll see.

And yet, as I listen to the agents making plans to further surveil the deli in Brookline, I can't shake the strange, unsettling suspicion that I'm missing something so obvious, it's staring me straight in the face...

AFTER A FEW HOURS, Evelson and Kaufman disappear to do... whatever it is they spend their days doing. Conor is fielding calls from the bedroom, helping coordinate the deli surveillance operation. After the Eastie incident, they're taking extra precautions. Planning a strategic strike. They can't just storm in, guns blazing, and hope like hell the Evanoffs haven't rigged the place with another homemade explosive.

Not without putting more agents lives in danger.

I suck down my second cup of coffee as I flip absently through the files on the coffee table. Most of them are stamped with big, bold *CONFIDENTIAL* notices on top, which means I probably shouldn't be reading them... but there isn't exactly a lot else to do here at the safe house.

My eyes snag on the name HUNT sticking out the top of one folder. I yank out the page, my eyes widening as they scan down a crib sheet of Paul's criminal activity. I knew he was in deep shit with both the SEC and the FBI for his myriad financial blunders... but this is far worse than I'd imagined.

Fraud, embezzlement, money laundering, insider trading.

The list goes on, predating even his involvement with Petrov. Some of these charges are for crimes committed while he still worked at LP Consulting, dating back nearly a decade. Which means, even he makes it out of this alive... he's not going to be a free man for a long, long time. There are so many federal felonies listed here, he'll make Bernie Madoff look like a freaking Boy Scout if he ever goes to trial.

"Not quite the perfect future you were expecting, is it?"

My head whips around at the sound of Conor's voice. He's standing behind me, staring at the sheet of paper in my hands. I set it down carefully on the table.

"When it comes to Paul, I learned pretty early on that expecting perfection was a surefire way to wind up disappointed."

Conor's eyes narrow on mine. His arms are crossed over his chest and he appears to be debating whether or not to say something.

"Look," he says finally in a strangely empty voice. "I know I made you a promise that I'd get him back for you. And despite what happened between us... despite what I feel for you... I will do my best to honor that promise."

Confusion spirals through me. "Huh?"

"I want you to be happy, Hunt. Even if it's not with me."

"I repeat... *Huh?*"

He shakes his head, not hearing me. "But you saw that rap sheet. And that's just a draft. Preliminary charges. Once he's in custody and formal charges are filed..."

I simply blink at him, wondering what the hell he's talking about. I'd be less lost if he started speaking in Swahili. "Um..."

"Shelby, you have to know... even if I manage to extract him from this, to get him away from Petrov and the Evanoffs... there's no way you'll ever have him back. Not in the way you want. Not as a husband or a life partner."

"But.." I splutter, utterly dumbfounded. "But I don't *want* him back."

Conor tenses. "What?"

"I don't want Paul," I tell him, eyes wide.

I want you, I think but don't say.

Scrambling to my feet, my hands plant themselves on my hips as I level him with a severe look. "What, exactly, led you to believe I'd ever in a million years want to get back together with my ex?"

Conor's face is a flat mask, his tone is carefully cool. "My observations over the past few days, mainly."

"Such as...?"

"Back at your house the other night... you were crying as they led him away in cuffs." His jaw clenches. "Then, after the firefight, your reaction when I told you he'd been grabbed by the Evanoffs. Again when you saw him earlier today in those photos... It's pretty clear to me. You're not over him."

My eyes press closed as puzzle pieces click together in my mind. This totally explains why he's been acting so hot and cold. Freezing up whenever the conversation shifts to Paul.

He thinks I want to get back together with my shithead husband.

I'd laugh, if I could summon even one ounce of amusement over this ridiculous misunderstanding.

"Conor, no. *No.*" I shake my head. "You're completely off base. What you saw... the way I've reacted when talking about Paul... it's..."

"What?"

"It's not what you think."

"Then explain it to me. Because from where I'm standing, your reactions look a lot like you're still in love with him."

"Are you serious?! Did you forget about the fact that I've been attempting to divorce the man for six months?"

"A legal separation isn't the same as an emotional one."

"I cannot believe this! You have lost your damn mind, Gallagher." I laugh ludicrously, taking a few steps in his direction. "And I suppose the fact that I've filed a restraining order against him, and kicked him out of my house, and done everything physically possible to move on from him... that doesn't count for anything in your book?"

His jaw clenches and unclenches rhythmically. I can see he's conflicted — torn between trusting my words and listening to his own instincts.

"*Conor.*" His name is a plea. "Do you honestly think, after everything that happened between us last night, that I still..." I trail off, too hurt to even finish the sentence.

"I don't know what to believe, Shelby. You're not exactly an open book when it comes to your emotions. You don't confide in anyone — least of all me. You don't let anyone in behind that wall you've built around yourself.

And you know what? That wall might keep you protected, but it leaves everyone on the outside flying blind, having to guess everything you're thinking and feeling." He exhales sharply. "I like to think I can read you pretty well by now. But when it comes to this, I can't rely only on instinct. I can't play some guessing game with you until you're finally ready to trust me. It's too important. And it's bigger than just you and me and your idiot ex."

"Oh, that's rich! *You*, Mr. Closed-Off, lecturing *me* about keeping people at arm's length."

"And yet, I'm not the one keeping secrets."

"No, you're the one throwing false accusations!"

"Look... if I'm off base, if I read things wrong... I'll own it. Hell, I'll throw a fucking parade to celebrate it." He shakes his head and a lock of dark hair falls into his eyes. "But this situation isn't exactly clear-cut. To put it bluntly, it's a fucking mess. You and him are—"

"There is no *me and him*!" I snap. "Except, apparently, in your delusional alpha male brain!"

"You think I like thinking about this? You think I don't hate the idea of you being with him? You think the thought of you going back to him doesn't make me sick to my fucking stomach?" His words are ragged with emotion. "But Shelby, you were married to the man for ten years. That doesn't just *end* because you take off your wedding ring and file some paperwork."

I flinch back, deeply offended. "You don't know a damn thing about what my marriage was like! About what he's done to me! And, based on this conversation, I'm starting to think you don't know a damn thing about me either!"

"Maybe I don't." He takes a step toward me, until only a foot remains between us. His eyes narrow dangerously. "Or maybe you're just too embarrassed to admit you could ever want him back in your life after everything he's done. Maybe you don't want to be one of those weak, stand-by-your-man wives who never grows a backbone, even after being treated like a piece of property rather th—"

My hand flies out and slaps him clear across the face. It's not a conscious action. It's more of a reflex to hearing all those awful things — the same ones I've whispered to myself over and over in the mirror for years — coming out of his mouth instead of my own.

I just... I snapped.

And slapped.

I'm not sure who's more stunned by the strike — me or him. My mouth falls open as I watch a bright red handprint blooming across his skin.

"Conor..." I breathe, instantly remorseful. "I'm so sorry, I didn't—"

"I think we should hit pause on this discussion," he growls tightly, turning away from me and striding from the room.

"Wait!" I call. "Conor, hold on!"

He keeps walking.

"*Conor!*" I yell, racing after him through the kitchen. I beat him to the door and plant myself against it, blocking his path.

"Hunt. *Move.*"

"No." My chest is heaving. My eyes are locked on his. "Not until you listen."

He's watching me carefully. "You planning on slapping me again?"

I shake my head.

"You planning on evading with a cutesy dodge? Hiding behind more walls? Because I don't have any interest in that."

"Okay. How about the truth, then?" I swallow. "Do you have any interest in hearing that? Or are you only concerned with your skewed version of events?"

An angry muscle ticks in his jaw, but he doesn't try to push past me. I take that as a sign he's listening.

He wants a peek inside these high walls?

He wants me to trust him with my secrets?

Fine.

Here goes.

"The reason for the tears when they led Paul away wasn't because I was sad to see him go. It was because I was ashamed," I say haltingly. "Not of him. Of *myself*. Of the things I was feeling in that moment."

Conor's mouth opens, but I cut him off.

"*No*, not the feelings you accused me of. Not love or regret or sadness. Not some wifely duty or spousal obligation." I shake my head. "You once asked me why I have this need to be perfect all the time. Why I like order and organization. Why I'm such a control freak." My voice gets smaller, softer. "It's because, for most of my marriage, I wasn't the one in control. I was the one *being* controlled."

His eyes darken. "Shelby—"

"Let me get this out, okay?" I swallow to clear the lump in my throat. "I was an insecure kid who grew into an even more insecure woman. I got married too young, to the first man who ever told me I was beautiful, because he checked all the right boxes of what I thought I was supposed to find in a husband. *Good job, good provider, good head on his shoulders.* He built me a home and gave me the support I needed to finally feel secure in my own skin. And, after a childhood spent as the chubby girl with mousy brown hair and highly critical parents... it was amazing to have someone who finally loved me for exactly who I was." I pause and suck in a steadying breath. "But... a few years passed. I got older. I started to grow into a real person. A real *woman*, not the naive girl he married, with new interests and new friends and new aspirations. New confidence in myself. And... Paul didn't like that so much. He didn't like *me* so much. And he showed me. With his words. With his fists, too, when things got really bad."

Conor makes a low sound of anger.

"You see, he wanted me to stay in that little box marked *wife*. To keep cutting myself down, inch by inch, until I fit the role he'd carved out for me." My eyes have started watering. It's a struggle to hold the tears at bay, so I tilt my head toward the ceiling. "And for a while, I tried. I let him keep me small. I let him keep me timid. I allowed him to take away my control, my autonomy, my dreams, telling myself it was for the sake of saving my marriage. But eventually... I couldn't do it anymore." My voice breaks. "Eventually, I realized I shouldn't have to shrink to fit a relationship I've outgrown. A *man* I've outgrown. I shouldn't have to make myself smaller just so he doesn't feel insignificant when he's standing beside me."

A rogue tear escapes down my cheek. Before I can reach up to brush it away, Conor's hand is there — cupping my face, warm and strong, his thumb stroking so gently it makes my breath catch. He doesn't pull away, even when the tear is gone.

I hold his eyes and force myself to tell him the rest.

"These past few months... and especially these past few days... I don't feel small. I don't feel powerless. I don't feel like I have to diminish parts of myself to make anyone else comfortable. For the first time in my life... I feel like me."

He pulls in a sharp breath. "Shelby..."

"You saw me crying when they led Paul away. Again

when I learned the Evanoffs had taken him. I know you think that means I was upset, or heartbroken, or grieving the loss of a man I still love... but the truth is, I was *relieved*. Relieved that, without Paul in my life anymore, I can finally move on. Can finally be *free*." I crack a small smile, through my tears. "Free to set my own course. Free to be the person I'd like to be. And, maybe someday... free to be with someone else. Someone who understands me. Someone who actually does love me for exactly the person I am."

The air goes still as I trail off. There's a poignant beat of hesitation while I wait for his reaction. While I wait to see if letting him get a glimpse behind my walls is enough to send him running for the hills, or bring him back into the circle of my arms.

"*Shelby*," he says simply.

And then he's kissing me. Kissing me so fiercely, it makes me want to cry and scream and sing. Kissing me like I'm the air he needs to live, a vital ingredient for his means of survival.

"I'm sorry," he breathes against my lips when he finally pulls away. "I'm sorry for what I said, for jumping to conclusions... for all of it."

I remember the first time I saw him, thinking he was a man who didn't know how to apologize. That he'd never in a million years take responsibility for his actions, even when he made a mistake.

I've never been so happy to be wrong.

"You know..." I bump my nose against his. "I believe you promised me that if we fought today, there would be hot makeup sex afterward. A package deal, if you will."

His eyes gleam. "I think that can be arranged..."

CHAPTER 13

BAD EGG

I CAN'T SLEEP — my brain is far too crowded with thoughts to power down for the night, despite the fact that Conor is snoring softly beside me. His face is the picture of exhaustion. There are deep circles beneath his eyes and a tension that never fully leaves him, even in sleep.

Not wanting to disturb him with my restless tossing and turning, I slowly untangle my naked limbs from his and slip out of bed. I grab his shirt off the floor and tug it over my head, smiling as his scent washes over me. Breathing it in like a drug. I smile even wider as I remember the moment I ripped it off his body earlier, when we stumbled into the bedroom after dinner.

He made for a delicious dessert course...

I walk out of the bedroom and shut the door behind me with a soft click, grinning at the thought. Passing through the dark living room, I make my way to the kitchen and flick on a light. My eyes widen when I see the state of it.

When I suggested cooking dinner together earlier, I figured it would be a fun way to pass the time while waiting for an update on the Petrov situation. I did *not* foresee our foray into homemade pasta-making would descend into a full-on food fight, complete with spattered egg yolk grenades and hurled handfuls of flour — most of which has now congealed into a sticky, lumpy mess that coats the floor, the countertops, the walls. Even some of the ceiling.

What a mess.

It's going to take a small eternity to clean. Still... it was worth it. I laughed more today with Conor than I did in a decade with Paul. And after our fight this afternoon, it was refreshingly normal to simply *hang out*. Like a real, actual couple, rather than two people thrown together in a high-stakes game of Russian roulette, running for our lives. It was almost as if the gods smiled upon us, as though someone up there decided to grant us a one-day-furlough from the madness of our situation.

Thank you, I toss vaguely upward into the great unknown, not even sure who I'm speaking to. *For giving us today. And... for giving me him.*

Shaking my head at my uncharacteristic show of faith, I grab a roll of paper towels and a bottle of bleach spray, then set to work scrubbing down the disaster zone that used to be a kitchen.

———

BY THE TIME the kitchen is clean, it's well past midnight and my arms are aching from hours of swabbing the decks. I collapse onto the couch in the living room with a deep sigh. I don't want to risk waking Conor by turning on the TV, but I know any attempts at sleep will be useless.

I'm still too wired.

My curious eyes slide to the files on the table. Before I can talk myself out of it, I pull one into my lap and start to read. And thus begins my proper education on the life of Alexei Petrov.

I read about his childhood in an orphanage outside Moscow, where he and his sister Ekaterina were placed together after the death of their parents. I read about his wild teenage years on the street, how he fought his way up from a skinny runt of the litter to the top dog of the most notorious gang in the city. I read about his first forays into the criminal underworld, running drugs and weapons over the Ukrainian border for an aspiring mafia boss he would one day surpass in both power and ruthlessness.

From what I can tell, his rise through the underbelly of the Bratva was damn near meteoric. By the time he was thirty, Alexei Petrov — a street rat from the gutters of Moscow — was the most feared man in all of the city. Maybe all of Russia. His lack of anything resembling a conscience was well-documented and highly effective when it came to eliminating his existing enemies and preventing new ones from cropping up. Few challenged him for control of his ever-expanding crime syndicate... and those who did were simply never heard from again.

Honestly, it has all the makings of a classic coming-of-age novel. An origin story for one of the world's biggest super-villains.

Keep your pretentious Russian literature, your Tolstoy and your Dostoevsky... the story of Alexei Petrov is far more interesting than anything I've read in ages.

My eyes devour file after file, stunned by the level of detail. It's excruciatingly thorough. Decades worth of research. A million facts and figures and anecdotes, all at my fingertips.

It's the ultimate binge-read.

And I'm undeniably hooked.

I learn about Alexei's propensity for expensive prosti-
tutes and fancy hotels. I even learn about his favorite food —
borscht, how very proletariat of you, Alexei — and his
favorite place to vacation — *a villa on the Baltic Sea* — and
the name of his first two wives — *both, coincidentally, called
Natasha.*

By the time I reach for one of the last folders in the
stack, my eyes are drooping closed. Deciding to call it quits
and head to bed before I go blind, I toss the folder back onto
the table. Thanks to my halfhearted aim, it skids off the top
of the pile and hits the floor instead, exploding in a flurry of
papers and photographs.

Damn it to hell.

Heaving a heavy sigh, I bend to pick up the scattered
contents and start shoving them haphazardly back into the
folder, vowing to reorganize them first thing in the morning
using more care. I'm rising to my feet when I see one last
sheaf has fluttered to a stop beneath the legs of the coffee
table.

Dropping back to my hands and knees, my fingers close
around a glossy black and white photograph. I glance fleetingly at the picture as I prepare to shove it away, expecting
yet another image of a suspected mob-hit, some bloody
crime scene or gruesome murder.

Instead, I see something highly unexpected.

Something that sends my pulse spiking like a seismo-
graph in the middle of an earthquake. Something that
makes absolutely no sense at all... and yet, somehow,
provides the exact solution I've been searching for all this
time. The answer to the question we've been asking
ourselves over and over and over for the past week, like a
riddle with no remedy.

Here is the remedy.

Right here in my hands.

I stare at the black and white image more intently.

Not a crime scene.

Not a mug shot.

An egg.

A golden egg, to be precise, inlaid with dozens of sparkling sapphires and brilliant rubies and glittering emeralds. I know this to be the case, even though the photograph shows no color at all. Because I've seen this egg before. I've held it in my hands, turned it over in my fingers with disdain before tossing it away in the bottom of a jewelry box, thinking it no more than some cheap bauble made from synthesized crystal that Paul picked up on a whim. Just one more gift in the long series he sent, trying to win me back.

But this...

This is no cheap bauble.

No useless trinket.

No inexpensive paperweight.

This is...

"A Fabergé egg," I marvel aloud, feeling like my head might explode. I wait one, two, three long seconds before I set the photograph carefully on the table, suck in a deep breath, and bellow at the top of my lungs.

"CONOR!"

"A FABERGÉ EGG," I say, pacing like a madwoman across the living room. "He stole a Fabergé Egg."

"I know, Hunt. You've said it six times, now."

"Not just any Fabergé Egg, either. A freaking Tsar Imperial Fabergé Egg."

Conor sighs.

"And not just any Tsar Imperial Fabergé Egg. One of the *long lost* Tsar Imperial Fabergé Eggs."

"Hunt—"

I shake my head. "I should've figured it out the other night, when he started speaking French. Paul doesn't speak French! And yet, I didn't blink a freaking eye when he kept saying '*nécessaire*' like a damn sommelier." I pause. "Of course, at the time, I thought he was telling me it was necessary to run. I didn't know *Nécessaire* was the name of the damn Egg. An Egg no one has seen, by the way, since 1952. At least, according to the brief Google search I conducted ten minutes ago while you were on the phone with Evelson."

"Not sure you're in the right state of mind to be Googling anything at the moment, Hunt."

I ignore him. "Surprise, surprise! *Nécessaire* is not lost to history after all. Unless by *history* you're referring to three months ago, when I tossed it in the bottom of a jewelry box like it was a freaking pair of fifteen dollar earrings."

"Hunt—"

"Did you hear me? I *threw it*. I actually *threw* a Fabergé Egg. A freaking relic."

"Shelby. *Breathe*."

I whirl to look at him. "Breathe?! How can I breathe, Conor? My no-good, dirty-rotten, lying, cheating ex decided it would be a good idea to steal a priceless object from his uncle, then sent it to *me* — presumably to keep it hidden for him until he could find a way to get the Evanoffs off his tail and come collect it again. Like I'm his own personal, illegal artifact storage facility. A drug mule, if you will. Except I'm more of an egg mule. Which isn't a thing. At least, so far as I know." My head tilts. "There could be a black market for eggs, I suppose. *Free-range, organic, cage-free, Cadbury, Easter, over-easy...*"

"Hunt." His lips are twitching. "I can't tell if you're joking or if you've had a stroke."

"Me neither, to be honest." My voice breaks. "I just didn't see this happening."

"Your newfound obsession with egg varieties?"

"No. Unknowingly possessing a priceless object that's made me the target for several Russian hitmen. And, for the record, when I say *priceless* I don't mean it in the, '*Aw, shucks, look at that family having a picnic, what a priceless moment*' sort of way. I mean it in the very literal, '*you cannot put a price tag on this item because it is irreplaceable*' sense of the word." I pause. "Though, if you *could* put a price tag on it, it would probably say something in the $20 million range."

"You're freaking out."

"Of course I'm freaking out! Why aren't *you* freaking out?"

"Not really my style."

"Well, it's not usually mine either, but I'm making an exception in this particular case." I blow out a breath. "Did you know that there were only fifty-two of these Eggs ever made? And that this one was made for the Tsar of Russia, as a gift for his wife?"

"Google tell you that factoid?"

"Maybe."

"That's it. I'm restricting your internet privileges."

"Too late! The damage is done. I already memorized the Wikipedia page. I am a freaking fount of knowledge. Ask me anything."

He stares at me blankly.

"Go on! Ask me something."

"You want some whiskey?"

"I meant something about the Eggs."

He shrugs. "You want the whiskey or not?"

"No! Yes. *Maybe.*"

"Way to be decisive, babe." Conor smirks and walks into the kitchen. When he comes back, he's got two low-ball glasses of whiskey in his hands. He passes one to me in silence and raises his other in solidarity. "Cheers."

"What on earth do we have to celebrate, in this moment?"

He takes a small sip. "You."

"*Me?*"

He nods. "You've been so busy spiraling into panic, I don't think you realize what this all means."

"Um... that we're utterly fucked? Because if you think Alexei Petrov is going to let a $20 million, one-of-a-kind antiquity slip through his fingers..."

Conor shakes his head. "Before, we were walking around blindfolded, hoping to stumble onto whatever your husband stole by dumb luck alone. That's like fighting with your hands tied behind your back. Thanks to you, we know exactly what Petrov is after. We know why he's so determined to get it back. And we even know where it is — presuming you didn't throw that jewelry box in the trash." He actually cracks a smile. "Don't you see? Now, we have a chance at closing this case on our terms. We'll get the Egg from wherever you stashed it, use it as bait to draw Petrov and his boys out, and finally catch the bastards." He lifts his glass again. "And *that*, Hunt, is definitely worth celebrating."

I eye him nervously. "Yeah... you might not want to celebrate our victory *too* prematurely."

His brows go up. "Why's that?"

"When I said I had the Egg, I meant it. I *had* the Egg. Past tense."

His silence is profound. I hear him take a sharp intake of breath, steeling himself. "Hunt, please tell me you didn't throw our only shot at stopping Alexei Petrov in the garbage."

I wince. "Not exactly."

"Then where is it?"

I keep my eyes closed as I tell him the location of the Egg. And, as I listen to him curse like a sailor on leave, I raise my glass to my lips and drain my whiskey in one long sip.

I'm going to need a little liquid courage for what comes next.

"YOU'RE NOT COMING WITH ME."

"Like hell I'm not," I growl. "You can't expect me to sit around here waiting. Not when I can finally be of use for something."

"It's too dangerous."

"No more dangerous than me sitting around here like a sitting duck while you rush headlong into the fight. *Again.*"

"I rush headlong into danger because I've spent years training for it." He shakes his head. "I can't protect you out there."

"I'm not asking you to protect me! I'm asking you to let me help you."

"Shelby—"

"You don't even know what the Egg looks like, besides what you've seen in some faded black and white photograph. And more importantly, you're not the one who's responsible for giving the damn thing away as a re-gift because she didn't have time to go shopping before her boss' 50th birthday party!" My cheeks heat with mortification. I'm still struggling to wrap my mind around the fact that I accidentally gave Aimee — the aura-reading, earth-loving woman who owns the small studio where I occasionally teach yoga — a priceless Fabergé Egg... under the pretense that it was a healing crystal to help 'channel her spiritual energy flow', no less.

Anyone else in the world probably would've realized their good fortune and sold the Egg to the highest bidder. It's pure dumb luck that Aimee happens to be the least materialistic person on the planet. I doubt she has any idea of the Egg's value. And, if she did, there's a solid chance she might not even care.

His jaw clenches. "You aren't coming with me. It's out of the question."

"This is my fight, too! You aren't the only one who wants this over and done with."

"I'm aware of that."

"And yet you expect me to sit here and do nothing."

"No, I expect you to sit here and be *safe* while I go out and get the Egg from your friend."

"I'll go crazy waiting, Conor." My eyes are suddenly stinging with tears. "I swear to god, if I have to stand here and watch you walk out that door one more time..."

He steps closer, bending until we're eye to eye. His voice is uncharacteristically soft. "Shelby. I will be fine."

"You don't know that! Evelson said the Evanoffs left the deli. That they're *in the wind*, whatever the hell that means."

"It means—"

"Oh, I know what it means!" I say crossly, cutting him

off. "I just don't think it's very specific, seeing as he's supposedly the master of surveillance. You'd think he'd be able to pin down their location a bit more precisely."

"The Evanoffs are highly trained at staying off the grid. How else do you think they've managed to evade capture after decades on the Most Wanted list?"

"Not dumb luck, I'm guessing."

"No. Nothing dumb about it. They're virtually untraceable when they want to be. Like ghosts."

"Coldblooded killer ghosts," I mutter.

"Yes. They are. Which is precisely why you're staying here, where they can't get to you."

"But—"

"*Shelby.*" His jaw is set stubbornly. "I cannot do my job effectively with you out in the open, exposed. Don't you understand? I won't be able to think about anything except keeping you out of harm's way."

"So you're saying I'm a liability. That I'm your Achilles heel. Your kryptonite. Your weakness."

His face softens. Leaning forward, he brushes his lips against mine in a gentle kiss that makes my heart flip over. "I'm saying that I am in love with you."

The world stops turning.

The air freezes in my lungs.

The muscles in my body go completely rigid.

"*What?*"

"You heard me," he says starkly. "I love you. I am *in love* with you. I have been for months, probably since the first time I saw you on Christmas night, sporting a black eye but still somehow smiling. Sitting on the floor of a dirty dog kennel, celebrating the holiday with a dozen mangey mutts."

I suck in a breath.

He was there for that?

I'd felt so alone, that night. The whole rest of the world was with family and friends, singing carols and spreading holiday cheer... but I was alone, with nothing at all to celebrate except the ending of my marriage. I sat on that kennel floor replaying my morning over and over in my mind. Paul's rage and my terror and the shriek of squad cars racing down Merriweather Street.

That was the moment I swore to myself I was done with love for good.

Coincidentally... the *same* moment Conor looked through a window at a lonely girl on a dirty floor and fell in love with her.

You can't say fate doesn't have a sense of humor...

At the time, I thought that was probably the worst day of my entire life. But now that I know it brought me straight to Conor...

I glance up. Right at him.

His eyes are warm. Ultra warm. Practically burning.

He loves me, I think, stunned. *Conor Gallagher loves me.*

At least... he thinks he does.

For now.

The panic hits so fast, it levels me — stealing away my fragile hopes in an instant. Suddenly, my mind is reeling like a merry-go-round. My heart is pounding far too fast to possibly be healthy. I think I'm going to need a cardiologist at the ripe age of twenty-nine.

Cause of death: sheer and utter panic.

"Shelby." His voice is soothing; he can totally see me freaking out. "Take a breath."

My head is shaking, thoughts tumbling over each other so fast it's a struggle to force one through my lips. "What the hell are you thinking, telling me you love me? You can't possibly *love* me. You don't even *know* me!"

"I know you."

"You only think you know me," I whisper, shaking my head. "There are things you don't know, things that might change how you feel or—"

"Shelby Quinn Hunt."

My words dry up. "Y-yes?"

"I know where you grew up and why you got out. I know you like dogs more than cats, especially strays that don't have homes to call their own. I know you prefer buying your groceries at a Farmers Market stall over a grocery store aisle. I know you have friends who love you, even though you keep them at arm's length sometimes." His mouth twists. "I know you can put your legs behind your head in a crazy ass yoga pose — and that it looks even better when you're doing it naked, while I'm deep inside you and you're screaming out my name."

Oh, boy.

I think he's done, but he's not.

"I know the way you take your coffee, the places you run to clear your head, your favorite takeout spot. And I know you're terrified out of your damn mind to hear me saying all these things to you right now, because the last asshole who told you he loved you ended up being the worst sort of liar."

I'm stunned silent.

Utterly speechless.

"But *because* I know you..." His hands come up to cup my cheeks. "I also know that, in a few days, when you finish having whatever internal freak out you're currently experiencing and let everything I just said sink in... you'll realize that I'm right. That I know exactly who you are. And that I love you for it."

I'm crying again.

Damnit.

I glare at him through the tears. "You know, if this was just some elaborate scheme to get me to stay here while you go running off to hunt down bad guys—"

His smiling mouth hits mine, swallowing the rest of my sentence. And I don't even care. Because I'm kissing him back, my chest full of a lightness I've never before experienced, and there's no need to say another word.

He loves me.

"DID YOU HEAR THAT?"

"Hmm?" I blink, still flying high from the drugging effects of his mouth on mine. "Honestly, when you're kissing me, most of my executive functions stop working..."

He pulls back from me abruptly and walks into the kitchen. His muscles are tight, his senses on high alert.

"Conor, what's goi—"

"Shh." He holds up a hand to silence me, listening hard.

The only audible nose is the faint ticking of the clock on the wall, which informs me it's just past six in the morning. At least, that's the only sound to my ears. Clearly, Conor's are more highly attuned, seeing as he reaches down and slowly slides his gun from its holster.

No, no, no.

"Thought I heard something outside." His voice is almost inaudible."I'm going to check it out. Lock the door behind me. And if I'm not back in two minutes, get inside the pantry and bolt the steel door."

I make a small sound of protest, but I'm afraid to speak. Too afraid that, if there really is someone lurking out there, any noise I make might tip them off.

And get Conor killed.

His eyes cut to mine, holding for a long moment. He gives a small nod — as if to reassure me everything will be just fine, before walking to the door. At the last minute, he pauses, turns, and holds up two fingers.

Two minutes.

I nod.

He winks.

And slips outside, into the pink-edged dawn.

TWO MINUTES.

You wouldn't think they could possibly drag on so long. That one hundred and twenty ticks of the second hand could be so torturously drawn out. Leaning against the kitchen counter, I hold my breath as I wait — my eyes fixed on that thin, jerking dial as it makes its slow orbit around the clock face.

Forty seconds.

He's not back.

A minute.

Still no Conor.

A minute thirty.

No sign of him.

The tempo of my pulse kicks up a notch as it nears the two minute mark. I strain my ears, listening hard for any sound outside. There's nothing — not the rustling of tree leaves, not the rattling of a trash can lid, not the sound of footsteps or — god forbid — gunshots ringing out in the early morning sky.

Two minutes.

Sighing deeply, I turn on leaden feet to face the pantry. The last thing I want to do is barricade myself in there… but even without him here to yell at me, I can feel the weight of Conor's disapproval looming large over my head.

Bossy, infuriating man.

I'm halfway to the pantry when I hear the soft rap of his knuckles on the back door.

Oh, thank god.

He's back.

I race across the room to let him in, fully prepared to scold him for scaring the shit out of me for no reason. After I kiss him. With tongue. And maybe a little butt-groping.

What can I say? The man has a killer ass.

"Two minutes on the nose," I say, smiling as I pull the door wide. The smile falls off my face when I see the man standing just outside, grinning back at me.

"Shelby Hunt," Lefty says in a faint Russian accent. "We meet again."

A millisecond later, his hand rears back and slams into my face, knocking me out cold in a single punch.

CHAPTER 14

GONE HUNT(ING)

WHEN I WAKE UP, I'm in a dark, enclosed space. It takes me a moment to realize it's the trunk of a car. A car that's *moving* — I can hear the distinct rumble of tires against the road beneath me. Where we're headed, I have no idea.

Probably straight to Alexei Petrov, if I had to guess.

I try to scream, but there's a piece of duct tape covering my mouth. I try to struggle, but the zip-tie binding my hands together makes that virtually impossible.

I suppose there's a lesson to be learned in all of this about opening the door for strangers... but my head is pounding too hard to discern what it is. Probably due to the golfball-sized welt on my left cheekbone, swelling more with each passing moment.

Ow.

Lefty really clocked me.

I try to slow my breathing rate, dragging air in and out of my nose as I take stock of my situation. There's nothing in the trunk that can help me escape. And, even if there were, I probably couldn't reach it in my current predicament.

I'm barefoot, wearing nothing but a thin pair of yoga

pants and one of Conor's baggy t-shirts. It still smells like him, which might be a comfort if I knew whether he was alive or dead, right now. I'm relatively certain nothing in the world will be able to soothe me until I know the answer to that question.

So help me god, if the Evanoffs laid so much as a hand on him... I will make them pay.

Brave words for a girl tied up in a car trunk.

If I knew how long I was unconscious, I'd have a much better idea of where we might be headed. As it is, I'm cut adrift without any sense of time or place.

Minutes? Hours? Days?

If the latter, I could be anywhere in the world by now. Hell, I could pop out of this trunk and find myself in Moscow. (Okay, so, it's more likely I'll pop out and find myself somewhere like Malden or Medford... but the point remains the same.)

My head feels like it's been detached from my body, put inside a dryer, and set to a sixty-minute tumble cycle. Everything is jumbled up. I try to focus on finding a way to escape, but it's not an easy task. Between the blow to my face and the not-so-minor fact that, for all I know, the man I adore is lying somewhere in a pool of his own blood... my thoughts are one great sloshing wave of panic, ebbing and receding with each passing moment.

He is not dead, I tell myself over and over as the car rolls onward to destinations unknown. *I refuse to even contemplate that possibility.*

I spend the remainder of the ride screaming in vain against the duct tape while attempting to kick out the tail lights of the vehicle, hoping I might catch the attention of a passing driver at a stoplight or intersection. All I succeed in doing is wearing out my vocal chords and bashing my bare toes until they're bruised and bleeding.

After a small eternity the brakes finally engage, slowing the vehicle to a stop. I flinch as I hear the sound of car doors opening, the crunch of boots on gravel as the Evanoffs make their way to the rear of the sedan. The trunk lid springs open and my eyes are immediately flooded by brilliant light from the sun blazing directly overhead. I blink away sunspots as I'm hauled out with all the gentleness of a farm-hand tossing a bale of hay and slammed into a vertical position, the soles of my feet jolting hard against hot pavement.

My head is spinning and I've barely found my footing when a hand slams into the base of my spine. I careen forward like a rag doll, nearly face-planting onto the ground but catching myself at the last minute. For a second, I remain bent over as the world tilts around me — head bowed low, bound hands hanging by my knees. Hauling breaths through my nose in desperate puffs.

"Let's go," Lefty sneers, grabbing hold of my shirt collar and dragging me back into an upright position. "*Now.*"

"If you can't walk, I'd be happy to drag you by your restraints," Righty offers. I notice his accent is slightly thicker than his brother's. Less polished. I wonder absently if he's Viktor or Vladimir before a voice from the back of my befuddled brain reminds me it doesn't matter.

They're about to kill you, crazy pants. Who gives a crap what their names are?

They drag me away from the car, across the scorching hot pavement. I squint my eyes, trying to see where we are, but every time my head lifts one of them shoves me from behind again, sending me stumbling. I lose track of how many times I almost crash onto my face. They chuckle every time this happens, enjoying themselves quite a bit at my expense.

The little I can make out about my surroundings isn't very helpful in narrowing down my location. I'm up on some kind of roof, judging by the flat expanse of poured concrete all around me.

The top level of a parking garage, perhaps?

No, that can't be right. We're not nearly high up enough for that. And there are no other cars anywhere in sight.

Where the hell are they taking me?

I'd ask, if not for the tape over my mouth. We reach a set of stairs and, evidently, even sociopaths have their limits when it comes to humiliation, because the Evanoffs stop playing their little Shove-the-Shelby game long enough for me to hobble down the steps. I keep my eyes on my feet to avoid falling face first down the flight, noticing belatedly that I'm leaving bloody footprints behind on the cement with each unsteady tread.

Funny. I can't feel any pain at all.

At the bottom of the stairs we come to a shaded space, completely out of the hot sunshine. It takes me a moment to realize we're now underground, standing in what appears to be the foundation of a large industrial building site. A project in the early stages of production, from the looks of it. Construction materials are littered everywhere, from cement mixers to excavation machinery to blasting explosives.

I guess this explains where they found the ingredients for their bomb...

Heavy steel beams lay in neat horizontal stacks, the bones of a building's future skeleton. Fifty feet away, a half-poured elevator shaft rises upward out of the earth. I can't help thinking it's the picture perfect place to commit a murder.

No one around to hear your victim scream, and a pre-dug grave so deep no one will ever find the body.

A sudden sound from my left sends my head swiveling around— the sharp rap of approaching footsteps, echoing in the vast space like gunshots. My eyes drag from the source of the sound — a pair of ultra-shiny black shoes — up the navy suit, all the way to the heavily-bearded face of a man whose picture I have studied in so many case file photographs and FBI mugshots, I could probably draw it from memory.

He's older than his pictures. His beard has gone gray, his dark eyes are slightly sunken in to his shrewd face. But it's him. Of that, I have absolutely no doubt.

At my back, I hear both Evanoff brothers shifting on their feet, standing a bit straighter as their boss comes to a stop about ten feet away. His eyes are locked on my face, full of cold curiosity.

"Niece," Alexei Petrov says in an empty voice.

I begin to shiver despite the hundred degree day. Of all the things I expected him to say to me, *'niece'* was not one of them. Hell, it wouldn't rank even in the top *hundred* things I expected him to say. (Mostly because I figured he'd pull out his gun and put a bullet in my head without saying *anything*, but also because, last I checked, he wasn't too pleased with either me or his nephew.)

His eyes move past me to the men standing at my back. "Why is she injured, Viktor?"

"Alexei..." Lefty sounds nervous. It freaks me out. I didn't even think it was *possible* for someone like him to get nervous. "We knew she would struggle when we removed her from the safe house. Rather than draw unnecessary attention... I thought it best we keep her silent for the journey."

Alexei says nothing for a long time. He merely stares at Lefty — Viktor — as his nostrils flare with rage, until the man is practically squirming by my side. He physically flinches when Alexei takes a step forward.

"She is married to a Petrov," he says in a searingly chilly voice. "You do not spill family blood without my permission."

"I'm sorry, boss. After the beating you had us give her husband, I didn't think you'd care if we roughed her up a bit..."

"My nephew is a separate matter. He stepped out of line and needed to be punished accordingly. However, I do not punish the innocent without cause." Alexei's eyes slide to mine. "I am not a monster."

I could laugh.

I *don't*, since I value my life... But I *could*.

Because Alexei Petrov telling me he's not a monster is like hearing a fire-breathing dragon who's just roasted a whole village alive swoop down on the destruction he's unleashed and tell the sole survivor that he's innocent of any wrongdoing... before eating him in one bite.

A thousand images flash through my mind — all the horrendous crime scenes he's had a hand in, every mob-hit this man has ordered. Every awful thing he's done over his four-decade reign of terror. All the lives he's ruined, whether directly through his actions or indirectly, through the sale of illegal arms, drugs, and trafficking victims.

I suppose it's par for the course: true monsters never see themselves as such.

Alexei takes a few more steps until only a handful of

feet separate us. At this proximity, his dark eyes are even more expressionless.

"Do you know who I am?" he asks lowly.

I hesitate a beat, then nod.

"Good."

At that, he reaches into his suit pocket and pulls out a switchblade. I start to panic, backpedaling straight into an Evanoff-shaped wall. They clamp down on my shoulders, holding me still with viciously tight grips that halt my struggles. Subdued, all I can do is watch with wide, terrified eyes as that knife swipes out toward me...

And slices cleanly through the zip-tie around my wrists.

I'm so stunned to be, well, *breathing*, I barely have time to brace myself as Alexei reaches up and rips the duct-tape off my mouth in a harsh tug that makes me gasp in pain. Tears spring to my eyes. It takes all my strength to keep them from falling; to straighten my spine and shake off the bruising grip on my shoulders.

When our eyes meet again, Alexei nods his approval. "Now, then. We have much to discuss."

I simply stare at him, unsure of what — if anything — he expects me to say.

Hey, nice to meet you! Thanks for having your thugs kidnap me, dragging me to this creepy murder site, and generally just scaring the shit out of me. Bygones!

"You've been married to my nephew for nearly a decade," Alexei says. "Is that correct?"

I nod.

"And, during that time, were you aware of his connection to the Petrov family?"

I shake my head.

"And are you *INCAPABLE OF SPEECH?*"

His sudden switch from murmur to roar makes me

flinch along with both Evanoffs. The scream strikes the air like a thunderclap, hits the far walls, then echoes back at us like a shout from a disembodied ghost.

"N-no, sir," I force myself to say, doing my best not to cower. Or cry. "Quite capable."

"Good." He's back to normal volume, as though the outburst never occurred. "Now. Do you know why you are here?"

My mind spins as I consider how much I should reveal. Honestly, I never expected to live this long if confronted with Alexei Petrov. Thus, I've never before considered what I'd say or do if I someday found myself in his — it must be said — super freaking intimidating presence.

Given the fact that even Righty and Lefty are damn close to peeing their pants every time he glances their way, I decide it's best to keep things as vague as humanly possible. The less I say, the lower the odds of pissing him off.

I think.

Maybe.

"My patience is expiring rapidly," he informs me. "If you are honest with me, you have nothing to fear."

Nothing to fear except literally everything about this situation.

I take a steadying breath. "I know Paul has gotten himself into trouble at work. But until a few days ago, I didn't even know he'd left his job at the consulting firm."

"You weren't aware he was working for me?"

"Forgive me, but... I didn't even know who you were until a few days ago. Paul didn't tell me about his family connections."

Alexei ponders that for a while, seemingly weighing my words for truth. "Paul was not raised as a Petrov. My sister took him from Russia when he was a small child. If he had been raised in Moscow, I would've reared him in my own image. He would be a man. He would run the family business by my side." His eyes narrow a shade. "Instead, he was raised here. And so he is still a boy. Soft. Weak. Spineless." He spits on the ground to emphasize his point. "And yet, the Petrov blood runs in his veins. I have no sons of my own. So when he reached out to me several years ago and confided about his money problems, I was happy to offer him a position working for the family."

"That was..." I search for something safe to say. "Very gracious of you."

"Yes, it was." His lips flatten into a harsh line. "But my nephew did not repay my kindness with loyalty. After only a year, he told me he no longer wanted any part in the family business. That he wanted to be a better man. Do you know why that is?"

"No, I'm afraid I don't."

His eyes sharpen like knives. "For *you.*"

I suck in a breath.

"You say you had no knowledge of the Petrov family. And yet, despite your ignorance, it seems you still managed to convince my nephew to abandon his obligations to it." He pauses heavily. "I find that... curious."

With effort, I keep my voice steady. "I assure you, I view family as the most important thing in this world. I would never encourage my husband to cut off communication with you, or anyone in his family."

"His mother assured me of the same thing many years ago... just before she fled Russia with her young son." Alexei's eyes are very, very cold. "Perhaps, if I'd trusted my instincts about Ekaterina, all this may've been prevented."

Oh, boy.

This isn't going very well.

This isn't going very well *at all*.

"During my nephew's last trip to Russia, your husband stole something from my estate. Something very precious to me. I believe he smuggled it back on my private jet and brought it home with him. Home to *you*, niece." There's a pregnant pause. "Do you happen to know what object I'm referring to?"

And this is where it gets tricky...

Do I lie and tell him I know nothing?

If I do... he'll have no further use for me. He'll most likely kill me and dump my body down the elevator shaft for the construction workers to find whenever work on this building resumes.

Do I tell him I know exactly where his precious Egg is hidden?

If I do... he'll probably be so angry, he'll kill me on the spot and dump my body inside one of the cement mixing vats for a wacky take on Han Solo in Carbonite.

Shelby Hunt in Cement!

Neither option sounds particularly appealing to me. In fact, they sound about as appealing as walking through a field of unexploded mines. Blindfolded. In six-inch heels. While drunk.

"Well?" Alexei prompts.

I make a split-second decision, praying it doesn't get me killed. "It's embarrassing to admit, but... Paul and I have been having some marital problems. He was traveling frequently, working all the time, and... well... it put a strain on our relationship." I let tears glisten in my eyes, praying they appear convincing. "We haven't been spending much time together lately. So, if he did steal something from you... I'm afraid I'd be the last person he would confide in." I swallow hard, trying to make my voice upbeat. Innocent.

Not like I'm lying my face off. "But I have hope things can get better between us. For the past few months, he's been giving me the most beautiful gifts — trying to make up for his absence."

There's a long, silent beat. "What kind of gifts?"

"Oh! Flowers and chocolate, of course. Some lovely pieces of jewelry. And the prettiest little paperweight to keep on my desk in the study."

"This paperweight." His eyes gleam with interest. "Could you describe it for me?"

Yes. Take the bait, you bastard.

I tilt my head, as though recalling distant information. "It's gold and oval-shaped, with lots of little gemstones all over it. Really beautiful. I don't know where he bought it, but I'd love to find another one someday."

Alexei's eyes shift to the Evanoff brothers. "I thought you searched the house."

"We did!"

"And?"

"I swear, boss — we looked but we didn't find it." Righty sounds like he's about to shit himself. "She's lying. She's stashed it somewhere."

I flinch. "Lying about what?"

"You know exactly what, you manipulative bitch!" Lefty lurches at me. "Where did you stash it? Tell us!"

"Why would she lie?" Alexei asks softly. "She may not know the value of a good *paperweight*. However... the two of you do."

"Wait... are you saying... you think my paperweight is stolen property?" I keep my brows high, as though I have no idea what's happening. As if I don't know precisely where his precious Egg is — somewhere *very* far from my study desk, that's for damn sure.

"It's possible," Alexei says noncommittally. His gaze moves back to the brothers, growing scarier by the second. "You assured me you searched the house from top to bottom. You expect me to believe you overlooked the *Nécessaire* when it was sitting out on a desk in plain view?"

"No, Alexei. It wasn't there!"

Alexei doesn't respond. He's looking very displeased with his minions.

Excellent.

Maybe they'll all kill each other and you can walk out of here scot-free.

HA!

A girl can dream.

"I assure you, Alexei. If the *Nécessaire* was there, we would've found it." He pauses, his voice growing less confident. "Unless... Unless we somehow missed it... though I thought we were thorough..."

Alexei's eyes narrow. "Or... perhaps you recognized its value and decided to keep it for yourselves."

"No, Alexei." Lefty falls to his knees, head bowed in subservience. His brother soon follows suit. "We would never betray you. On our honor, we are faithful to you and to the Bratva."

Alexei lets them sweat it out on their knees for a long time, saying nothing. "Viktor, I see two possible scenarios, here. Neither is agreeable. Either you are incompetent, or you are a liar. I can afford to keep neither in my service."

"Please. Give us another chance. Let us go back. We'll search the house again. We'll rip up every floorboard, if we have to."

"And how will you do that, with the FBI watching our every move? They are monitoring *everything* in this cursed city. They've already discovered your hideout at the deli.

They have my nephew in custody, thanks to your sloppiness!"

So Paul is safe, then.

Safe... and likely in handcuffs...

But I suppose handcuffs are still preferable to death.

"The FBI is stretched thin. They can't cover every location at once," Lefty says.

"And yet, they have driven us to do business out here—" Alexei gestures around at the construction site. "—like common thugs. It is an affront to the Petrov pride."

Ah.

So that explains the creepy locale. No street cameras or surveillance.

Somewhere far overhead, I sincerely hope Evelson is watching via satellite. Like a bald guardian angel in a kevlar vest.

"Alexei, you have seen us operate in the past. We can get back into the Hunt house without detection."

"Getting in isn't the issue. It's getting *out* again that will require a magic trick. The FBI will surround you within moments." He pauses. "I myself am worried about accessing my jet. They will be staked out at the airport, as well."

"It's true enough that they'll surround the house. But all we need is a suitable distraction. Something to occupy the FBI while we grab the Egg... and something to use as leverage for our extraction."

"A distraction," Alexei murmurs, interest peaked. "I assume you mean something similar to the Belarus incident last spring?"

"Exactly," Lefty says, sounding pleased with himself. "And we already have all the supplies we need to build it right here. Just waiting to be put to good use."

To build what, exactly?

Alexei's eyes flicker to me. Goosebumps break out on my arms as his lips curl into an eerie smile. "That is... an intriguing idea, Viktor."

"It will work. The FBI always prioritizes saving civilian life over anything else — even a criminal pursuit." His words are intent, almost frenzied. "Give us this chance to prove our loyalty."

"I really should kill you both for this display of gross ineptitude." Alexi looks like he means it. "But I will grant you one more chance. If you can return the Nécessaire to me... all will be forgiven. If not..."

The threat hangs in the air.

"We won't fail you, Alexei."

"See that you don't." His eyes eventually move back to mine. "As for you, niece... I see no reason why you cannot return to your life. You will not be punished for my nephew's mistakes."

Oh, thank god.

He's not going to kill me.

My relief is tempered by a strain of disbelief. I'm stunned that my plan actually worked. As Conor would say... it feels almost *too* easy.

A red flag is waving in the back of my mind.

Alexei Petrov is not an idiot. He did not rise to the top of the largest crime syndicate in Russia by playing fast and loose. He is a man of plans. Strategy.

Which is why I know it should've been far, far harder for the Evanoffs to convince him to agree to their half-baked plan. And far more difficult for me to convince him of my ignorance concerning the Egg.

Something isn't right.

My suspicions are confirmed a heartbeat later, when

Alexei smiles again. "You may return to your life... just as soon as you do us one small favor for us."

There it is.

The catch.

All my hopes of escape, of *survival*, deflate instantly — hissing out of me like air from a balloon. I try to take a deep breath, but there's a lump of nerves blocking my airway.

"You are family, after all." His eyes gleam, as though he's the only one in on a particularly amusing joke. "And what is family for, if not to help in times of need?"

"Right," I say weakly, heart thundering. "Anything for family."

You are not my family, you pretentious prick.

Alexei watches silently as the Evanoffs scramble to their feet. I try not to balk as they close ranks around me; as two very large sets of hands wrap around either bicep, squeezing hard enough that I see stars.

Alexei's chuckle is cold as ice. "It seems we find ourselves in need of a rather... *explosive*... distraction. Just to keep the FBI agents occupied while Viktor and Vladimir retrieve my property. And *you*, dear niece, will be absolutely perfect..."

CHAPTER 15

OMG LITERALLY DEAD

I AM GOING to die today.

I'm not exaggerating or looking for a pity party. I'm just stating a fact.

Today is the day that I, Shelby Hunt, will shuffle off this mortal coil.

Looking back, it's hard to believe I actually thought I'd get to walk away from this situation alive. How naive I was — thinking I could manipulate one of the most notorious criminals on the planet. A little girl playing with toys far above her maturity level, in a game with rules that have been rigged against her from the start.

"Can't you go any faster?" Lefty barks at his brother, cocking his gun.

"Not unless you want the police on our tail before we get there." He presses his foot against the gas pedal and the van picks up speed. "We're right around the corner, anyway. Get ready. Even if they don't have agents posted outside, we won't have more than ten minutes before this whole area is swarming."

I watch my neighborhood pass outside my window and

wonder if it will be my last time ever seeing it. When the blue sign comes into view, feel my heart clench as I read the familiar words.

Merriweather Street

We barrel down the cul-de-sac, toward a sprawling blue Victorian with a wraparound porch. It's the perfect house. Prettiest on the block by a mile. Any stranger seeing it from the outside would automatically assume the family dwelling inside it is equally perfect.

But looks, like life, are often deceiving.

Righty jerks the wheel violently and the van jolts up over the curb, onto my perfectly manicured lawn. He slams on the breaks so hard I get whiplash as we screech to a stop with the tires straddling my front walkway, just outside the front stairs.

"Go time!" Righty says, leaping out of the front seat. He's holding a semi-automatic assault rifle, gesturing madly for us to follow as his eyes scan the street for threats. "Let's move!"

Lefty throws open the door and drags me out of the van, up the steps, onto the porch. He holds me like a shied as he runs after his brother, arm banded tight around my shoulders.

"Keep moving, bitch," he hisses in my ear. "Or things will go *boom* before you can blink."

I pick up my pace, heart thundering inside my chest.

When we catch up to Righty, I see he's already bashed out my pretty bay window with the butt of his gun and is stepping over the sill, into my dining room. Lefty follows, dragging me inside after him. I feel my bare arms catch on broken shards of glass in the window frame. My feet receive similar treatment from the razor-sharp pieces scattered across the floor.

On a normal day, it would probably bring tears to my eyes. But I'm feeling strangely numb, in the face of my imminent death. I guess it's just hard to get worked up about a bit of glass when there's a bomb strapped to your chest and a crazed Russian holding the detonator.

Oh.

Right.

Did I not mention that, before?

IT TURNS OUT, the Evanoffs reputation as expert bomb makers was not exaggerated in the slightest. The speed at which they rigged a vest full of plastic explosives was truly astonishing. They could do infomercials.

Dirty bombs in two hours or less or your money back!

Ignoring the weight of the bomb around my chest, I listen to Righty and Lefty tearing violently through the study. Drawers are overturned, furniture flipped over. A constant stream of angry Russian curses peppers the air.

"Do you see it?"

"It's not here!"

I can't help smiling a little.

Oh, boys. You got played even worse than I did. And that's really saying something, since I'm about one sneeze away from triggering an accidental explosion.

My eyes slide to the window. I feel a thread of hope weave through me at the sight of the black SUVs pulling to a stop at the curb.

"We've got company!" Righty shouts. "Fuck, that was fast. Not even two minutes. How the hell do they already know we're here?"

"Almost like they knew we were coming," his brother

hisses, grabbing me by the arm and jerking me around to face him. His skin is mottled purple with anger. "Listen, you little bitch. We need your fucking *paperweight*," he spits the word. "Where is it? We've checked the desk."

"Oh... Hmmm..." I stall.

"Don't trifle with me, bitch! Or I'll—"

"You'll what?" I snap, fed up with his threats. "Blow me up? Please, if you're going to... make sure to do it while I'm standing right next to you."

"Shut your mouth, you little whore!" He waves the detonator darkly. "I promise, nothing will give me more pleasure than the moment I get to snuff out your life."

"I'm your only bargaining chip to get out of here, now that they've arrived." I jerk my chin toward the window.

I think his head might pop off, he's so furious. "We need that fucking paperweight! Do you understand me? Now *find it* so we can get the fuck out of here before more arrive."

Unhurriedly, I walk over to the bookcase, reach inside, and pluck an item off the bottom shelf. I turn and extend it toward Lefty.

"Here," I tell him sweetly. "This is the only paperweight I own."

If I'm going to die, might as well do it with flair.

A dangerous glint creeps into his eyes as he stares at the gold and glass orb I got in a Yankee Swap two Christmases ago from one of the other yoga instructors at Aimee's studio. While it's very pretty... we had a $20 limit.

Slight difference from the $20 million Fabergé Egg he's looking for.

I see the moment my duplicity clicks inside his head. Taking me by the shoulders, he shakes me so hard my teeth clack together. So hard, I'm worried he's going to trigger the bomb around my chest and blow us both to hell.

"You played us! You fucking played us!"

Righty appears, looming beside his brother. *Double trouble.* "What are you talking about Vik?"

"She lied! The fucking Egg isn't here!"

"Egg?" I ask innocently. "What egg?"

He shoves me aside with a growl and paces toward the window. His face gets even redder when he steals a glance outside and takes in the sheer number of agents on my street. In the distance, four shots ring out in quick succession.

"*FUCK!*" Lefty bellows. "They just shot the van's tires."

"Vik, relax. SWAT won't come in here without the bomb squad. They learned that lesson the hard way last week," Righty says, smirking as he grabs his gun off the table.

It's a huge semi-automatic rifle with a long scope and a curved magazine clip. My mouth goes dry at the sight, envisioning the kind of damage a weapon like that could do to a person.

"Vlad, they've got snipers taking up positions on fucking roof across the street!"

"Then I suggest you get away from the window, Vik." He exhales. "Look, if we stick to the plan, we'll be fine. That's why we have *her*, isn't it?" His chin jerks at me. "She's our ticket out of here. They can't kill us so long as we have a hostage."

"Yes, but Alexei *will* kill us if we go back without the Egg. And now we don't even know where it is, thanks to this *suka's* lies."

"We'll get back to Moscow and explain—"

I laugh. I can't help it.

Both brothers look at me darkly. "What the fuck are you laughing about?"

"Sorry to interrupt." I snort, shaking my head. "I just can't believe you two idiots still haven't figured out what's going on here. I mean, there's *slow*, and then there's the two of you."

They stare at me.

I sigh. "You're never getting back to Moscow."

"What?" Lefty hisses.

"Alexei needed you to create a distraction, something to draw the FBI's attention. Right?" I shrug. "*This* is the distraction. *You* are the distraction. Not me and my little bomb vest. *This entire thing.*"

They stare at me, clearly not understanding.

Poor Vik and Vlad. They may be talented bomb makers, but they're not particularly bright.

"Your boss sent you here to be his fall guy. A diversion to distract the FBI so he can get out of this country unscathed," I say slowly, as if I'm talking to third graders. "My guess? He's speeding down the runway as we speak in his private jet, sipping a cold glass of champagne. Or whiskey. Vodka? Hell, I don't know what Russian crime lords drink."

Lefty strides back to me, his expression full of wrath. "*That is not true.*"

"Isn't it, though?" I blink up at him, eyes wide. "He insisted you come here, even though he knew the FBI was all over this place. You said it yourself — they got here *so fast*. Almost like someone *tipped them off.*"

"Alexei would never do that! Not to his own men."

"See, I think you're wrong. I think he'd do *exactly* that. And I know, from reading about his past exploits, this wouldn't even be the first time he's done it." I shake my head. "He let his first wife take the fall for him back in the '80s when he was charged with tax evasion. He implicated his own business parter for fraud in '94 when he wanted an excuse to turn their partnership into a sole-proprietorship." I tilt my head, glancing from one brother to the other. "Alexei Petrov evaluated this situation and did exactly what he *always* does — he ensured his own survival. Then, he cut his losses and headed for the hills."

"But.. The Nécessaire..."

"Oh, I'm sure, when things calm down, he'll send someone else to retrieve his precious Fabergé Egg." I sigh. "But I'm afraid, by then, it'll be long over for you boys."

Lefty's mouth is pursed, his nostrils flared. As much as he doesn't want to believe what I'm saying, I can see by the look in his eyes that he does.

"It's not true," Righty murmurs, but his voice is unsure. "Don't let this bitch get in your head, Vik."

"Think about it," I murmur. *"Two birds, one stone.* He escapes home while the FBI cleans up the mess for him by getting rid of..." Eyeing them, I make a *tsk* sound. "Two assets who, let's face it, have totally bungled this whole Egg fiasco up right from the beginning."

With a growl of rage, Lefty punches me in the face.

I knew it was coming. Hell, I didn't even try to brace for it as his fist hits me square in the mouth. I taste the copper tang of blood and blink away tears as stars spin before my eyes.

At least I didn't pass out, this time.

The Evanoffs are talking rapidly in Russian. Bickering, from the sound of it. Which was exactly my intention. I may not have many cards left to play, here... and I'm probably going to die regardless of what I do... but damned if I'm going down without a fight. And maybe, if I can stall them long enough for the FBI to get in position... then at least I'll go out knowing the Evanoff boys will never be free to hurt anyone else ever again. I'll meet my maker with the knowledge that I tried my best to level the playing field.

For Sykes, lying unresponsive in a hospital bed.

For three SWAT team members blown to pieces.

For five Americans in an Embassy ten years ago.

And for me.

My head is still reeling when I hear the sound of a bullhorn blasting from the street. My heart clenches when I recognize the voice as Kaufman's.

"EXIT THE HOUSE WITH YOUR HANDS IN THE AIR!"

Wiping a trickle of blood from the corner of my mouth, I look from one brother to the other and strive to keep my voice light. "If you turn yourselves in now, I promise this will go better for you."

"You'd like that, wouldn't you, bitch?" Lefty hisses.

"Since you asked — *yes*. Yes, I would."

"You've got a smart mouth. But I think you're forgetting about this." He shakes me by the arm, holding up the detonator for emphasis. "One push, you're pink mist."

I go still.

It's easier to be brave about this whole situation when I don't think too specifically about the bomb belted just beneath my boobs, like the worst push up bra *ever* created.

"SEND OUT YOUR HOSTAGE!" Kaufman's voice blasts into the air again. "THEN COME OUT WITH YOUR HANDS UP!"

Lefty's eyes narrow. "You think this is over? You think you won? *Think again.* I've already killed four FBI agents this week. If I'm going down... I plan on taking a few more with me."

Grabbing his gun in one hand and my arm in the other, he drags me down the hallway. I hear his brother close on

our heels, saying something, but my mind is spluttering
inside my skull, caught up on one word.

Four.

He said *four* FBI agents.

But...

That's not possible.

That *cannot* be possible.

Because I know for a fact that only *three* died in the
bomb blast in East Boston. And as of this morning, Sykes
was critical-but-stable in the ICU.

Which means...

Someone else is dead.

A fourth FBI agent.

A face flashes in my head before I can stop it — messy
black hair falling into dark blue eyes. Killer smile, on the
rare occasion he lets it show. Mouth that melts me into an
emotional puddle, whether he's using it to kiss me or telling
me he loves me.

All day, since I opened that safe house door and saw the
Evanoffs standing there instead of Conor, I have refused to
entertain the possibility that he might be... that he's...

I can't even *think* the word.

My brain instantly rejects the mere idea of it, like a
vending machine spitting out a crumpled dollar bill.
Because a world without Conor Asshole Gallagher would
simply be...

Unbearable.

I don't know when it happened, or even how. I cannot
trace the exact moment, cannot pick out the precise instant
my heart changed from despising him to something entirely
different. Something like...

Devotion.

I know it's crazy. A week ago he was a stranger. He

burst into my life, full of bossy demands and dark scowls and gruff orders, and flipped it upside down. And every day since, he has pushed me. Challenged me. Inspired me. Infuriated me.

He has sparked my temper and delved my deepest secrets. He has expanded my emotional limits and fucked my body beyond the brink of pleasure. He has awoken something inside me I didn't even know was there until he coaxed it out.

Not with gentle hands and false promises; with stark truths and brute force.

Maybe at first, I didn't want to see it. Didn't want to acknowledge how much I needed him. How much I wanted him. How similar we are, from the unrelenting stubborn streak to the disapproving parental figures to the tendency for self-imposed isolation. But now, as I stand here on the brink of losing him, I see it. I see it so clearly. And all I feel is regret that it took me so damn long.

I should've told him.

I should've said it back.

I shouldn't have been so fucking scared of getting hurt again that I pushed away a man so well-suited for me, it's like I dreamed him into existence one detail at a time.

I shake my head in disbelief.

He can't be dead.

Then why is it Kaufman on the bullhorn? a small voice questions. *If he could call out to you right now... don't you think he would?*

I shove the voice away, banish it to the back of my mind. Shove it away in a box and lock it up tight with a thousand loops of unbreakable chain.

In a daze of shock, I don't struggle as the Evanoffs drag me through the house, avoiding windows and open expanses in case the snipers decide to try their luck. We make our way to the garage door off the kitchen and Lefty grins as he grabs the keys to my convertible from the hook.

I have a distinct feeling that whatever's about to happen will *not* be good. But somehow, in the sudden numbness of shock over Conor's unknown fate... I find it hard to drum up a suitable amount of concern for my own.

Stepping into the attached garage, Lefty scans the space, looking from the retractable door to my sporty black coup and finally back to me.

"Sorry. Only two seats in this ride." He smirks at me and holds up the detonator. "Looks like you've reached the end of your road, Shelby Hunt."

THERE'S a harsh grating sound and a mechanical buzz as the garage door slowly begins to peel open. I stand before it like a statue, watching as the gap widens from a sliver to a foot. From one foot to six to twelve. I hold my breath until it's rolled all the way up in the ceiling, praying like hell the snipers don't take me down.

The door falls silent and my eyes focus on the world beyond.

There's a sea of black police vehicles facing the house, their doors ajar to shield the agents sheltering behind them. I see gun barrels braced against car hoods and window frames.

I wonder how many sights are trained on me right now.

I'd swear, there's a collective intake of air as I raise my arms slowly above my head and take my first step out of the garage, into the driveway — the sound of fifty FBI agents spotting my explosive vest all at once. I take another few steps, coming to a stop when Lefty honks the horn sharply from inside the garage.

You will do exactly what I tell you, he told me ten minutes ago, his eyes gleaming in a scary, unhinged sort of way. *And the second you don't comply... boom goes the dynamite. Got it?*

I don't doubt his intentions for a second. Nor am I surprised by them. As soon as this plan came into being back at the construction site, I somehow knew I'd wind up here. One button-click away from blinking out of existence. Standing entirely on my own.

Alone.

Even now, in the end.

It shouldn't bother me. For my entire adult life, I've perfected the art of being alone. I've been so good at it, sometimes I've scare myself with my own freakish self-sufficiency. In the question of what I'm more afraid of — *being alone or being rejected* — the answer was always so clearly rejection.

Because being alone was easier.

In fact, for a very long time, it was almost *too* easy.

But now, as I stand here on my own, with the sun streaming down around me like a freaking halo of light, glinting off the dark panels of plastic explosives on the belt around my waist...

I don't want to be alone, anymore.

I'd give anything to *not* be alone.

I would happily face a hundred rejections from Conor if it meant there was even one half-chance at having even a bit more time with him. If he could be here now, his arms holding me close, his mouth pressing against mine.

Maybe it's better if he's not here, I lie to myself. *It would be much harder to say goodbye with him standing in front of you now, at the end.*

"I'm Shelby Hunt!" I call out, my voice stretched thin as it tries to fill the void of silence surrounding me. "They say they'll detonate the bomb in my vest if anyone shoots. They say they want free passage out of the city. Otherwise... I die."

The world stops turning.

I stand with my hands above my head, afraid to move. Afraid to breathe too heavily, lest I somehow disturb the homemade explosives. My eyes sweep the crowd of FBI agents, seeking out familiar faces.

One in particular.

But he's nowhere. Not with Kaufman and Evelson by the bullhorn. Not with the plainclothes officers standing to the sidelines. Not with the uniformed BPD officers at the far end of the street, setting up a strict traffic cordon.

Conor Gallagher is nowhere to be found.

A tear streaks down my cheek — the first one I've allowed to escape all day. And while I'm sure everyone in the crowd of onlookers thinks I'm crying with fright over my own incendiary predicament...

It's not about me at all.

It's about him.

It's about the truth I can no longer deny, or look away from, or lock up in a box inside my head.

In my heart I know, the only reason he's not here right now, standing in that crowd... is because he can't be. Because something is keeping him from me.

I hear Lefty's voice.

I've already killed four agents...

He's dead.

Conor Gallagher is dead.

The bomb hasn't exploded yet, but my heart — oh, my aching, breaking heart — detonates into a zillion pieces inside my chest.

FOR A LONG TIME, no one seems to do a damn thing.

I have a feeling there's a flurry of discussion going on behind the scenes — pros and cons being weighed, ideas being proposed, strategies being suggested — but from my perspective everything has gone totally quiet. Only the faint sound of the engine rumbling behind me inside the garage; the restless shifting of men in heavy body armor ahead of me.

A sudden screech of tires splits the air.

My head whips toward the sound. In fact, every head in a two block radius whips toward the sound. All I can do is watch as a black Jeep Wrangler flies down the street, around the police barricade that's been set up to cordon off any incoming traffic. Whoever is driving appears to be a total maniac — hopping curbs and front lawns, dodging mailboxes and parked cars with seemingly no regard for traffic rules, let alone the fact that there's a very active hostage situation unfolding right now.

My heart is in my throat as the Wrangler slams to a stop at the end of the driveway. And a tremble moves through my whole body, from the tips of my fingers still pointed at the sky to my bare, bloody toes pressed against the smooth stone. Because there's a man hopping down from the driver's side, dressed all in black despite the summer day — from his shirt to his pants to his badass motorcycle boots. A man with the darkest blue eyes I've ever seen. A man who is unquestionably, heart-stoppingly...

Alive.

Those deep blue eyes are fixed firmly on mine as he walks up the driveway with steady strides, only the faintest hint of a limp revealing the injury concealed beneath his clothing. My stomach lurches as I realize he's hurt. It turns to lead when I notice the pallor of his skin, so unlike his usual coloring. As though he's lost half his blood.

Christ.

Was he shot?

If so, how the hell is he walking, right now?

His face is a mask of composure, but I know him well enough to recognize the fury churning through him. It's there in the fissure between his furrowed brows, in his tight-locked jaw, in his clenched fists. I see the strain in his shoulders and know he's desperate to break into a run. That if he could, he'd close the distance between us in less than a second and rip the bomb from my body with his bare hands, if necessary.

But he'd never put me in that sort of jeopardy.

From the garage, Lefty blares the car horn in clear warning.

Close enough.

Conor instantly stops moving. He's ten feet away, now. I can see every muscle in his throat working roughly, as if he's struggling to find the right words. His eyes never shift away from mine as he calls out, "I'm not armed! I just want to talk."

His voice is loud enough to carry inside the garage.

Waiting for a rebuttal from the Evanoffs, we stand there drinking each other in. I can see the desperate fear in his eyes. The sight of me in danger is killing him.

I'm sure my own eyes are a perfect match, but I try to smile anyway.

His frown gets more pronounced. "*Don't.*"

"Don't what?"

"Don't you fucking smile at me like that." His voice is low, gruff with anger and terror. " Like you're giving me some nice last memory to remember you by. You're not going anywhere, Hunt. You hear me?"

I suck in a breath at his words. I so desperately want to believe him. To believe that I'm going to walk out of this. To believe that we'll walk away, hand in hand, and live happily ever after, just like in those fairytales I've always derided and dismissed.

I pull in a breath. "Just so you know, I was only smiling at you because I'm so damn happy you're alive. But if you're going to give me attitude while I'm wearing an explosive vest—" My voice breaks, despite my best intentions. A tear slips out, spilling down my cheek in a rush.

Conor watches it fall to the ground, flinching when it makes impact. As though it's hit his skin instead of the stone.

The horn beeps again — twice in succession.

Conor's eyes narrow on the car with lethal intent. His voice is clear and controlled. "I don't speak beep, Evanoff. You want to talk? Let's talk. No guns. No snipers. Just you and me." He pauses. "I'll even come to you."

"*What do you think you're doing?!*" I hiss at him. "*You're going to get yourself killed, Conor!*"

"I think you'll want to negotiate with me!" he calls out, ignoring me. "Especially since I have something you want."

My eyes widen as he pulls the Fabergé egg from his back pocket.

CHAPTER 16

CUFFING SEASON

CONOR HOLDS THE *NÉCESSAIRE* ALOFT.

It's dazzling in the sunshine, refracting a hundred rainbows in every direction.

I can't help gasping — at its beauty, but also at the fact that he has it in his possession. I'd thought it lost for good, after my poor treatment of it.

Before I can ask how the hell he managed to track it down, the door to my convertible opens. I flinch at the sound of Lefty's voice.

"Kitchen. Five minutes. Come alone." He pauses. "Any weapons, the girl dies."

With that, the garage door begins to close with a shriek of metal gears. Tense with nerves, Conor waits until it's fully shut before rushing forward in a burst.

"Don't!" I exclaim, holding out my hands to stop him. "It's not safe."

He ignores me — *what else is new?* — closing the distance between us in three massive strides. He hovers scant inches away, as close as he can physically get without touching me. His eyes are locked on the vest.

"*Okay*. Okay, we're going to get you out of there soon, Hunt."

I nod. "That would be good. Before my bladder explodes."

His eyes fly to mine.

"Bad joke," I say weakly.

"Not funny. At all."

"I really do have to pee."

"You're gonna have to hold it for a bit." He reaches out for the vest.

"Hey!" I step hastily out of reach. "What do you think you're doing?!"

"Can't figure out how to get you out of the damn vest if you don't let me look at it a little closer."

"No! You could get yourself blown to smithereens, standing too close to me."

"That's not going to happen."

"Sure. Fine. Whatever." I pause. "Now back off. Ten feet, minimum."

"Hunt, don't be stubborn."

"*Me*, stubborn? What about you?"

He ignores me, brow furrowed as he stares at the vest with intent eyes. "Strange. I've never seen a circuitry pattern like this before..."

"And you're suddenly some bomb expert?"

"Not remotely." He swallows hard. "But everyone at Quantico receives basic training. Plus, I did three years with the counterterrorism unit before I switched to organized crime. Seen more than one suicide vest in my day."

"Oh," I murmur, swallowing. That's oddly comforting.

"The wires on this belt... I'd need the bomb squad to confirm, but there's not enough time... we have about forty seconds before we're due in that kitchen." He glances up at me. There's an edge of desperation in his eyes. It scares me. But quite not as much as the deep rasp of his voice when he asks me a question.

"How much do you trust me?"

I don't hesitate. "Conor Gallagher, I would trust you with my life."

"Good." His hand reaches out and wraps around mine. With a squeeze, he turns to look at the house. "But let's hope it doesn't come to that."

WITH THE EGG passed off safely into Kaufman's big hands, Conor and I step through the front door of my perfect house. We walk hand in hand to the kitchen, not speaking. I can feel the tension radiating through his body, just as I'm sure he can feel the fear thrumming through mine.

The Evanoffs are waiting for us.

Righty is gripping his assault rifle. Lefty has both hands wrapped around his Glock. I'm certain they're going to shoot us stone-cold-dead as soon as we step over the threshold.

Thankfully, I'm wrong.

There's a terse silence as the four of us face off from opposite sides of the kitchen.

"Didn't I already kill you?" Righty asks Conor, smirking. "I could've sworn I shot you in the chest this morning, outside that safe house."

"Can you really call it a *safe* house, though, Vlad?" Lefty's voice is smug. "It wasn't too hard to torture the location out of that Fed we caught following us yesterday." He pauses, and leans forward, his eyes on Conor. "You know, you should really train your men better. Any Bratva would die before betraying his brothers." He pauses. "Then again, your agent died as well. I know, because I watched the life drain out of his eyes after he told me where to find the Hunt bitch."

I glance sharply at Conor, horrified by this news. I don't want to believe it's true, but I know it must be. Lefty's earlier words are ringing in my ears.

I've already killed four FBI agents this week.

Conor's face is utterly blank, but his eyes are lethal. I'm stunned by his self-control. Stunned he doesn't pull out his gun and shoot these assholes where they stand.

But he can't.

Not without losing me.

"Next time you try to kill me, I suggest you make sure I'm actually dead," Conor tells them in a scary voice. "Or I promise you, I will take great pleasure in hunting you to the edge of the fucking earth. I will make sure my face is the last thing either of your see before I send you straight to Hell."

I shiver at the burning conviction in his voice. I have no doubt he means every word of that vow. Judging by the way the Evanoffs start shifting like skittish horses, I'm not the only one, either.

"Where's the Nécessaire?" Lefty barks. Even from here, I can see the sweat on his brow. Despite his angry tone and show of bravado, he's nervous.

"If you think I'd just walk in here with it and hand it over, you're sorely mistaken." Conor shakes his head. "We're going to settle a few things, first."

Righty aims his gun directly at Conor's chest. "And what's to keep me from killing you right now? I'll be sure not to miss this time."

I stop breathing.

"I assumed you wanted the Egg." Shrugging lightly, Conor somehow manages to sound totally unruffled. As though they're discussing their favorite sports teams or TV shows. "If you kill me, that will never happen. My agents will storm this house. You will either die or be taken into federal custody. You'll never see Russia again, let alone breathe free air."

Grudgingly, Righty lowers his gun again.

I resume breathing.

"What are you proposing?" Lefty snarls. "Let me guess — you want us to surrender quietly."

Conor shakes his head. "No. I want to offer you a trade."

"A trade for what?"

"The Egg. And your chance to go free — without being gunned down in a firefight you cannot possibly win." His eyes cut to Lefty's hand. "In exchange for that detonator. For her life."

Every muscle in my body freezes.

No.

He cannot actually be considering this. Allowing these monsters to walk out of here, after everything they've done. All the people they've hurt. All the chaos they've caused.

"Conor," I breathe. "Conor, no, you can't—"

His eyes cut to mine. "I can. And I will."

Lefty's scoff pulls our attention back. "You expect me to believe you want *this*..." When his hand contracts around the small remote, I nearly have a heart attack, thinking he's about to kill me with a careless jerk of his fingers. "Badly enough to make that trade? Badly enough that you would let us walk free?"

Conor's jaw is clenched tight, but he gives an affirmative nod.

Lefty's eyes are wary. He shakes his head at Conor, clearly suspecting a trap. "You would give up the *Nécessaire* for so little? For one *suka* with a big mouth..."

"Maybe he doesn't know what it's worth," Righty grunts.

"Maybe he's going to try to pass us off a counterfeit replica," Lefty hisses. "But if he thinks he can fool us so easily, perhaps we should show him how serious we are..." His eyes cut to me and he waves the detonator again. "One push..."

I try not to flinch when his finger starts to descend over the red button.

"*Enough.*" Conor cuts in sharply. "No counterfeits. No tricks. You have my word."

"And why would we trust the word of a Fed?" Righty sneers.

"Vlad, let's just kill them both. This is a scheme to stall us. They will never let us go." Lefty's right hand tightens on his gun. "Better off taking them out now, then as many as their friends as possible."

Righty contemplates this plan for a long moment, then nods. "Okay, brother. We fight to the end. Side by side. No surrender."

I watch their fingers sliding toward the triggers and know we're about to die if we can't somehow change their minds about going out in a blaze of glory.

"*Wait!* You'll never get back in Alexei's good graces without the Egg!" I yell desperately. "Remember what he said — this is your *one* chance. You know you'll never get another."

The Evanoffs glance at each other, hesitating.

"But if you take this trade... you could go home. Not just that, you could return the Egg to Alexei. He would welcome you with open arms. You would be heroes." I swallow hard, struggling to maintain an even tone. "Or... you can kill us right now, then die yourselves... and be remembered by no one as anything except failures."

The air is thick with tension. Righty and Lefty are staring at each other and I know my words have had the intended effect. They're hesitating. Not only that... they're actually considering taking this deal.

"My offer," Conor says softy. "Expires in thirty seconds. *Decide.*"

Lefty's head shakes. So does his voice. "One life in exchange for the priceless *Nécessaire?* For something worth a limitless fortune? It's absurd. Ridiculous! I cannot believe any man in his right mind would ever make that deal." His eyes cut to me, full of disbelief and indecision. "No one girl is worth that much."

There's a beat of silence. Then, after a moment, Conor says very simply, "That depends entirely on the girl."

My heart clenches.

One girl, for a limitless fortune.

"Your thirty seconds are up," Conor informs them.

The Evanoffs glance at each other. They're suspicious, but they're also desperate. And the chance of walking out of here with not only their lives but also the Egg... the chance to restore their position by Alexei's side and return to Russia as heroes...

It's too good to pass up.

"We want all your snipers pulled from the roofs," Lefty says.

"Done," Conor agrees immediately.

"We want the barricades removed, so we can drive out of here."

"Fine."

"And we want every agent in a five-mile radius gone."

"That'll take some time. But I'll make it happen."

The brothers look at each other again. They seem almost baffled by their good fortune, but they realize there's no other choice. This is their best shot at freedom. Their only shot at freedom, really.

Lefty looks back at Conor. "When the area is clear of your agents, you will send the girl to the garage." He jerks his chin at me. "She'll give us the Egg. We'll hand her the detonator."

"I will make the exchange," Conor snaps, letting his anger show for the first time. "She is not going anywhere near you without my protection."

"Then there will be no deal." Lefty smirks. "She comes alone with the Egg. No weapons. No protections. Those are the terms."

"And how do I know you won't shoot her on the spot, as soon as she hands over the Egg?" Conor's fury is bleeding into every word.

"You'll have to trust us." Righty looks thrilled. "Just as we have to trust you'll actually pull back your snipers and call off your agents."

There's a tense silence.

Trust them.

What an absurd concept. I'd feel more secure trusting Paul with my investment portfolio.

"Well?" Lefty prompts. "Are we doing this or not?"

"I'll do it," I agree, heart pounding like a wild animal inside my chest. "I'll come alone."

"Like hell you will," Conor grits out.

"Conor." My eyes hold his and I see the stark fear swimming in their blue depths. "This is how it has to be."

"A compromise." Lefty nods. "You have my word. After

the exchange, we agree not to shoot the girl... so long as we are allowed to drive away without pursuit."

Conor's jaw is locked tight. A muscle is ticking in his cheek. I can't tell what's bothering him more: the idea of letting these two go free, or the thought of me being the one to make the exchange.

"Do we have a deal or not?" Righty asks impatiently.

"*Conor*," I plead, when he doesn't respond.

He exhales sharply. "We have a deal."

IT ALL HAPPENS SO QUICKLY.

One minute the street is full of agents and police vehicles and barricades. The next, it is a ghost town. Completely evacuated. Every house has been emptied, every trace of law enforcement removed. There are no sounds or signs of human life anywhere to be found. It's eerie. Like something out of a post-apocalyptic horror film — one starring Conor and I as the sole survivors.

We stand in the middle of the quiet street, sheltered partially by his Wrangler.

Waiting.

Worrying.

Our hands are laced so tight together, I've nearly lost circulation. We both look up at the sound of the garage door opening.

"Are you ready?" Conor asks in a tight voice.

Inhaling deeply, I nod and pick up the Nécessaire off the front seat. Now that I'm truly looking at it, I can't believe I ever mistook it for some cheap trinket. The craftsmanship is truly incredible — the product of months of painstaking work by Peter Carl Fabergé. The rubies and emeralds are positively dazzling in the hazy evening twilight. It's one of the most gorgeous things I've ever held in my hands. (And certainly the most expensive.)

"Go," Conor says, leaning down to kiss me. It's a stern, no-nonsense sort of kiss — perfectly matching the tone of his next order. "And then come back to me."

Bossy, bossy, bossy.

The walk up the driveway seems endless. I keep my eyes fixed dead ahead, listening to the roaring of my own pulse as I close the distance between me and the garage door, which is now fully open.

The Evanoffs are standing by my convertible, still fully armed, watching me approach. They both have their fingers on their triggers. The sight makes my stomach turn over.

They won't risk their own chance at escape. Not now that they're so close to getting everything they want, I tell myself, trying not to freak out. *They gave their word they wouldn't shoot me.*

I can't lie — I'd feel a lot better about trusting that highly-questionable *word* if I knew there was a team of snipers on a roof next door, watching us through a scope right now.

Ten feet from them, I draw to a stop.

"The *Nécessaire*," Lefty growls. There's a gleam of excitement in his eyes as they lock on the Egg in my hands. "Hand it over."

"As soon as you slide me the detonator," I counter. "*Carefully.* Unless you'd like your Egg to go boom as well."

He doesn't move.

"I came alone, like you said. I'm not armed. I kept my part of this bargain," I point out. "Time to keep yours, Evanoff."

"Vik," Righty grunts. "Give it to her so we can get the fuck out of here."

Looking like he's just swallowed a glass of vinegar, Lefty leans over and slides the detonator down the sloping driveway. It skids to a stop by my feet and, for the first time in hours, I feel a smidge of relief.

Maybe I'll actually walk out of here in one piece.

My hands shake as I bend over and carefully lift the small remote, careful not to put my fingers anywhere near the red detonation button.

"The Egg!" Lefty snaps, impatient as ever. "Now!"

My eyes swing up to his. "Sure. Of course. Here."

Without wasting another breath on them, I toss the Egg straight up, as high into the air as I can manage. Gasping in horror, both Evanoffs scramble to catch it before it crashes to the ground.

While they're momentarily distracted — and, thus, unable to change their minds about shooting me — I take the opportunity to turn and bolt fast as I can without disturbing the belt of explosives still wrapped tight around my chest.

Back to the street.

Back to safety.

Back to Conor, who's waiting for me by the Jeep.

There's an intense look in his eyes as he sees me coming — one I've never seen before. One that steals my breath, hits me straight in the chest. One with so many different layers, it's hard to decipher all of them at once.

Impatience, anger, worry, longing, fear.

And love.

Most of all, love. It's there, so clear I can't deny it. Burning so bright, I can't mistake it. Undeniable. Inescapable. And as I take it in, as I feel it rushing over me like a warm wave that starts in the left side of my chest and radiates outward, until every part of me feels set aflame, alight with the power of it...

For the first time, I find myself believing. Believing that it's actually possible. That he really did mean those three little words he spoke to me.

This man truly loves me.

Me.

The woman I am. Not the woman he wishes I could be or the woman he thought I might be. Not the illusion I always thought I had to show the world — the perfect woman who lives in the perfect house with the perfect life.

The imperfect one.

The real one.

The real me.

Conor Gallagher loves me.

Truly.

Deeply.

Unconditionally.

More than a limitless fortune.

And I love him in return.

TEN MINUTES LATER, thanks to Conor's careful work, I'm breathing freely for the first time in hours. The weight of the bomb is gone from my chest. And the Evanoff brothers are long gone as well — we watched their brake lights disappear down the block as soon as they had the Egg in their possession.

The sun is setting, now, and the street is still abandoned. Before, I found it rather eerie. But now that the standoff is finally over, I look around at my empty neighborhood and think it's actually rather peaceful.

Just me and Conor.

The only two people in the entire world.

"I can't believe it's finally over," I whisper, looking over at him. We're leaning against the side of his Jeep, arms locked around each other's waists, watching the sun sink slowly across the sky in a gorgeous pastel tableau.

"Believe it," he whispers, pressing a kiss to my temple. "You're alive. Paul is in custody. Alexei Petrov is long gone. And the Evanoffs are halfway to the New Hampshire border, by now."

I shake my head. "I still can't believe you did that."

"What?"

"Let them go. Gave up everything — the Nécessaire. The chance to arrest the Evanoff brothers, after everything they did, all the people they hurt... just for me. That's crazy."

"What was the alternative?" he asks lowly. "Let them kill you?"

"Yes! Rather than sacrifice all that... rather than give up everything..." I bite my lip, feeling tears prick at my eyes. "I don't know how you could do it."

"Shelby." He turns to look into my eyes, taking my face between his hands. "Haven't you been paying attention? There's nothing I would not do for you. Nothing I would not sacrifice."

"But—"

"No buts. No limits," he whispers. "*I love you.*"

I stare at him. One, two, three long seconds. And then, without any fear whatsoever, I whisper, "I love you, too."

CHAPTER 17

AFTER PARTY

"HOW ARE YOU FEELING?"

"Honesty? I'm pissed," Lucy Sykes says, sitting up in her hospital bed. There are bandages on her arms, a cast encasing her left leg, and some bruises on her face, but otherwise she looks remarkably good for someone who's recently come out of a coma.

"Pissed?" I blink. "Why — do you need more painkillers? I can call the nurse."

"Don't you dare," she grumbles. "Bad enough I missed all the action over the past few days. Now you're going to call Nurse Ratched in here to force another pudding cup down my throat."

Conor snorts.

I roll my eyes. "Trust me, it wasn't that exciting."

"Says the girl who had a bomb strapped to her chest while she faced off with the Evanoff brothers." Her eyes narrow as they move from me to Conor. "Tell me you've got some surveillance footage I can check check out from the scene. Or at least give me some files to go over, while I'm stuck in this damn hospital bed."

"Lucy, has anyone ever told you you're a workaholic?"

She grins. "Only those who know me well."

"Sykes." Conor crosses his arms over his chest. "Just focus on getting well. We'll need you to testify at the trial — it would be nice if you were alive and able to do so."

"Oh, trust me, I'll be there. Even if they have to roll me in on a stretcher." Her ice blue eyes gleam. "Nothing in the world will stop me from witnessing the moment Viktor and Vladimir Evanoff are sentenced to life in prison without even the faintest possibility of parole."

I can't lie, I'm looking forward to that day as well. Knowing they're locked up behind bars is comforting, but I'll feel even better when we've thrown away the key.

Dasvidaniya, boys.

I'll never forget how relieved I was to learn that, during our tense negotiations in the kitchen, Evelson had climbed through a small window in the garage and sliced an undetectable — but extremely effective — hole in the brake lines of my convertible.

Riding off with the Egg, the Evanoffs made it approximately two blocks from my house before their luck ran out — along with the remainder of their brake fluid. They plowed through an intersection and slammed into a tree, thus putting an end to their glorious plans of returning to the Motherland as heroes.

They tried to shoot their way out, of course, but the FBI tactical teams were on them before they could so much as scramble out of the car with their guns in the air. Kaufman and Evelson had them on the ground and in handcuffs within seconds.

As for the *Nécessaire*... I'm sure it will look quite beautiful when we see it again next month — safely behind glass this time, during its grand debut at the MFA's new

Romanov Exhibit. And there it will remain for the foreseeable future... At least until Alexei Petrov sends more thugs to try to steal it back.

When he does, we'll be ready.

"You know, you guys didn't have to check on me." Lucy's eyes move from me to Conor and back again. "*Together*, I might add."

"Was there a question buried somewhere in there, Sykes?" Conor asks.

"No question." Her lips are twisted in a smile. "Merely an observation."

I fight a blush. "Oh. Well... the thing is..."

"You're together." Lucy rolls her eyes. "About damn time, too."

"Excuse me?" My brows go up. "I've known him for, like, a week! What do you mean, *about damn time?*"

"Oh, please. The only people who didn't know you two were going to end up together... were the two of you." She shakes her head. "Kaufman, Evelson and I actually had a pool going to see how long it would take. Hundred buck buy-in."

"*What?*" I gasp, nose scrunching. "And, not that I condone you betting on our love life, but... who won the pool?"

"Kaufman," she mutters darkly. "Optimistic bastard. Pegged you two falling head over heels in about three minutes. I, on the other hand, am a cynic. Thought it would take a month, given all the drama with your ex." Her eyes light up. "Heard he finally signed those divorce papers, though. Congrats on officially being a free woman once more."

"Thanks." I grin. "Not being married has never felt so good."

"Mmmm. Well, we'll see how long that lasts." Her eyes are twinkling playfully as they shoot back and forth between me and Conor. "May be time to call Evelson and Kaufman, get a new pool going..."

"Apparently my agents have so much free time they're starting in-house gambling rings." Conor's trying to look stern, but his mouth is tugged up at one side. "Guess I'll just have to pile on the work when you come back to the office, Sykes."

"Bring it on. I'm bored to tears in this hospital bed. I can handle a heavy caseload but, so help me god, if I have to eat one more pudding cup..."

"Don't worry, you'll be plenty busy. You're going to have to juggle some extra cases."

"Oh? Whose?"

"Mine." Conor shrugs. "Since I'll be taking some time off."

"I'm sorry... it sounded like you just said you were taking time off, Gallagher." Lucy's blonde brows are by her hairline.

"Glad to know your ears weren't affected by the blast, Sykes."

She's still staring. "*You*. Conor Gallagher. Taking time off."

He nods.

"But you never take time off."

"You're right. Which is why I have about ten years worth of vacation days to use up. I intend to use them now."

"Doing *what?*"

"A two-month road trip across the country, for starters." His eyes cut to mine, full of warmth. "As long as my co-pilot hasn't changed her mind..."

"Nope. Assuming I still have veto-power over your

music choices, that is..." I wince. "I can *not* listen to Springsteen for five thousand miles, no matter how cute you look while singing *Dancing in the Dark* off-key in the Wrangler."

He shakes his head at me. "You have no appreciation for the classics, Hunt."

"You... but..." Sykes is having a hard time processing. "I can't believe what I'm hearing."

"Believe it."

"This is a whole new world I've woken up to, huh, Gallagher?" Sykes is still baffled. "I mean... won't you miss it? You live for this job..."

Conor never looks away from me. "I'm learning there are better things to live for, Sykes."

My eyes gloss over with tears. I reach my hand out to him. Lacing our fingers together, he pulls me up from my seat, into his warm chest. When his lips brush mine, they're still curved from his smile.

"*Ugh.* You two are disgustingly cute. Get out of my hospital room before I go into diabetic shock from this display of sweetness." Sykes shoos us toward the door. "Oh, and Gallagher—"

At the threshold, Conor looks back at her.

"In case I didn't say this before... I'm really happy for you." Her eyes slide to me. "For both of you."

"YOU READY?"

I glance at Conor as he loads the last suitcase into the Wrangler. "Ready."

We climb into the Jeep. Leaning over, he kisses me — a long, lingering one that makes my heart soar inside my chest and my blood race with desire. When he pulls back, we're both breathing hard.

"Maybe we should postpone this trip for a few hours," he murmurs, eyes full of heat. "I have some very important matters to discuss with you concerning our route..."

"Oh, really?"

"Mhmm."

"And where, exactly, would you like to discuss these important matters?" I ask. "Let me guess... in bed."

He grins — a carefree, almost boyish look of such pure happiness it makes my breath catch. Seeing him like that — knowing I'm the cause — never gets old.

"It'll be a very official, entirely legitimate vacation-planning session," he informs me. "We can discuss more of the places we want to stop... Go over our map one more time..." He pauses. "If we happen to be naked for said discussion, so be it."

"This is *exactly* what you said this morning! Which is *exactly* how we ended up in bed all day and missed our scheduled departure time!"

He chuckles.

I narrow my eyes at him. "Don't laugh, Gallagher! We are now officially late for our itinerary!"

"Know I'm new to this whole vacation thing, Hunt... but I'm pretty sure the whole point is to relax and *not* follow an itinerary."

"Just start the car, bossy."

"As soon as you strap your seatbelt, stubborn."

He grins at me.

I roll my eyes at him.

And as we pull out of the driveway and turn down Merriweather Street, leaving behind the perfect house where I spent so many years living a not-so-perfect life...

Conor reaches for my hand and a smile spreads across my face.

I don't look back.

Not even once.

There are far better things ahead.

THE END

NEED MORE BOSTON?

Not ready to leave Boston behind? Don't worry...

Go back to the very beginning with Chase & Gemma's story in **NOT YOU IT'S ME.** Fall for Nate & Phoebe in **CROSS THE LINE**. Don't miss Parker & Zoe in **ONE GOOD REASON.** Laugh along with Lila & Luca in **TAKE YOUR TIME**.

All books are now available in e-book, paperback, and audio!

THE BOSTON LOVE STORIES:
NOT YOU IT'S ME
CROSS THE LINE
ONE GOOD REASON
TAKE YOUR TIME

Never miss a new release! Make sure you've subscribed to Julie's newsletter: http://eepurl.com/bnWtHH

ABOUT THE AUTHOR

JULIE JOHNSON is a twenty-something Boston native suffering from an extreme case of Peter Pan Syndrome. When she's not writing, Julie can most often be found adding stamps to her passport, drinking too much  coffee, striving to conquer her Netflix queue, and Instagramming pictures of her dog. (Follow her: @author_julie)

She published her debut novel LIKE GRAVITY in August 2013, just before her senior year of college, and she's never looked back. Since, she has published more than a dozen other novels, including the bestselling BOSTON LOVE STORY series, THE GIRL DUET, and THE FADED DUET. Her books have appeared on Kindle and iTunes Bestseller lists around the world, as well as in AdWeek, Publishers Weekly, and USA Today.

You can find Julie on Facebook or contact her on her website www.juliejohnsonbooks.com. Sometimes, when she can figure out how Twitter works, she tweets from @AuthorJulie. For major book news and updates, subscribe to Julie's newsletter: http://eepurl.com/bnWtHH

Connect with Julie:

www.juliejohnsonbooks.com
juliejohnsonbooks@gmail.com

ALSO BY JULIE JOHNSON

STANDALONE NOVELS:
LIKE GRAVITY
SAY THE WORD
FAITHLESS

THE BOSTON LOVE STORIES:
NOT YOU IT'S ME
CROSS THE LINE
ONE GOOD REASON
TAKE YOUR TIME
SO WRONG IT'S RIGHT

THE GIRL DUET:
THE MONDAY GIRL
THE SOMEDAY GIRL

THE FADED DUET:

FADED

UNFADED

THE UNCHARTED DUET:

UNCHARTED

UNFINISHED

THE FORBIDDEN ROYALS TRILOGY:

DIRTY HALO

TORRID THRONE

SORDID EMPIRE

THE DON'T DUET:

WE DON'T TALK ANYMORE

WE DON'T LIE ANYMORE

Made in the USA
Coppell, TX
21 August 2023

20616623R00166